MW01125498

The Riddle of Billy Gibbs

No Longer
Property Of
St. Louis Public Library

SEP   9 2017

Also by Henry Kisor

Previous Steve Martinez Mysteries

Season's Revenge, 2003
A Venture into Murder, 2005
Cache of Corpses, 2007
Hang Fire, 2013
Tracking the Beast, 2016

Nonfiction

What's That Pig Outdoors: A Memoir of Deafness, 1990
Zephyr: Tracking a Dream Across America, 1994
Flight of the Gin Fizz: Midlife at 4,500 Feet, 1997

The Riddle of Billy Gibbs

Copyright *2017 by Henry Kisor*

First published as an original paperback and an e-book by Henry Kisor/CreateSpace, 2017

No part of this book may be reproduced, scanned, or distributed in any printed or electronic form or by any mechanical means without permission in writing from the author. This is a work of fiction. Names, characters, places, and incidents are the product of the author's imagination or are used fictitiously, and any resemblance to actual persons, living or dead, or to any businesses or locale, is purely coincidental.

www.henrykisor.com

THE RIDDLE OF BILLY GIBBS

The Riddle of Billy Gibbs

For Barb and Dave

THE RIDDLE OF BILLY GIBBS

ONE

A TALL AND LANKY figure in my office doorway blocked
the light from the squad room in the Porcupine County
Sheriff's Department, as always happens when Detective
Sergeant Alex Kolehmainen of the Michigan State Police
comes to call. I leaned back in my chair, folded my hands
and prepared myself for another of the detective's gnomic
observations, as he likes to call the smartass remarks that
always precede his hellos. Alex loves to lay these
comments upon me, but long ago I learned to ignore them.

This time there was no twinkle in Alex's eye.

"Just got a call from Selena Novikovich," he said
with unusual gravity. Selena is my counterpart in
Mackinac County, whose seat is St. Ignace, five hours and
275 miles from Porcupine City due east across Upper
Michigan. "And it's bad news."

"Let's hear it."

"This morning Selena and her deputies found a
male African American corpse hanging by the neck from a
tree in the woods north of St. Ignace," Alex said. "He has
no chest. Looks like someone fired a howitzer at near
point-blank range right through his back. Blood and tissue
on the clothes but none on the ground. Lividity had set in.
Body temperature the same as outside. The shooting was
done elsewhere, at least nineteen hours earlier, probably
more."

"Who's the victim?" I said, dreading the answer.

Alex took a deep breath before replying.

"Forensics hasn't yet finished the identification,"

Alex said, "but the driver's license in the victim's wallet belongs to Billy Gibbs. So do the credit cards. And five hundred fifty bucks in cash—five Franklins and a Grant."

"Holy shit." I shut my eyes. This was not news I wanted to hear.

"Holy shit indeed," Alex said, folding himself into the chair in front of my desk.

In my jurisdiction less than a month before, Billy Gibbs, who was just about the only African-American in all of Porcupine County, had been found not guilty of criminal sexual conduct in the third degree—forcible rape—in a two-day trial. Our little community had been divided even before the trial and its outcome, and feelings were still running high. This news was going to be a bombshell.

"Hanging from a tree?" I said. "Selena calling it a hate crime? Obviously not a robbery."

"Not yet. But it looks that way. Of course forensics is processing the clothes and the shoes and the fingernails and stuff, looking for clues about where the victim had been and maybe where he was killed, but Selena doesn't hold out much hope that we'll learn anything useful. But she'll be calling to ask you to canvass folks in Porcupine County and let her know if you find any leads."

"Sure," I said. "I'll get right on it."

Before I could do that, Sheriff Novikovich called. It was midafternoon, a few hours after Alex had left.

I like Selena, having encountered her on the job a dozen times during inter-county co-operation, as we officially call coming to the aid of a fellow sheriff in a troublesome case. Every year I hoist a Molson's or two with her at the annual gathering of Upper Michigan sheriffs, which we used to hold at the very grand Grand Hotel on Mackinac Island when county coffers were flush. Now, in these difficult economic times, we must settle for a nondescript chain motel in Marquette or Munising.

She is one of the most visually striking women I have ever seen, but not for the usual reasons. She is a shade under six feet tall, with broad shoulders, narrow hips, slim legs and a small round butt. The modest bulk she has packed on over her fifty or so years has gone all above the waist, giving her the look of a weightlifter who neglected her thighs and calves. Both of her young adult daughters are built the same way, except for the added weight. She wears her graying blonde hair in a long ponytail thrust through the vent of her sheriff's ball cap. Her still pretty features have softened into a comfortable face that can instantly transform into a slab of steel when she is angered.

She speaks in a smoky contralto that reminds me of Lauren Bacall at her most come-hither, but Selena is hardly a cougar. Rather, her normal manner is gentle and even grandmotherly, especially with first offenders and teen-agers.

Repeat customers, however, bring out brusque disapproval. One does not make sexist remarks or moves around her. Once, when a belligerent logger grabbed her breast outside a bar, she threw him across her hip into a brick wall and on the rebound cold-cocked him with her baton. A few of her sparring partners have sued, but she has won in court every time. She has been the sheriff of Mackinac County for ten years, winning re-election by wide margins, and for fifteen years before that was a deputy and an undersheriff.

In all that time I have known her to be a crackerjack investigator, thorough and careful, almost never taking a case to her prosecutor that she thought he couldn't win. She also has the rare talent of accurately sizing up a crime at first glance. But this time she was stumped.

"Steve, I don't know what the hell this is," she said as soon as I picked up the phone. "What's Alex told you?"

"Just the tree, the wound, the lack of blood, the contents of the wallet and the apparent name of the victim."

"Not apparent anymore," Selena said. "Forensics made the official ID just an hour ago."

I let out a long sigh.

"I heard about the case and the trial," Selena said, somewhat unnecessarily. Law enforcement in Upper Michigan keeps tabs on major felonies everywhere in the region. Every sheriff and deputy knew the fine details of the sexual assault charge, trial and release of the black man in Porcupine County.

"Hanging suggests a racial motive, a felony hate crime," I said. "But if it were a genuine lynching, the killing and the hanging would have been done at the same time, probably by a mob, wouldn't it?"

"No mob at the scene. We're still looking for evidence, but so far we've found only one set of shoe prints under the tree. Field & Stream field boots, size eleven medium. Gibbs was wearing Nike walkers and there are no prints from them, just drag marks. A single partial print made by a smooth-soled moccasin was found next to a bush several yards away, but it's anybody's guess when it was made. It could have been earlier or later. Impossible to tell what size it was."

"Field & Streams, eh?" I said. "That narrows the list of suspects to about, what, twenty-five thousand?" Field & Stream is one of the most common brands of work and hunting boots in the north country. "If we find the owner of those boots, maybe we've got the killer."

"Maybe not," Selena said. "Maybe just the hangman."

"You think more than one person is involved?" I said.

"Who knows?" Selena has never been known to jump to a conclusion.

"Size eleven?"

"Fairly big guy, huh?"

"Anything else?" I said.

"We found a buckshot pellet embedded in the back of Gibbs' leather belt," Selena said. "From the size of the entry wound between the shoulder blades and the slight specking of burnt powder it appears that someone fired at least two loads of Double-Oh from not more than ten feet away. Probably twelve gauge."

"Murder in the first degree," I said. "That was no accident."

"Obviously," Selena said, but she was not being ironic.

"Is that it?"

"No," said Selena. "There was black stamp sand in Gibbs's pants cuffs. Forensics hasn't yet done an analysis, but one of my deputies says it looks like it comes from the beach just west of Houghton."

That stretch of the shoreline of Lake Superior is famous for the coarse sand, a byproduct of the ore stamping mill at the once booming village of Freda. The mill crushed trap rock separated from native copper dug up at mines near Painesdale in Houghton County in the nineteenth and early twentieth centuries. The mill closed in 1967 and Freda has all but dried up, as have so many former copper towns in the Upper Peninsula.

"What about the other black sand beaches?" I said. During the heyday of Upper Michigan's Copper Range, similar mills had operated on Keweenaw Bay just south of Houghton, a bit north of Baraga and on Torch Lake near Hubbell, all within nine miles of each other. They had also dumped ore stampings, often containing toxic chemicals, into the water.

"My deputy grew up near Freda and swears the sand is from there," Selena said. "Houghton LEOs have already started searching the lakefront and countryside near Freda, asking if anyone saw Gibbs there and when, and are looking for evidence of a shooting. They'll work their way south and east. It'll be a few days before forensics can confirm where the sand came from. No time to lose. Needle in a haystack, but we've got to do it."

"Yup." Sheriff Novikovich was doing exactly what Sheriff Martinez would have done.

"You got any usual suspects at your end of the Yoop?" Selena asked. "People who might have done it?"

"I can think of a few," I said. "Maybe more."

"You have much trouble with racists?" she said.

"Not really," I said. "We're pretty well behaved here. At least in that regard."

It was the answer she expected.

"It's all below the surface, eh?" she said. "Like in a mine."

"Yup."

"Hold on. The medical examiner's calling. He seems to have done the autopsy quickly."

I waited for a long moment. Finally Selena came back on the line.

"Holy shit," she said.

That was the third time that day I'd heard the phrase. That was not good.

"Hmm?" I said.

"Cause of death was strangulation, the med examiner says. Petechiae in the eyes and fluid in what remains of the lungs. The noose didn't break his hyoid. A length of twine did. Fragments of binder's twine are embedded in the skin of his neck."

"Holy shit," I said.

"Yes. Gibbs was killed *before* he was shot and hanged. Examiner says the gunshots came within seconds after the strangling. The arteries were still pumping."

"But why?"

"God knows. Somebody really had it in for this

12

guy."

"It *could* be a lynching," I said. "All that violent stuff fits the historical pattern." Over the centuries, unreasoning rage has driven people to extremes in killing their enemies, real or perceived. They have shot, stabbed, hanged, beheaded, burned and dismembered their victims, scattering the limbs to the four corners.

"Or not," Selena said.

"Any defensive wounds?" Victims often fight back, bruising their knuckles and tearing their fingernails.

"None at all. Just rope burns on his wrists. Clothesline, it looks like."

"He could have known his killer," I said.

"Or killers."

"There's those bootprints. Could one person have done all this? Gibbs was no wimp. He was strong and athletic. If it really were just one person, then maybe Gibbs knew him and let down his guard and was taken by surprise."

"You got something there."

For a few moments we poked and prodded our thoughts, trying to make sense of what we knew and needed to know. Then Selena spoke.

"I'm thinking the strangling and the shooting were done in a blind rage, but the hanging was a deliberate and considered act that took place some time afterward. Maybe it meant the killer *wanted* us to think his motive was racial. Maybe it really wasn't, that he was covering up something else."

"Yes," I said. "But."

"But what?"

"Billy Gibbs was a black man in white country. He was accused of raping a white woman and was found not guilty. That's reason enough for plenty of people in Porcupine County and elsewhere to want him dead."

Selena fell silent. "There's that," she finally said.

13

"Oh, Jesus. This is giving me a headache."

"We'll do our best," I said, meaning her fellow policemen and women from all over the Upper Peninsula. Sheriffs, deputies, state troopers, tribal officers, conservation officers, even Forest Service and state park rangers. We all lent our aid, especially when everybody was short-staffed and needed help in major cases.

"I'm hoping the killing went down outside Mackinac County," she said. "That would make it somebody else's problem and I can stay the hell out of it and go back to doing my usual job. That's hard enough."

Yet Selena, I knew, would be there for me, loaded for bear, if Billy Gibbs had been murdered in Porcupine County. And if he had, I would need help. Lots of it. Because it seemed to me that there was a better than even chance that the motive for murder had been racial.

"Got your back," I said. "I'll get cracking right now."

"Thanks," she said, and we hung up.

TWO

OVER THE TWENTY years of my law enforcement career, it has been obvious to me that most Porcupine Countians would be astonished, and even angered, if it were suggested that they harbored racism in their hearts.

"There's no racism in Porcupine County," a surprisingly clueless professor from a third-rate university once declared all down my shirt front at a cocktail party, barely missing me with the olive from his martini, "precisely because there's no diversity."

He was right about the last part of that sentence. For several censuses the county consistently has been ninety-seven per cent white, and also is about that proportion Christian, much of it evangelical. Because of that the county has been well insulated from the racial unrest that has overtaken much of the rest of the country, especially the big cities. My department, unsurprisingly, has never been charged with misconduct against racial minorities. There simply are none in Porcupine County. Almost.

"Indeed?" I said to the professor all the same. I'm a full-blooded Lakota born on the Pine Ridge rez in South Dakota, as black-haired and mahogany-skinned an Indian as you can get. The professor did not even blink at the irony, so fuddled was he by his self-inflicted ignorance.

Growing up in a nearly utterly white community doesn't necessarily foster overt hate, but it does tend to result in lack of knowledge and experience about people of different colors, creeds, and cultures, especially when a resident of that community never travels outside it.

Not long before Selena called me, a personable young man from Porcupine County had asked me for a recommendation for a civilian job with the state police in Lansing. He was a hard worker and had done well at Gogebic Community College in the neighboring county to the south and west of my jurisdiction, and had both the skills and the personality to start work on the reception desk at state police headquarters. I was happy to give him the recommendation, delighted that he was invited downstate for an interview, and surprised that he didn't get the job.

"They wouldn't tell me why," he said. "Everything was going well but they stopped the interview after only an hour. Later in the afternoon they told me the job had been filled and wished me the best of luck."

Something, I thought, had gone wrong. I called the state police personnel director, an old acquaintance who now and then called to offer me a job as a trooper, and asked what had happened.

"He aced the aptitude and psych tests and charmed everybody. Then we got to one of the last questions in the interview. It was 'You will be encountering, working with and helping people of all races and religions all day long. How do you feel about that?'

"And his answer was, 'I don't have anything against colored people.'

"We were appalled. And disappointed. We really liked him."

"If he had only said 'people of color,' " I said.

"Yes. His heart was in the right place, but he was just too green. We just couldn't take the risk of him saying the wrong thing at the worst possible moment in a police facility."

These days, I reflected, you must not only walk the walk but also talk the talk.

On another occasion, a worldly Methodist pastor further illuminated the issue late one night in his parsonage. "Porcupine County has one extended Japanese family and a couple of Ojibwas who have been here for generations," he said. "They're a familiar part of the local furniture. Some of them have married whites. They're accepted. But nobody knows their stories."

"The prejudice of ignorance," I said.

"Pretty much," said the pastor. "Of course people have heard the news about Detroit and Ferguson and Baltimore, and some have lived for a while in the Deep South and soaked up old segregationist attitudes. But without close neighbors who are appreciably different from them, they just don't think much about the subject from day to day. Sometimes they do, if it's splashed around the broadcast media. There are a lot of right-wing talk radio fans up here in the U.P. who use dog-whistle racial code in their conversations such as 'welfare,' 'taking from the few to give to the many,' 'Kenyan,' 'Muslim,' 'illegals' and 'that man in the White House.' They get riled easily, and reduce people who are not like them to cartoonish stereotypes. They are especially noisy about the possible federal resettlement of Muslim refugees in the area, going on and on about Sharia law. They lack empathy simply because they lack experience. These people are not always aware of their biases, but those on the receiving end most assuredly are."

Part of the problem is that Porcupine County is aging as fast as the population is disappearing. The median age is fifty-three. The paper industry has vanished and mining is all but dead, despite struggles to reopen old sources of ore. Most of the people remaining are still processing their grief, refusing to accept the reality that things will never be the same. Should they keep their roots deep or pull them up to replant in more fertile fields? Young families increasingly are leaving for where the jobs

are, most recently the once booming oil fields of North
Dakota. True, many of their elders who grew up in this
beautiful semi-wilderness and quickly headed for the
bright lights are increasingly coming home to retire,
bringing in some fresh views, but in the main, old attitudes
hang on, unleavened by those of youth.

A year or so ago, my department fielded a flurry of
phone calls from Porcupine County citizens worried
because three young men had come to their doorstep with
clipboards, asking if they'd be interested in subscribing to
a new cable television venture in Porcupine County.
"They're all *black*," the callers said. "Maybe they're trying
to find out what we've got in our houses."

"Did they have identification?" we asked.

"Yes," the callers said. "But, you know, it could be
fake."

"We'll check it out," we said, "but we doubt very
much that anybody's casing the joint."

A short phone call to the cable company established
the young men's bona fides, and from then on we
reassured further callers that they had nothing to worry
about.

So far as racism is concerned, the practical truth is
that most Porkies are no more—and no less—bigoted than
those who live anywhere else in America. Like most of
their apparently enlightened countrymen, they don't wear
hate on their sleeves. They profess love for everyone. And
most of the time they get along with everybody.

But when they are goaded, cracks often appear in
their smiling walls of benevolence. In a place where
unemployment is high and money is tight, wounded white
male pride and nostalgia for the mythical good old days
often leads to racial grievance. In the living rooms of my
constituency, as well as its cafes and taverns, I have heard
plenty of hateful remarks about African Americans, Native
Americans, Mexicans, Jews, Muslims, Arabs and Asians—

even from the most upstanding citizens of the county.

Wealthy summer people, too. At one gathering in a lakefront log mansion, I listened as the talk turned to sensational revelations of Latinos suffering in semi-slavery on Florida cane plantations, and the hostess squelched the conversation with an airy "Oh, they don't matter. They're only Mexicans." It was all I could do not to throw my glass of wine in her face and stalk out of the party.

Still, Porkies are not Klansmen. They clean up too well for that. They do not wear white sheets and march with torches. True, there are noisy poor white supremacists in Porcupine County, but thankfully there have been few of them. No organized militias have cropped up here so far, although perhaps half a dozen backwoods families are known to be chummy with neo-Nazi and skinhead groups downstate and in Wisconsin. In the main I have not worried overmuch about them, although I have kept an eye on their antics with the help of friends at the Southern Poverty Law Center, the national clearinghouse of information about hate groups, and will investigate suspicious activity.

I think about racism not only because I am a cop and naturally worry about it, but also because I am a member of a minority group that historically has suffered a lot of it. Maybe that makes me oversensitive, as my lady love Virginia Anttila Fitzgerald thinks. Ginny is a gorgeous redhead of Finnish extraction, as fair-skinned as I am dark-hided. Like Sergeant Alex Kohlemainen, who never misses a chance to crack an airy joke about my Indian-ness, she thinks I get too prickly when people bring up my Lakota heritage for no good reason at all.

As when a blue-haired tourist at the historical museum where Ginny presides gushed, "Oh, are you the Native American sheriff?"

"The *Porcupine County* sheriff," I said, as gently as I could, but I couldn't keep a slight edge out of my voice. It wasn't about the term "Native American," an academic coinage that once annoyed most Indians but now has become so common it's accepted with a shrug. It was about being pigeonholed by race.

Quickly she said, "Oh, I'm sorry, I didn't mean—"

"It's all right, ma'am," I said. "No offense taken."

I felt guilty for embarrassing her and covered by taking her by the elbow and ushering her to a display case where I spent the next few minutes telling her about the antique Fresnel lens from the old lighthouse that had guided sailors into Porcupine City harbor a century ago. I probably went into far too much detail, but she gamely pretended to be fascinated.

"Are you a *real* Indian?" small children will often ask, but it is of course impossible to bristle at youthful blue-eyed innocence. I'll just lean over and whisper with a wink, "Yes, but I left my tomahawk on my pony." They dissolve in glee.

When I tell Ginny about these encounters—what good is a girl friend if you can't unload upon her?—she just pats my hand and gives me a hug. "People are people and you can't control what goes through their minds," she will say, quite reasonably. Now and then she adds with a sly wink, "I hear Indians make the best bedmates," and leads me by the hand up to her four-poster. Who can take umbrage with that?

On the other hand—there is always an "on the other hand" when discussing social issues—there also are strong countervailing undercurrents in Porcupine County. Many if not most Porkies may at first look askance at groups whose skins and religions are different from theirs, but they also have long been willing to give individuals a chance to prove themselves. Performance often trumps prejudice. I myself have been the beneficiary of that trait. They've elected a Native American—me—to office three consecutive times, the last two unchallenged.

What's more, enough Porkies take such deep pride in keeping open minds and considering all the facts that juries of reasonable men and women can be convened in both civil and criminal cases of great racial sensitivity. Such a jury had passed judgment on Billy Gibbs. And it was all white.

THREE

BILLY GIBBS HAD been a transplanted Porky for a year before we met. People often talked about him. Everyone knew that Frank Czecko, owner of the county's biggest trucking company and a champion of employing recently returned veterans, had hired him right out of the army Ordnance Corps at Fort Lee in Virginia as the war in Afghanistan began to wind down. Soon Gibbs owned an enviable reputation as a gifted mechanic who could also decode and program automotive computers. Everybody knew who he was.

He was the only black guy in town and he was also a wizard with a wrench. He lived alone, in a furnished rented double-wide on U.S. 45 south of town, but was a familiar figure after work in the county's cafes and bars. He cheered at schoolboy hockey games and flipped burgers at fund-raisers like any other member of the community. He had arrived in town in a brand-new and loaded Ford Super Crew Cab pickup that must have cost upwards of seventy thousand dollars, and as he settled in often bought drinks for the house. He was generous with both his free time and his money, donating both labor and cash to community organizations, and he made friends easily among both men and women.

In his late twenties he was tall, lean, athletic and handsome, with a shaven head and a striking resemblance to Michael Jordan. From time to time he was seen in the company of adoring young women—yes, all of them white, but that's the only color we have—and among the men about town there were envious rumors of two-legged cougars prowling around his place. Joe Koski, my corrections officer, chief dispatcher, town gossip and one-man intelligence service, said he had heard that shortly after his arrival Gibbs had been propositioned in a bar by a couple of wealthy swingers, Milwaukeeans with a summer house on the beach. Many horny young Porkies would have jumped at the chance to make group whoopee, but Gibbs wasn't going to be anybody's Mandingo notch on the bedpost. If that was true, I had thought, the young man had both sense and dignity.

He was just beginning to be known familiarly as "Billy Gibbs" instead of "the black guy" when he briefly became a guest in my jail.

Late one January night Chad Garrow, my large and capable No. 1 field deputy, had gone off duty and was destroying a three-quarter-pound Superburger with fries at Maxie's Grill and Tavern on River Street when he heard two patrons down the bar engaging in an altercation. They were Ralph Michael and Billy Gibbs, and of course they'd had way too many beers.

Ralph, who worked close alongside Billy in the Czecko garage, had been expounding noisily upon the urban blight in Detroit, his home town, which led to a different but related topic, and Chad just heard Ralph say something about "welfare queens" when Billy snarled "Why don't you go get a nice glass of shut the fuck up?" and kicked aside his stool. He unleashed a roundhouse right that missed, sending him into an untidy clinch with Ralph. Swiftly Chad moved in and with two massive hands pried apart the pair, gripping each by his collar, before they could do damage to each other or the furniture.

At the sheriff's department that night I was sitting in for Joe Koski while he took a day off. We are chronically shorthanded and I often have to fill in for my deputies. My chess game in the squad room with Freddie Fitzpatrick, a regular lodger and our favorite trusty, suddenly was

23

disturbed when the front door flew open, letting in a gale of snow, and with massive paws in the two drunken mechanics' collars Chad escorted them down the hall and into a pair of cells.

"Are they under arrest?" I said.

"No," Chad said. "Just a sleepover."

Prosecuting a drunk-and-disorderly usually costs more than the fine the county takes in, then there is the time-consuming paperwork to fill out and file, doubly annoying when we're so shorthanded. If neither property nor person has been harmed, there is no official complaint, and if the miscreants are first-time offenders or otherwise generally behave when sober, we'll just let them sleep it off and send them on their way in the morning. A titanic hangover is usually punishment enough, but sometimes we have heart-to-hearts with our guests, especially if they're young and, we hope, impressionable. At any age they usually aren't. Porkies are nothing if not hard-headed.

Late in the morning I opened the door to Gibbs' cell. It wasn't locked. He was sleeping quietly on his back, mouth closed, hands on his chest. They were striking hands, large but not coarse, the fingers long and graceful, their nails clean and closely trimmed. I could imagine them coiled around either a cylinder of greased steel or the neck of a violin. If he was not yet a man of parts, the raw material seemed to be there.

I coughed discreetly and Gibbs' eyes slowly opened.

"How're you feeling?" I asked as he struggled to sit up on the bunk, shading his eyes against the morning sunlight streaming through the barred windows. I handed him a foam cup of coffee. We don't use crockery in the jail. Crockery can be fashioned into weapons.

"Shitty," he said, but he took the cup.

"Quite a toot last night. Do you know why you're here?"

"Kind of."

"Billy, I'm sorry," said the inhabitant of the next
cell. "I shouldn't of . . ."

Gibbs didn't turn around, but said calmly, "Forget
it, Ralph."

He gazed up at me through bloodshot eyes and
sighed. *You know how it is,* his eyes said. *You're also a drop of
color in an ocean of white.*

"Clean yourself up," I told Gibbs, "and stop by the
kitchen on your way out. Ralph, you're free to go, too.
Neither one of you is going to be charged."

"Thanks, Sheriff," Ralph said. "Appreciate the
hospitality."

"Don't abuse it," I said. "We don't care for repeat
guests."

"Yes sir," he said, and was gone, no doubt in search
of a bottle of aspirin.

In a few minutes Gibbs knocked on the jamb of the
open door to the kitchen, which served as our
interrogation chamber as well as lunch and break room.
Our jail is small and cramped, and we have to make do. I
sat at the cracked linoleum table, nursing a coffee in an
equally lumpy mug.

He looked better, though his eyes were still red and
his clothes rumpled.

"You wanted to see me?" he said.

"Yes, have a seat. More coffee?"

He took both.

"I'm curious about you," I said, leaning my chair
back against the refrigerator, "just for personal reasons, not
official ones. You don't have to answer if you don't want
to. This is a conversation, not an interrogation."

"Yeah?" Gibbs said. "What do you want to know?"

"For starters, where are you from?"

"Chicago. Born and raised on the South Side. Went
into the army right out of high school. You?"

That answer, I could see, was not defensive, as

25

THE RIDDLE OF BILLY GIBBS

answers at this particular table tended to be. Nor was it challenging. Rather, it felt like a subtle declaration of equality. If I was curious about Gibbs, he was about me, too. That was fine with me.

"Born on the Lakota reservation at Pine Ridge, South Dakota," I said. "Adopted as a baby and brought up in Upper New York State." I didn't offer the added history that my adoptive parents were whites and brought me up as one of them. That could come later.

"I've heard about that," Gibbs said. My personal history is no secret.

"How'd you end up here in Porcupine County?" I said. "We don't see many black people, let alone Indians like me."

It was an open and frank question, and Gibbs chose to answer it openly and frankly. A subtle us-against-them appeal often loosens reluctant tongues.

"I was in the Ordnance Corps down in Fort Lee, Virginia," he said in a soft and calm baritone. His voice had emerged from its shaky hangover. "My unit had rotated home from Afghanistan and I wanted to get out of the army. I'd seen and heard enough IEDs and what they did to soldiers and machinery. There was an ad on the bulletin board of the company mess hall. It was from Frank Czecko. He was looking for mechanics and offered pretty fair pay. I called the number and, to make a long story short, six weeks later I arrived."

I leaned back in my chair and chuckled. "I did the same thing at Fort Leonard Wood," I said. "Down to the ad on the bulletin board, no less."

Almost a quarter of a century ago Operation Desert Storm had ended and my army military police unit had returned from Kuwait, where it had been herding Iraqi prisoners of war. I had received a Dear John letter and in unthinking despair grabbed the first opportunity that came down the pike. It was for a poorly paid deputy's job out in

the middle of nowhere, hardly suitable for a first
lieutenant not long out of Cornell ROTC and City
University of New York criminal justice school.

"I was young and foolish," I said. "But I have no
regrets, none at all. I've come to love this place. Maybe you
will, too."

"Maybe," Gibbs said. He did not sound either
doubtful or hopeful. He was keeping an open mind, I
thought.

"Now why would *you* want to take a job in the
middle of the biggest nowhere?" I said. "Of all the places
in the world where you could have ended up, why
Porcupine County?"

"Good question," Gibbs said. "I needed a change. A
real change."

"All right," I said. "How're they treating you? Other
than last night."

"Okay," he said, "for the only black guy in town."

"What did Ralph say?"

"He called my mama a name. He was drunk as hell.
Didn't know what he was saying. But nobody calls my
mama names."

I wasn't going to ask what the name was. It didn't
matter. If Gibbs wasn't going to be specific, that meant he
wasn't going to hold a grudge.

"Ralph's not a bad guy, is he?"

"No, no. We get along. On the job and off."

"I understand you're very good at what you do," I
said. "That counts for something, doesn't it, with the
people in town?"

"I guess. Yeah, it seems to."

"One thing I've noticed about the white folks of
Porcupine County," I said, "is that they respect hard work
and a good job done. I think that's how most of them look
at you. And me, for that matter."

It was Gibbs' turn to chuckle, and he did so,

27

although it probably made his head hurt all the more. "Yeah. Up to a point. But you have to *earn* the respect. They don't give it to you easily, the way they would if you were a white guy. You have to meet them more than halfway. You have to work hard for what oughta be yours from the beginning."

I knew what he meant and did not contest the notion. He gazed at me and laughed ruefully.

"The first day I arrived in Porcupine City," he said, "I stopped at Frank's Supermarket for some groceries and a checker came up to me and whispered so nobody else could hear that I was in the wrong line for food stamps."

"She was just trying to be kind," I said. "She didn't want you to be embarrassed. Food stamps are a stigma. Some of Frank's checkers also try to protect the feelings of poor white folks who need them, and there are a lot of those in this county. There but for the grace of God, et cetera."

"So it goes," Gibbs said, but without rancor.

"Yeah," I said. "Even now some folks will ask if I carry a medicine bag."

"Don't you?" Gibbs said with a sly grin. "I thought all of you *nay-teeve A-murr-i-kins* did."

I smiled back. The polite term makes many Indians laugh, because it is so patronizing. Liberal white folks who use it can be both well-meaning and clueless.

Gibbs' expression darkened. "It's not always funny. When I'm out with a white girl, I can feel the hard looks. Nobody's said anything yet, but somebody's bound to."

Even at this late date in history, something atavistic rises in the hearts of even the most liberal and educated white citizens at the specter of black sexuality. But they have the sense to keep quiet and sometimes have the grace to be ashamed of their thoughts. The poor, the uneducated and the unemployed — and there are unfortunately lots of those in Porcupine County — don't always suppress their resentment at outside competitors for women and jobs, and throughout American history black men have always been easy targets for their anger. I was surprised that Gibbs hadn't yet been challenged by a disgruntled backwoods lout. Or if he had, that I hadn't heard about it.

"You plan to stick around long?" I asked.

"For now," he said.

"Still giving it a go?"

"Yes. We'll see what happens."

I nodded, stood up and extended my hand. "Got to go do some sheriffing," I said. "I'll see you around. I hope things work out for you." *For both of us,* I thought.

"Me too," Gibbs said, and was gone.

"Who was that?" growled a voice from the office next to mine. It belonged to Gil O'Brien, my crusty undersheriff and the longest-serving employee of the Porcupine County Sheriff's Department. Gil, a former army drill instructor, is getting on in years, rarely goes outside the office even though he is an expert crime-scene director, and is a bit of a martinet with the deputies. Still, I am happy that the leathery old lawman runs the place. He is a first-class administrator and a wizard at prying loose dollars and equipment from the federal and state grant bureaucracies. We need them.

"Just a couple of overnight visitors," I said.

"Did they have breakfast?" Gil said.

"No."

"Good."

"Why?" I knew the answer and Gil knew I knew, but he said it anyway.

"We can't afford it."

"Right." Each meal for inmates is catered at Merle's, the town's leading café and vendor for the jail's population. We don't serve our guests Cordon Bleu cuisine, but we don't give them kitchen slops either. Maintaining humane conditions costs money, and Gil watches every nickel.

FOUR

ONE BRIGHT MONDAY morning in late May, Deena Stenfors called the sheriff's department.

We all knew Deena. She was a sophomore at Michigan Tech University in Houghton, an hour to the east, and worked two half-time summer jobs — one of them waiting tables at George's Supper Club in a chain motel at Silverton thirteen miles west of Porcupine City, and the other as a housekeeping maid at the motel. She had a reputation as a hard, willing worker, and restaurant patrons liked her outgoing personality. Whenever Ginny and I dined at George's and Deena was our server, we exchanged pleasantries just to bask in her sunshine, often asking her about her studies, which she loved. She was a good kid, as we call our young people who manage to stay out of trouble and try to make something of themselves. She also had the blonde good looks of her Swedish forebears, though the years had yet to shape her still soft blue-eyed features.

"I've been raped," she announced to Sheila Bowers, the department's office manager. Sheila had done such a good job as our only secretary, or rather administrative assistant as she insists on being called, that I'd talked the county commissioners into giving her a ten-dollar-a-week raise and a new title. She deserved ten times that, but even ten dollars was a stretch for the county budget.

Sheila immediately and expertly set things into motion.

"Are you all right?" she asked Deena. "Any

injuries? Are you being threatened?" At the same time, she threw a tennis ball into my office, where it bounced off the wall and captured my attention. Sheila often does that when she wants me to pick up my extension and listen without alerting the caller that I'm there. Gil, that stickler for decorum, hates the act but doesn't want to pay the extra money for an extension with a flashing lamp bright enough to catch my eye.

"No," Deena said. "I'm okay." I could hear the tension in her voice. She had not wanted to make this call.

"When did it happen?" Sheila asked.

"Saturday night."

That meant thirty-six hours had passed since the event, almost too long for sufficient evidence to have survived. No time was to be lost.

"Deena, we can offer you a medical examination for sexual assault," Sheila said. "It won't cost you anything. It's your decision. But if you choose to have the exam, we've got to get you to the hospital in Baraga right away."

Porcupine City has a hospital with a first-rate emergency room, but it has no qualified SANE, or Sexual Assault Nurse Examiner, a registered nurse trained in forensic exams of rape victims. Baraga Hospital, forty-five minutes east, does.

"Okay," Deena said in a frightened voice.

I placed my palm over the mouthpiece. "Send her with Annie," I said.

"Where are you?" Sheila asked Deena.

"Jenny's," she said. Jenny's is a coffee shop on the corner of River Street, the main drag, and U.S. 45, the major highway into town from the south. "I couldn't call from home. My car's parked outside."

"How old are you?"

"Nineteen." That meant we would not need to get permission from her parents for the examination. Eighteen is the age of consent for medical care in Michigan.

32

"We're sending Deputy Annie Corbett over right now," Sheila said. "She'll drive you to Baraga. Leave your car at Jenny's and Deputy Corbett will return you there."

I stepped into the squad room and quickly enlightened Annie. Our most recent hire, she had just passed the twelve-month deputy's probationary period with flying colors. Short, brunette and slightly chubby, she is still remarkably fit, working out for an hour every morning at the fitness center in town. She is not only strong, but also serious, capable and a quick study. Having come directly to the department from graduation at Michigan Tech, she was only three years older than Deena but probably light-years ahead in maturity. She had studied chapter and verse of the sexual assault procedure, but I chose to repeat the key points.

"Don't talk to her about the case on the way over," I said, quite needlessly for Annie but mostly for my own benefit. After all, it was her first rape case and I wanted to make sure she followed the book. "Just tell her what to expect in the hospital and, before asking if she wants to proceed with a complaint, wait until the exam's over and she's decided what to do. Take my Jeep."

"Will do, Steve," Annie said. She knew that a civilian vehicle would attract less attention from bystanders than one of the department's official Ford Expeditions. We try to give rape victims as much privacy as possible. And we needed to find out the physical facts before asking Deena if she wanted to file a complaint. Until then, we wouldn't ask who had committed the assault, if indeed an assault had taken place.

I called Dave Manning, my counterpart in Baraga County, and let him know as a matter of routine that one of my deputies was going to be working in his jurisdiction in a rape case. As a matter of routine he said fine, and to let him know if he could help.

For the first twenty minutes of the ride to Baraga, Annie told me later, Deena sat silent, sometimes weeping, sometimes twisting a handkerchief. When Deena suddenly said angrily, "He didn't even . . . !" Annie replied, "I think it'd be better for you not to tell me anything at this stage. You can tell the nurse everything, and then later, if you want, we can talk about it."

Annie had made a tactical decision. Many police officers wouldn't cut off a witness' spontaneous statement that way, but she wanted to keep Deena focused on the events that shortly were to follow. She knew Deena was going to have to tell her story more than once. The young woman settled down and remained quiet all the rest of the way to the hospital.

The nurse examiner, Nicole Weber, a veteran at her calling, was waiting at the entrance as the young woman and the deputy arrived, and quickly ushered them into an examination room. As soon as the door closed, Annie turned to Deena and said, "Do you want me to come in with you? I can wait outside instead."

Annie wanted Deena to feel that she had some control over what was happening — that she was being helped, not pushed around, by the law. The young woman hesitated for only a moment and said, "It's okay. I'll be okay."

"Fine," Annie said. "I'll be here when you come out. Nicole will take care of you. Do answer her questions. Tell her everything."

Deena nodded and Annie left the room. She knew the procedure would take at least an hour, maybe more. First Nicole would take a complete medical history, asking about things like allergies, immunizations, past medical procedures and medications, whether she had any STDs — the standard questions any new patient is asked. She would ask Deena if she had showered since the event, douched, or changed clothes. Then she would do a pelvic exam, using swabs, a comb, and a camera to gather evidence and placing whatever she found into jars and glassine envelopes for later forensic analysis and matching with whatever evidence, if any, was found on the scene. After that she would offer Deena whatever treatment the examination suggested, including day-after contraception.

Finally she would discuss Deena's options. She could choose to do nothing, and the incident would be closed and forgotten unless at some time in the future she wanted charges to be brought. She had at least twelve years to do so. If the charge was the lowest, third degree sexual assault, the statute of limitations was ten years after the victim turns twenty-one. For first degree rape there is no statute of limitations in Michigan.

She could choose to wait until the results of the analysis came back from the lab in about thirty days. Waiting would mean a better idea of the possible outcome of a complaint. Waiting, however, might also mean that outside evidence — things still remaining at the scene of the event — could disappear. Witnesses could vanish. So could the rapist.

Or Deena could choose to file a criminal complaint immediately and start things in motion. It was her choice, and her choice alone.

Deena looked pale and shaky, Annie said, when she and the nurse emerged from the examination room. They went to a bank of vending machines where the nurse treated the young woman to a bottle of lemonade and a candy bar.

Then Deena turned to Annie. "I want to prosecute," she said firmly, head high, gazing directly into the deputy's eyes.

"Very well," Annie said, and glanced at Nurse Weber, who returned to the room and emerged with a box containing the rape kit.

"Sign here, Deputy," the nurse said, "and I'll drive

it right to the crime lab and ask for a quick turnaround. We'll preserve the chain of evidence."

The nurse said nothing else, but Annie shot her a questioning look.

Nurse Weber returned her gaze and nodded, as if to say, "Run with it."

As soon as Annie and Deena pulled away from the hospital building, Deena said, "Do I tell you what happened?"

"Yes," Annie said, "but let's wait until we get to the sheriff's department so you only have to tell me the story once."

"Okay," Deena said.

Annie glanced over at her. Deena seemed to have collected her wits and was gazing calmly out the window at the passing countryside, as if her ordeal were finally over and she could enjoy life again. Annie knew that Deena's troubles were only beginning.

She remained calm and even pointed and laughed when the Jeep sped past a meadow full of sandhill cranes clumsily pecking for insects under freshly mowed hay. Then, as they approached the outskirts of Porcupine City, her eyes began to puddle and her chest heaved with sobs.

When Annie and Deena pulled up in the department's little parking area, I met them at the door.

"You're safe with us, Deena,' I said, ushering them to the kitchen. "Coffee? Coke? Water?"

When everyone was settled around the table I said, "Deena, Deputy Corbett will be here with you while you tell us the story. Tell us everything you remember. Don't leave anything out. Every detail is important. If you forget something and remember it later, that's fine. Just do your best, and we'll do our best, too."

I reached across and squeezed her hand. I intended the human touch not only to relax her, to give her

THE RIDDLE OF BILLY GIBBS

confidence, but also to let her know that we were on her side, that we cared. Trust builds truth.

"We're going to record the interview. If anything isn't quite right we can always go back and fix the transcript and add details to it if necessary." Normally the investigating officer just takes notes, to which prosecutors and defense attorneys both have access during the pretrial discovery process. Given the importance of this case, which I thought could blow the roof off Porcupine County when the story got out, I wanted every detail to be taken down. This wasn't just to thwart possible charges of sloppy police work. I knew Deena's life was going to be upended and wanted to protect her from unfounded rumor. The truth would be hard enough.

Deena nodded and I went to my office, where Sheila was waiting. She turned on the speaker connected to the microphone in the kitchen. We'd hear everything Deena and Annie said. Sheila would type up the tape transcript later, but I wanted her to hear everything as it unfolded.

"It was Billy Gibbs," Deena said almost as soon as the kitchen door closed. She loosed a ragged sigh.

"Are you certain?" Annie said.

A moment of silence, then Annie said, "You nodded. I'll take that as a yes."

"Yes," Deena said.

"You might as well begin at the beginning," Annie said. "That might make it easier to remember things."

"Last Saturday night," Deena said, "my friend Mary O'Rourke and I went to Hobbs' Bar. There was a party going on for somebody from Czecko Trucking who was moving to North Dakota."

"Who was that?" Annie said.

"Ralph Michael."

"He was there?"

"Yes."

"Anyone else you know?"

"Lots." Porcupine City is a small town, after all. And there would be plenty of witnesses.

"Go on," Annie said.

"Ralph was sitting with Billy Gibbs. They were doing shots, having a good time. The music was loud."

"You knew them both?" Annie asked.

"Oh, yes. Everyone does. Billy was buying for everybody, the way he always does. He said he'd had some good luck."

"What kind?" Annie said.

"He didn't say."

"What happened then?"

Flirting started, as always happens when young people party, and soon everyone was enjoying a good buzz. Music pounded and dancing started, the wild hormonal ritual of Saturday nights everywhere.

"We did D-Mac and Wu-Tang," Deena said, "and then somebody put on 'Get Ur Freak On,' and we were all grinding. I was grinding with Ralph, and then with Billy."

I looked over at Sheila and raised an eyebrow. Neither of us had ever heard of the first two dances, but we knew all about the grind. Its chief move was rubbing of female buttocks against male crotch. The kids said it was like having sex standing up with your clothes on, and in the past the dance had been major fuel for brimstone in Porcupine County pulpits. Even though more than a decade had elapsed since it first appeared in the big cities in the early twenty-ohs, the grind was still popular among young people.

"We had a lot to drink," Deena said. "I really liked Billy. He made me feel like somebody. He asked me what I wanted to do after college."

"What did you say?" Annie said.

"That I wanted to go into the army, like Billy. He said he thought that would be a waste of time, that I ought to go to grad school of some kind and get out of here, go to

Chicago or something. He said he might move back there and we could live together. I thought he was just kidding."

Deena said that she could not remember what time it was when Billy whispered, "Let's blow this joint and go to my house."

"Did anyone see you leave?" Annie said.

"I don't know. Everybody was partying."

"Did you go in his car?"

"No. I followed him in mine."

"What happened then?"

"We got to Billy's. We sat on the couch in his living room and had some wine, listened to some music. Then we started making out."

Deena fell silent.

"Go on," Annie said quietly.

"Our clothes came off. We started touching each other. Do I have to say?"

"It would help. Just tell me what happened."

"He was touching me and I was touching him."

"How?" Annie was gentle but insistent.

"His fingers were in me and I was jacking him." Deena began to weep. "It wasn't my fault."

"No, it wasn't," Annie said.

"He pushed my head down on him. I started to, for a minute, but then I changed my mind. I said no, no, *no! Stop! Stop!* Then he pulled me over on his lap and he was in me. I kept saying *no, no, no,* but he kept going, and I was afraid he was going to hurt me. He was strong and grabbed my butt. I dug my nails in his shoulders but he wouldn't stop. Then he finished."

Deena sobbed uncontrollably for several seconds, then took a deep breath.

"We sat on the couch for a few minutes. I wanted to tell him thanks for raping me, but I was afraid he might do something. Finally I put my clothes on while he just sat there staring at me."

"What did he say?"

"I don't remember — oh, something like 'I thought we were having a good time.' "

"Did he seem upset?"

"Kind of."

"Did he use a condom?"

"No, I'm on the pill."

"Did you tell him that?"

"Yes. Back at Hobbs'. We were all talking about sex and I told everybody."

"Deena, why did you change your mind?" Annie said.

"I don't know. It just didn't seem right."

Annie did not press the question. The answer was irrelevant. It was the act, not the reason for it, that was important.

"What happened then?"

"I went out to my car and managed to drive to Ellie Holstein's house and asked if I could stay with her." Ellie was the same age and a practical nurse at the hospital.

"You didn't think about going home?"

"My father would have killed me. He still might."

"Do you have trouble at home?"

"Daddy hits me sometimes when he's mad and drinking."

"Deena, we want you to be safe," Annie said. "We want to put you in a place where nobody can get at you. Will you let us do that?"

"Yes."

"Okay, that's it for now," Annie said, and turned off the recorder.

I watched as my deputy and the young woman walked out to my Jeep and headed for Jenny's to pick up Deena's car, then drive in tandem to the women's shelter at Bruce Crossing in the southern part of the county. At any one time it housed half a dozen or so victims of domestic violence. The residents, I knew, would take Deena to their collective bosom and help her gain strength to face what was coming.

"Chad!" I called into the squad room. The big deputy jumped up from his desk and loomed in my office door. Quickly I filled him in on what had happened that morning.

"Go over to Czecko's garage and get Billy Gibbs. Tell him I want to talk to him about something. Try not to make an arrest. Keep it low and quiet if you can."

I should have instructed my deputy to do things by the book and slap the cuffs on him, even with everybody watching. But somehow I wanted to keep the lid on the pressure cooker I thought was about to explode and shower Porcupine County with an awful mess. I should have stayed detached, but sometimes I care too much.

FIVE

RIGHT AFTER CHAD left on his mission, I phoned Garner Armstrong, the county prosecutor.

"Garner, we've got a troublesome rape case on our hands. You'd better come over to the department."

"Why troublesome?"

"White woman, black man."

"Who?"

"Deena Stenfors, Billy Gibbs."

"Holy shit," Garner said. These days "holy shit" seems to have replaced "holy wah" as the standard Yooper exclamation when calamity comes to call.

"Yes. Chad's out bringing Gibbs in. You want to sit in on the interview?"

"Absolutely. I'll be right over."

Within five minutes Garner arrived—the county building lies less than a mile from the sheriff's department—and there was barely time for me to fill in the prosecutor on what Deena had told us before Chad shouldered open the squeaky front door and rolled in, Goibbs just behind him. Immediately we ushered Gibbs to a seat in the kitchen. I hung back to talk with Chad.

"No arrest," Chad said in a whisper. "I told Billy you wanted to see him about something, and he didn't even ask what it was. He just shook his head and said, 'I know what this is all about.' Right away he agreed to ride with me. No cuffs."

"Okay." Gibbs was being cooperative. Maybe he would keep on doing so.

42

Chad, Garner and I sat on three sides of the square kitchen table, with Gibbs on the fourth. The arrangement of four equal sides often relaxed suspects, as if it symbolized an evenhanded search for truth rather than a two-sided confrontation.

I switched on the recorder while Chad, whom I had designated as investigating officer, began the proceedings.

"Billy, we've asked you to come in because Deena Stenfors said you raped her Saturday night," Chad said. "You have the right to have a lawyer present before you answer questions."

That was true, but the Miranda warning was not required at this point in the interrogation, for Gibbs was not yet in official custody. I had asked Chad to gild the lily, not only to see how much Gibbs would cooperate but also ensuring that a defense lawyer could not claim that his client had been coerced. We sometimes did that to help fashion an airtight prosecution.

"Never mind that," Gibbs said calmly. "I didn't rape her. I don't need a lawyer."

"Are you sure?" Garner said.

"Yeah. Go on."

I couldn't tell if Gibbs' refusal of counsel was bravado or conviction. I think it's always stupid to refuse. Agreeing to answer police questions without a lawyer is like throwing oneself to the lions. In any case, at the arraignment the following morning Judge Rantala would assign a public defender to the case. I hoped Gibbs wouldn't turn his back on that, too.

"Well, then," Chad said, "please tell us what happened Saturday night."

"We were at Hobbs' Bar," Gibbs began, "having a sendoff party for Ralphie Michael."

Ralphie? I thought. *Looks like those fellows made their peace.*

"We were having a good time when about ten p.m.

43

a bunch of girls came in and joined the party. Deena Stenfors was with them. We all had some drinks together, talked for a while."

"What did you talk about?" Chad asked.

"The Lions, the Vikings and the Pack," Gibbs said. "Movies. Rockers. Sex. The usual."

"What did you talk about with Miss Stenfors?"

"I asked her what she wanted to do after she graduated. She said maybe the army."

That would not have been surprising—many Porky High seniors go directly into the services after graduating, partly to learn a useful trade and partly to put off inevitable civilian responsibilities—but those few lucky enough to get into and afford college generally have loftier goals.

"Why do you think she said that?" Chad said.

"I was in the army," Gibbs said. "A little hero-worship sucking-up, maybe. I don't really know. I didn't pursue it."

"Then what happened?"

"We did a few shots, then we started dancing. She's a pretty good dancer."

"Go on."

"After a while we were grinding. Know what that is?"

"Yes."

"Both of us were getting hornier and hornier, and I leaned over and said, 'Let's go to my house.' Her eyes opened wide and she gave me a big smile."

In their separate vehicles they drove the six miles out of town down U.S. 45 to Gibbs' double-wide, he said, and dashed inside gaily.

"Both of us had quite a buzz on," he said. "I put on some Ella and popped a bottle of chardonnay. After a while Deena snuggled up to me on the couch."

There was a long pause, during which all of us,

Gibbs included, recognized that he had just admitted to driving while intoxicated. But we were investigating something more serious.

"What happened then?"

"Pretty soon we were more comfortable."

"What do you mean by that?"

"You know." Clearly Gibbs was growing embarrassed with his own narrative.

"Please be specific."

"We were naked."

"Go on."

"One thing led to another, and then she was, uh, going down on me. She was really into it."

"Did you force her into that?"

"No, no, no. We were both getting frantic."

"Go on."

"Before I knew it she was on top of me and bucking wildly."

"Your penis was inside her vagina?"

"Yes. She was moaning and hooting and carrying on. She seemed to like it a little rough. She dug her fingernails into my shoulders."

Gibbs stood up, stripped off his T-shirt, and turned around. We could see deep indentations in the skin over his shoulder blades. One long shallow scratch ran down his back.

"Thank you," said Chad. "Please put your shirt back on."

Gibbs did so, then sat down.

"At any time during this event," Chad said, "did you hear her say 'no' or 'stop'?"

"Not at all."

"What did she say?"

"I don't really know. She was making jungle noises. And they call *us* jungle bunnies."

"Then what happened?"

"Then it was over and we were sitting side by side catching our breath."

For a long moment everyone sat silently, waiting for Gibbs to continue. Then he took a deep breath and said, "She started crying. I asked her what was wrong. She wouldn't say. Then she suddenly stood up and threw on her clothes. I kept saying 'What's the matter, baby? Tell me.' She wouldn't look at me. Then she was gone."

"Why do you think she did that?" Chad said.

Gibbs gazed mournfully at his hands in his lap. "I don't know. Maybe she realized that she had been fucked by a black man and was ashamed of it. I don't know."

"So her reaction was racial?"

"I don't know. Maybe. Lots of other girls have come to my place and this never happened before."

"Do you have anything else to say?" Chad asked.

"No. Can I have that lawyer now?"

Chad looked at me and at Garner. I nodded and we stood up. "Stay right here," I said. "We'll be back in a few minutes."

Chad, Garner and I went into my office, and I closed the door.

"Classic 'he said, she said,' " Garner said. "When the results of the rape kit come in I don't think we'll learn anything new. His DNA will be present, but he does not deny having had sex with Deena."

"He's convincing," I said. "But so is Deena."

"We'll leave it to a jury to decide," Garner said. "Jungle noises or not."

I thought that was the most logical move for us to make. Although all we had to go on was Deena's deposition, it was powerful evidence, enough to bring charges. Technically, not to act upon it would hardly be dereliction of office, but an election year was coming up. It wasn't just that the jobs of the present prosecutor and sheriff would be endangered if we chose to dismiss

---

46

Deena's story. It would also be that the case might occupy the minds of most Porkies to the detriment of all the other issues, especially the economic ones, that we faced.

I nodded. Chad nodded.

"We're agreed?" Garner said. "Criminal sexual conduct in the third degree, involving penetration, coercion and intoxication of the victim?" The charge was his decision as the prosecutor, but he believed in collegiality. So did we.

"Yup," Chad and I said in unison.

"Okay," Garner said, standing up. "Let's go."

Back in the kitchen we faced Gibbs.

"William Gibbs," Chad said in a stern voice, "you are under arrest for the criminal sexual assault of Deena Stenfors."

Quickly he turned Gibbs around by his shoulders and snapped on the cuffs. The act was not only symbolic—the event was happening in the sheriff's department—but an arrestee might bolt for the door.

"I was afraid of this," Gibbs said. He did not resist.

Chad had no reply to that, but began reading again from his Miranda card, just to be sure. "Do you understand your rights?"

"Yes," Gibbs said.

"You will be arraigned in county court tomorrow morning," Chad said. "If you have a lawyer, you may telephone him now. If you do not have a lawyer, you will be assigned one by the judge."

"I get a phone call?" Gibbs said calmly.

Michigan is not one of the few states that mandates arrestees' rights to phone calls. In practice we let them have any number of calls because that is the humane thing to do. Not only do they need a lawyer, they might need someone to pick up the kids at school or let loved ones know where they are. Phone calls, however, are a privilege, not a right, and if the arrestee becomes violent or antagonistic, we'll cut them off.

"Yes."

"May I?"

Chad handed Gibbs his cell phone.

"Ralphie?" Gibbs said when his party answered. "Take my truck home with you tonight. I'm at the sheriff's department. In jail. It's bullshit. No, it'll be a while."

He hung up and handed the phone back. Chad gently but firmly marched him to the lockup where his prints would be taken as well as a DNA swab of his cheek and photographs of the wounds on his back. The DNA would be compared not only to that collected by the rape kit, but also to that in the leavings from unsolved sexual assault cases. Serial rapists were sometimes identified that way, if state forensic labs did their job — and often they didn't, resulting in a huge backlog of cases. But I doubted that Billy Gibbs was a habitual offender.

As they left I turned to Garner.

"I need a warrant to search Gibbs' place," I said.

"I'll call the judge," Garner said. "It'll be just a few minutes."

Twenty minutes later I was on my way. I wanted to do the job myself because I knew that at the trial, Annie as one investigating officer would testify about what Deena had told her, and Chad as the other would be asked about Gibbs' story on the stand. It might help if each was clear on the facts as given by the interviewed party, without the story of the other muddying the water of what they knew that they had heard. I had heard both sides and just did not know which to believe.

At Gibbs' house I unlocked the front door with a key borrowed from his landlady and walked into his living room. A semi-shabby, corduroy-covered couch of indeterminate manufacture and a couple of old imitation teak tables occupied the tidily kept space. I stepped over to the couch. Its cushions bore several dried stains, probably semen. Slipping on latex gloves, I photographed the cushions *in situ* and stacked them by the door to take to the lab.

What interested me the most was the sound system. Bose home theater, Harmon Kardon turntable, tall Bang & Olufsen speakers in all corners of the room. Probably cost thousands of dollars. Except for his fancy truck and barroom generosity, Billy Gibbs had not seemed to live high on the hog, but this setup suggested a truck mechanic with a nice independent income. He could have saved his money in the army, or he could have inherited, or both. Or he could have had something on the side. I photographed the setup just in case.

Atop the turntable cover sat an old LP, Ella Fitzgerald's "Hello, Love," in what appeared to be its original jacket. It looked to be in great shape. A pair of white cotton archivist's gloves sat atop the jacket. Billy Gibbs took care of his toys. And so far his story was holding together.

I moved into the bedroom. Neat, freshly vacuumed, brushes and combs, electric razor and Dopp kit arranged in tidy rows on the dresser. Bed made with square military corners, no wrinkles in the spread. Bathroom the same, bottles lined up neatly in the medicine cabinet: Tums, aspirin, Right Guard, Benadryl tabs, Band-Aids, antibiotic ointment, razor and blades, and a small spray bottle of Deep Woods Off! No prescription drugs or suspicious pills.

In his mind, this guy was still in the army, though he had been out for a while. Uncle Sam teaches good habits, routines that are hard to shake until one settles down and relaxes a little. Former soldiers often never lose their reliance on military drill, and some of them, especially those suffering from PTSD, abuse others — including their families — just for not living up to the standard. I didn't think Gibbs was one of those. He had not been a combat soldier, although he had seen the bloody results of bombs and bullets and indeed risked them every time he set foot off his base.

No weapons were visible in the double-wide, but in one corner of a second and tiny bedroom stood an unlocked gun case. Another corner sheltered an almost brand new twenty-seven-inch iMac hooked to a DSL modem and a small laser printer. Billy Gibbs was well connected to the outside world.

I would have loved to learn what was on the computer, but the warrant — essentially a permit to search for evidence in a rape case — didn't allow me to snoop into its contents, so I left it alone. No gun had been cited by either party to the rape case, so the warrant did not allow me to take the contents of the gun case either. Only if the conditions of Gibbs' bail mandated that the guns be surrendered to the authorities would I be able to snap them up, and the arraignment and bail hearing wouldn't be until the next day.

I opened the gun case anyway. Inside lay a rifle and a shotgun, standard tools for every Porky hunter I had ever known. The rifle was a well-used but equally well-cared-for Winchester Model 70 .30-06, a standard deer gun everywhere in the nation, and the shotgun a Marlin twelve-gauge over-under, a favorite with upland bird hunters. Both were clean and oiled and did not smell if they had been fired recently. Nothing suspicious there.

At the bottom of the case sat a handgun, a familiar one to me: a nine-millimeter Beretta in a leather speed holster, both well kept and lubricated. There were no registration or purchase permits, but this was a rape case that did not involve firearms. Lack of documentation would be a comparatively minor technical infraction, especially if Gibbs produced or otherwise obtained the permits in the future. Michigan homes are full of undocumented guns that might have been handed down over the generations or bought at garage sales. They're impossible to keep track of.

The legend "M9" was engraved into the Beretta's slide, indicating that it had originally been a military pistol. By itself that meant nothing. Many surplus M9s had found their way into the civilian market. Most of these were so old and battered they were little more than loose and highly unreliable assemblages of parts. Gibbs' pistol, however, looked close to new. Maybe he had acquired the Beretta in the army and had taken it home, although military pistols are supposed to be logged in and out. The serial number might tell the truth, or it might not. Recordkeeping is often careless when the American military pulls out of a foreign theater. Although the warrant did not allow me to do so, I wrote down the number in a pocket-sized notebook I carry with me everywhere. Yes, a defense lawyer could demand that it be suppressed as evidence. But you never can tell when some tiny piece of information might lead to legally gathered evidence down the road.

As I left, I tacked up a few yards of yellow crime-scene tape over the doorway, legally sealing it from entry by persons unauthorized. I was beginning to think there was more to Billy Gibbs than being a mere truck mechanic.

When I got back to the department I asked Chad to check out his army record. Chad called the provost marshal's office at Fort Lee and found that Gibbs had been given a honorable discharge as a staff sergeant, military occupation specialty ninety-one-B, Wheeled Vehicle Mechanic. He had earned the usual theater decorations and had no black marks on his official record. That told me he had been a solid if unexceptional soldier.

SIX

THE NEXT MORNING Chad and I drove Gibbs to the courthouse for his arraignment. Normally arraignments were held in the kitchen of the jail via video links to a courtroom or judge's chambers, saving deputies time and the county money, but not on this occasion. The sensitivity of the case, we all agreed, demanded complete transparency, and so Gibbs would face the charges publicly.

Word of his arrest had leaked out by late evening the previous day, the bars and taverns rocked with shocked gossip, and I expected a crowd for the short perp walk from vehicle to courthouse door. A television crew from Marquette had set up shop on the sidewalk, but only about a dozen or so townspeople had gathered. They were more curious than they were angry, and their buzz fell silent as Gibbs walked past in cuffs and orange jail jumpsuit. As the TV reporter thrust her mike in front of my face, I shook my head and followed Chad and Gibbs inside.

Not that I had thought an angry mob with shotguns and a noose would greet us, but I was surprised at both the small size and restraint of the crowd. Its members actually were well behaved, even the town's noisiest right-wing religious scold, whose pulpit was the letters column of the Porcupine County Herald, which printed just about anything it was sent. His counterpart on the other side of the political spectrum, a fiery radical feminist and retired scholar of women's history, stood by demurely although she shot Gibbs an equally fierce look of hatred. Those two had made up their minds already.

Most of the onlookers managed to crowd into the courtroom, already nearly filled with the usual trial buffs, retirees with nothing else to occupy their time except to watch the fine grinding of the machinery of law. I suspect more than a few of them place small bets on the outcomes of the few civil cases that actually manage to go to trial. Most reach settlements in a short time. Porkies are thrifty with their litigation dollars.

Deena Stenfors was nowhere to be seen — she was keeping out of sight at the women's shelter — but her parents sat in the second row of benches. Her mother, Carla Stenfors, a shy, thin and washed-out woman, sat slumped and unmoving, eyes downcast, the picture of suppressed shame. Her father, Gene Stenfors, a ruddy, straw-haired man who always seemed angry, sat bolt upright and followed Gibbs with a stony glare as he was escorted into the courtroom.

The arraignment went as expected, a routine reading of the charge and appointment of counsel. That was Grady Craig, a veteran general-practice lawyer and a former assistant state's attorney from Peoria, Illinois. He entered a routine not-guilty plea on behalf of the defendant. To my surprise, Chief Circuit Judge Rantala announced that he was recusing himself because of his close friendship with the complainant's family, and that Probate Judge Andrea Cunningham, also a circuit judge who heard civil and criminal trials, would try the case instead. Judge Rantala stepped down and Andrea took the bench for the bail hearing.

She told Gibbs that if found guilty, he faced a fifteen-year prison sentence and registration as a sex offender with lifetime electronic monitoring. Garner offered a routine request for denial of bail because Gibbs might be a flight risk. Andrea said no, and set bail at fifty thousand dollars, ten per cent of which Gibbs would have to pay in cash for his get-out-of-jail card.

Lawyer and defendant conferred briefly, and Grady announced that Gibbs would waive his right to bail. That took me by surprise. In the Deep South not so long ago, a black man accused of raping a white woman would be far safer in jail than outside. At this time and in this place, however, a lynching was highly unlikely, although it would take only one armed and drunken meathead to ruin things for everybody. Maybe Gibbs had other reasons, but I was not going to ask about them. That was his lawyer's problem.

Andrea set a trial date for November 1, five months in the future, and the hearing was over.

Afterward we returned Gibbs to his cell and I sent Chad with a county crew to Gibbs's place to board up the windows and seal the doors as a crime scene. It would remain sealed until the trial was over.

"I'm glad Andrea's presiding," I told Ginny at breakfast the next morning. "Judge Rantala has been pretty good, but he's getting on. He's nearly eighty and really ought to retire."

"Can't argue with that," Ginny said. "Andrea would make a fine chief judge. I hope she runs this fall."

"She won't if Rantala decides to stay," I said.

Andrea Cunningham was a comparative newcomer to Porcupine County, having come up from Grand Rapids in lower Michigan about fifteen years before. She had had a successful general law practice there but wanted a change of venue in her life. Even though she was a native of Ann Arbor, where her father had been a history professor, and a law graduate of the University of Michigan, she liked small towns and small-town people.

Having raised their two sons, she and Ed, her husband and fellow lawyer, rolled into Porcupine City one day on a midlife whim and hung out their shingles. As a deputy at the time I was often in court and soon was impressed with the skill of their advocacy. They were always the best prepared of any attorneys I encountered.

What's more, they took to small-town life as if they had been born to it. Ed is a basically shy fellow and prefers to work behind the scenes, volunteering to clean up after fundraisers and the like. Andrea, on the other hand, was out front flipping pancakes and offering her labor at church suppers of all denominations. She soon drove up the bidding at charity auctions, coming home with stuff she donated to the needy. If an organization asked for help from the public, Andrea was nearly always the first to answer.

In the social order of Porcupine County, both Andrea and Ed are outliers. Andrea's *couture* is as *haute* as any I've ever seen in the North Woods, a place that favors warm, casual and rumpled comfort in dress. She is tall, slim and carries herself regally, often in power suits adorned with a simple strand of pearls. Ed always wears a suit in court, and even in weekend mufti his tailored blue chambray work shirts are pressed, the collars starched, his khakis with knife-edge creases. The Cunninghams are urban eccentrics who stand out in a community of rural eccentrics.

But they are about as well accepted as any non-natives can be in Porcupine County, where one's ultimate status is determined by one's place of birth. Joe Koski, a native Porky, has two grown children. The elder was born in Porcupine City and is considered the county's equivalent of a landed aristocrat. The younger was born unexpectedly in Rhinelander, Wisconsin, during a family weekend trip there, and although she grew up in Porcupine City like her sister, she is still viewed as a carpetbagger.

Andrea and Ed earned their acceptance because

even though they are not Porky-born or Porky-bred, they give themselves wholeheartedly to the community in the manner expected of the native-born. Within a few years Andrea's growing circle of friends urged her to run for office, and to no one's surprise she won the probate judgeship, easily defeating a retired prosecutor who had expected the job as a sinecure. In her three years in office she had won plaudits for her fairness in judgment. Everyone liked her. I don't think she had an enemy in the entire county.

"If there's any trouble at the trial," I said, "Andy will smother it immediately. Nobody wants to get on her wrong side."

"You think Grady Craig will try to impugn Deena's character?" Ginny said. She is no stranger to the law, having dissected any number of criminal trials with me over the evening meal.

"No. Andrea knows very well that these days healthy young men and healthy young women hit the sack at the drop of a hat. She won't allow defense counsel to try to brand Deena as a slut. Not that Grady would, anyway."

Michigan rules of evidence, as in those of most states, bar testimony about a rape complainant's prior sexual behavior.

"Deena's no slut," Tommy Standing Bear said from the doorway.

"Overheard us, did you?" I said. The Ojibwa lad, Ginny's former foster son, is nineteen and no longer her legal charge. But we are his de facto family and he lives with Ginny when he is not at Michigan State, where he is a sophomore on a full scholarship. I'm a more or less semipermanent lodger myself, mostly on weekends.

"Of course."

"What's your take on the case?" I said. Tommy wants to go into law enforcement, and I often contribute to his education by illustrating the fine points of criminal law.

Sometimes he sees things I miss.

"Like everyone else, I just don't know what really happened," he said.

"Deena was in your class at Porky High," I said. "You must know her pretty well. Did you ever date her?"

Their graduating class numbered only thirty-two seniors. It was not unreasonable to expect all the kids to be familiar with each other. Many of them had been on-again, off-again boyfriends and girlfriends and a few already had married each other and started families.

"Not really," Tommy said. "She was often in the gang when we all went out together. I don't know if she ever had a steady boyfriend, though."

"Why not?"

"Once," Tommy said, "I asked her to be my date to the class prom. She said sure, but the next day she stopped me in the hall and said she couldn't. Her father didn't want her going out with an Indian."

Tommy looked directly into my eyes. "Did that ever happen to you when you were growing up?"

"More than once."

"Hurt, didn't it?"

"Yes. But I got over it."

"So did I."

For a few beats we all sat silent. I knew Tommy had occasionally had to field racial insults. Many Porkies, especially the poorer and less educated, express extreme dislike for the reservation Ojibwa at Baraga and L'Anse, claiming they don't deserve both casino income and Bureau of Indian Affairs welfare, that they're all dirty and drunken and don't want to make something of themselves. The long and tragic history of Native Americans means nothing to these uneducated white folks. They live only in the present, and their resentment is immediate.

Tommy, however, not only knows the history and culture of his tribe but also takes great pride in it. He pities the ignorance of poor whites and understands, although he doesn't accept, their need to blame others for their troubles. He is also as good with his fists as he is in making friends. I have never worried about his psyche, although Ginny occasionally does in her maternal way.

Tommy broke the silence. "I haven't seen Deena since graduation last year," he said. "But in high school she always struck me as kind of timid. She wanted to do what all the seniors did, like having a beer now and then, but always held back, worried that she might get busted. Sometimes that was a drag. Now a couple of guys I know at Michigan Tech tell me she hits the wine pretty hard on weekends and is quite the party girl. Sounds like she's discovered liquid courage."

"That happens to a lot of nineteen-year-olds at college," I said. Tommy is not a teetotaler. He will have an occasional beer, but I have never known him to have more than one. His birth parents were reservation alcoholics, as mine were, and he long ago vowed never to fall into the cauldron that drowns so many of his fellow tribesmen and women.

"Yes, that's true," Tommy said. "They go on weekend binges. It's not pretty."

"Sometimes I wonder how Americans survive their youth," I said.

"I remember Deena once coming to class in high school with bruises on her face when she stayed out all night."

"Her father?" I said.

"I guess. She never said who hit her."

Domestic violence is the lot of a rural sheriff's department, especially one whose jurisdiction includes all too many people down on their luck. We often have to rescue children as well as wives from frustrated and unhappy men who lash out in their drunkenness. Some of them consider their families property to do with as they

58

please. Most show remorse after the fact but the pattern repeats itself again and again.

"I wonder," I said.

"Wonder what?" Tommy said.

"Never mind," I said. "Better get going." Tommy was working as a summer ranger at the nearby Wolverine Mountains Wilderness State Park, checking campers in and out of the Union Bay campground and laboring on back-country cabin rehab projects.

The door slammed as the lad dashed out to his ancient pickup and headed for the park ten miles to the west of Ginny's house.

"I wonder, too," she said.

"Wonder what?"

"The same thing you wonder," she said. "Did Deena suddenly cry foul because she's afraid of her father and what he'd do if he found out she was having sex with an African American?"

"That did cross my mind. But the more important question, if it did happen, is *when* it happened. Before the consummation, or after?"

"Who do you believe?" Ginny said.

"I don't know. But I think both of them are telling the truth, that they're telling what they believe happened."

"Or maybe what they *want* to believe happened."

Three weeks after the arraignment we received the results of the rape kit. Most of it was as we expected. Gibbs' DNA was found in Deena's vaginal secretions and under her fingernails. Handprints on her buttocks had been photographed, and there were two tiny tears in her vagina, possible evidence of forcible entry, but I knew Grady would ask the sexual assault nurse on the stand if the marks and tears were also consistent with rough sex and she would have to say yes.

Not much happened during the five months

between arraignment and trial. In jail Gibbs seemed to be happy with three meals a day on the county's dime, and kept his own counsel although he was affable enough with other inmates, joining in their poker sessions and pickup games of "horse" on the tiny basketball court outside. Whenever Joe Koski was on corrections officer duty, he and Gibbs often chatted about hunting and fishing in Porcupine County. Billy was simply a likable, quick-to-smile guy, the kind almost everyone felt comfortable with. Almost.

I made it a point not to talk with Gibbs except to offer polite pleasantries, for I might have to testify at the trial and did not want the legal waters muddied. He seemed to understand the problem and made no attempt to engage me in conversation.

Several times Gibbs' mother came up from Chicago to visit her son, and once in a while Ralph Michael came by for a chat. Gibbs had no other visitors except for Grady Craig. Billy asked that his home computer be brought to jail for his use, but we had to say no. Jails in wealthier counties do allow computers, but the machines have to be provided by the institution and their use, even for email, carefully monitored. We don't have the manpower for that. Gibbs did make occasional phone calls, but in the main he seemed self-contained and content. He did a lot of reading and complained to Joe that the jail library was short on good murder mysteries, especially the Yooper game-warden whodunits by Joseph Heywood. Other than that, Gibbs was a model inmate.

Just before Labor Day, Grady filed the expected motion for a change of venue. His client, he declared, could not get a fair trial before a jury that lacked African-Americans, because there were no other blacks in all of Porcupine County.

Quickly Andrea denied the motion. She was not going to allow anyone to besmirch the even-handedness of the good taxpaying voters of Porcupine County. That, she declared, would be inverse racism. Despite my reservations, I agreed with her. The trial would begin November 1 as planned.

And so it did, for a day and a half. When court was in session I stationed a couple of deputies in the courtroom to help the bailiff keep order, while Chad, Annie and I watched the hallways and the parking lot. Chad and Annie would have to testify, hence stayed out of the courtroom until called. There was a possibility I might be summoned, too, so I decided to join them on the outer skirmish lines.

To my great relief nothing untoward happened at the courthouse. An all-white jury of five women and seven men was quickly picked, with few challenges, and seated. ("Six Finns, two Croats, two Irish, one French and one Cornish," Ginny said. "Almost a perfect ethnic mirror of Porcupine County.") The courtroom was packed standing-room-only, including representatives of the press, and the overflow congregated in the hallway immediately outside. There was whispering but no raised voices.

By lunchtime Garner had finished the prosecution's side, and after lunch Grady began the defense. Nothing was said on either side of the aisle that everybody hadn't already known for many weeks. When Grady finished shortly before 3 p.m., Andrea gaveled the proceedings to a close for the day.

That night, however, there was plenty of heated disagreement at Merle's, Maxie's and other dining and watering holes. Both accuser and defendant had their noisy supporters, and the undecided said their pieces, too. "I've never seen or heard so many people so het up about a trial," Joe Koski said in the squad room that night.

But no fists flew. It seemed that everyone knew Porcupine County was on trial, too.

In the morning both Garner and Grady offered their summations, and, according to Ginny, who attended the entire trial, each attorney turned in an eloquent and persuasive conclusion for his side. Andrea charged the jury just after lunch, and everyone settled in to wait for the verdict.

Two p.m. passed, then three, then four. At five the jury sent a note to the judge asking for a precise definition of the term "beyond a reasonable doubt."

Just before six the foreman announced that a verdict had been reached. I stood by the door to the hallway along with Annie and Chad, ready for whatever might transpire. Court reconvened, and as everyone sat forward on their seats, the verdict was announced.

As the foreman intoned "Not guilty!" Deena slumped at her seat and Gibbs, who was standing as he waited for the verdict, let out a long sigh and embraced Grady. Andrea released the defendant from custody and gaveled proceedings to a close, then left the courtroom, and for the first time the spectators lost their restraint. As most of my department watched to make sure nothing got out of hand, a hubbub arose, but it was just that. No punches were thrown, no threats made, just expressions of delight or dismay rippling through the crowd. I watched as Deena left the courtroom with a group of friends of both sexes, their faces set in shock and anger. Her parents left by another door, Gene Stenfors' face white with rage. Other young men and women surrounded Billy, shaking his hand and slapping his back.

Outside, once the media had its quotes and photos, the crowd slowly trickled away, much if not most of it to watering holes to relive the trial and debate its outcome. Billy Gibbs strode over to me as I stood by the Expedition.

"Thanks, Sheriff," he said in a happy voice with a broad grin. "You were fair."

I nodded, trying not to betray my thoughts: it was the most sensible verdict the jury could have reached. When the precise truth is impossible to pin down, reasonable doubt should rule. And in this case, it did.

"Billy, your house is still sealed," I said. "I'll send a deputy right over to take off the boards and signs and tape."

"I'm not going home tonight," he said quickly. "Don't think that'd be a good idea."

"I won't ask where you're going," I said. "None of my department's business."

"Can you keep my place sealed for a while?"

"Yes, and we'll keep an eye on it until you get back."

"Thanks."

That was the last I saw of Billy Gibbs until Selena sent me the photographs she had taken of his corpse in the woods outside St. Ignace.

SEVEN

SELENA AND I finally broke the connection and I shouted through the door into the squad room. "Chad! Please get onto the Houghton police and ask them to check out Deena Stenfors at Michigan Tech to make sure she's okay and find out where she's been the last five or seven days."

"Right, boss," Chad said, reaching for his landline.

I next raised Alex on my cell phone. He was still in Porcupine City, stopping to have his state police Tahoe's squeaky brakes checked at Horton's Garage before heading back to his headquarters at the post in Wakefield, forty-five minutes away in Gogebic County.

"Alex, can you do me a favor?" I asked. "Somebody needs to go to Gibbs' doublewide and get his guns and computer, and have a better look-around than I did five months ago." Alex carries a full forensic crime-scene kit in his vehicle and is well equipped to go over everything with a complete set of fine-tooth combs.

"Ahead of you," he said. "I was there early in the afternoon with a couple of uniforms while you were talking to Selena and was about to call you to tell you what I found."

I was not in the least resentful. The trooper and I often thought alike and did things on our own initiatives, calling each other later to bring investigations up to speed. I often did simple searches but asked Alex to do the more complicated ones. He had better tools.

"And that was?"

"Pretty much nothing. I'm taking some stuff back to

the post for closer analysis. The guns you saw, the computer, items from his medicine cabinet. By the way, I got into the computer easily."

"How?"

"Gibbs used his Social Security number — backwards — as his password. Not too bright. "That was almost the first one I tried."

We'd obtained Gibbs' number the day we arrested him. It often amazes me how people think personal items like Social Security numbers can protect their computers from snoopers. Even complicated encrypting schemes can be broken by knowledgeable hackers. I used to lock up my home computers with passwords taken from the names of old horses my grandfather had owned, fortifying them with parts of old phone numbers. Now I kept my most sensitive stuff, like bank accounts and personal information, on an external hard drive that I stored in a bank lock box. Once a month or so I'd pick up the drive and take it home to update the accounts, then unplug it from the computer and return it to the lock box the next day. I felt vaguely paranoid until I learned that Ginny does the same thing. She is an extremely wealthy woman and has lots of financial stuff to keep hidden from prying eyes and sticky fingers.

"And what did you find?"

"A whole bunch of nothing," Alex said. "Nothing that stands out, anyway. "

"Bank accounts?"

"A checkbook for an account at Countryman's National. Eleven hundred dollars in that one. A couple of CDs, one for five thousand and another an IRA for seventy-five hundred. Both five-year deposits, interest rates lower than one per cent. Nothing out of the ordinary for a gainfully employed truck mechanic of his talents."

"Emails?"

"Several dozen saved emails," Alex said. "Mostly to

and from buddies suggesting fishing trips, beers at Maxie's and the like. A few rather sexy ones with girls reliving the previous night's whoopee. If this wasn't a murder case, they'd make me horny."

"How long do they go back?"

"Not far. A week or ten days before Gibbs' arrest. Nothing since."

"Gibbs policed his brass," I said. "He didn't want anything embarrassing on his computer."

"Or incriminating," Alex said.

"What makes you say that?"

"Just a feeling that there's more to this guy than we thought. He used software that wipes erased files on hard drive tracks. That's almost paranoid."

"I've had that feeling for a while, too," I said. "Fancy new truck, expensive audio system, a bit more than a guy talented with a wrench should be able to afford. Are you impounding the audio stuff?"

"Yes. They're on their way to Wakefield as we speak, with my guys. We'll hold them until the end of the investigation, then release them to Gibbs' heirs."

"He has one," I said. "His mother in Chicago."

She had been at the trial and had gone home immediately afterward, surprised and gratified at the outcome. Black Americans do not have much faith in white justice.

"Does she know yet?"

"I don't think so. I'll call Chicago police and ask them to break the news."

I was glad that task had not been left up to me. Informing next of kin is one of the hardest jobs on a cop's plate.

"Boss," Chad called.

"Yeah?"

"Deena's fine. Houghton police reports she's been on campus all week. Hasn't missed any classes. But her roommates say she's been depressed ever since the trial. Doesn't go out much. She's talking about quitting school and moving somewhere. The Houghton cops say they'll keep an eye on her and let us know if anything happens."

"Thanks, Chad."

I hoped Deena would not leave the area that had been her home for more than nineteen years, but was afraid she would, and not just because of her unhappy history here. To most young people in the western Upper Peninsula, greener pastures lie elsewhere.

The next morning, while Selena and her crew hunted for clues in Mackinac County and Sheriff Mark Coyle and his deputies searched the shoreline near Freda in Houghton County, I decided to start my investigation in the woods down near Ewen in the southern reaches of Porcupine County. Might as well begin with the most obvious suspects.

"Annie, ride with me," I called into the squad room. She buckled on her equipment and we walked out to the Expedition. Normally I go alone when making a routine call on a routine subject, such as asking a citizen a few questions, but this call had the potential of being anything but routine. I might need backup.

"We're going to visit Caleb Pennington."

"Who's that?" Annie said. She had not been a deputy long enough to have absorbed the personal histories of all of Porcupine County's citizens.

"A strange one," I said. "A member of the Red October nationalist movement in Wisconsin. Used to belong to the Christian Identity group in southern Michigan. A bunch of racist and anti-Semitic yahoos. He's been unemployed for years but we think he runs drugs, poaches and generally commits petty crimes. He did a couple of years at Saginaw for running a chop shop, and moved up here with his family after he got out. He's noisy, an obnoxious popoff. After Gibbs was arrested Pennington tried to drum up a posse at Eddie's Bar to raid the jail and lynch him." Eddie's Bar is a deplorable dive on Highway M28 just west of Ewen.

"He was stinking drunk, and his kinfolk had to drag him out to their truck."

"How'd you find that out?" Annie said.

"A little bird," I said. One of the barflies at Eddie's was a long-retired deputy in his eighties who still kept his ear to the ground and let me know things he heard. There are a lot of sources of information in my jurisdiction and for their safety I keep their identities confidential, even with my deputies, who have their own little songbirds to feed and protect.

"Is he dangerous?"

"Potentially," I said. "So far he hasn't been able to organize his way out of a paper bag, but it seems that some sorry high school dropouts have been listening to him. One of them is the grandson of a woman who lives in Silverton. She told me he was full of blather about forming a Patriot battalion to take over the Wolverines and blow up the bridges at either end of the park to keep outsiders from getting in."

"That's nuts," Annie said as the Expedition bounced off M28 and onto a gravel road leading south into the interior.

"It used to be that those people were so far over on the fringe that nobody paid attention to them. But now that the Tea Party has brought ultraconservative politics into respectable living rooms, these extremists are gaining a pretty good foothold on the far, far right wing."

"I've heard," Annie said.

Two miles south of M28, the county had stopped mowing the verge of the gravel track, and the forest closed in as the road grew narrower and became a single set of ruts through two inches of new snow. Autumn had denuded the deciduous trees and the first snows of winter had dusted the evergreens. Brush swished with an evergreen whisper against the sides of the wide SUV. Without a GPS and a topographic map it would have been impossible to tell whether we were on federal land, the Ottawa National Forest, or private property. The virgin timber had been cleared more than a century ago but secondary growth had turned the land back into thick woods spotted with brushy clearings where hopeful Finnish immigrants had tried to wrest a living from hardscrabble farms in the nineteen-teens and twenties. They were now mostly abandoned, their rude buildings tumbledown.

Census records told me that Caleb Pennington lived on one of these places along with three adult sons. None, I thought, had had more than a few years of schooling. They had erected a stout eight-foot-high steel chain-link fence around their two acres of brush-choked property, topping it with barbed wire. A tall two-piece swinging gate of the same construction greeted us at the entrance to the driveway. It was open. I drove through and covered the fifty yards to the old logger's cabin that sat in the center of the property.

As my Expedition approached the cabin, I glanced through the windshield. The cabin's roof was a patchwork of steel roofing, dried-out cedar shakes and salvaged asphalt shingles. One of the four windows on the driveway side was a freshly installed vinyl double-hung, the labels still on the glass. It looked as if it had been inserted into the frame backwards, with the sash handles on the outside. Some of the missing panes in the other windows had been stuffed with box cardboard.

"These aren't the sharpest knives in Upper Michigan's drawers," I told Annie. "Stay on your toes."

As Annie and I opened our respective doors and stepped out, so did Caleb Pennington, through a piece of heavy tent canvas that served as a front door. He was short, stocky, clad in stained jeans and leather jacket, and sported a wild and unkempt growth of the kind Chad liked to call "an old-man-of-the-woods beard." I was glad that Annie and I stood upwind of the apparition.

He was also cradling a M16 military rifle across his chest. Even from fifteen yards I could tell that it was the latest model, the M16A4, with a scope mounted above the receiver. It looked brand new, fresh out of the Colt factory. I wondered where he had gotten his hands on it. Probably the huge arms black market of America.

Behind him stood a startlingly attractive woman in her forties, tall, slim and blonde, wearing a long dress that appeared to be a hand-me-down from pioneer days. I knew Pennington's wife had died years earlier. Whether this was his daughter, a daughter-in-law, or maybe a concubine, I didn't know. She held something behind her back and squinted at us from eyes full of menace. Annie noticed, too, and nodded slightly to me. If something went down she'd cover the woman while I dealt with Pennington.

"Mr. Pennington," I said, "I'm Sheriff Steve Martinez of Porcupine County. This is Deputy Annie Corbett."

I glanced toward her and noted approvingly that she held her gun hand relaxed at her side, not on the pistol butt as many deputies do when in a tense situation. It's a small thing that can mean the difference between a peaceable result and a sudden shootout.

"What do you want?" Pennington said in a low growl, as if he were trying to imitate a wounded bear. He just sounded like an asthmatic old man.

I spotted a face in an upstairs loft window. It quickly disappeared. I had no idea how many Penningtons were in the cabin and how many in the woods, watching us through gunscopes.

"Just to talk," I said.

"You're on sovereign property," he said. "Belongs to the Red October Patriot Nation."

"It's still part of Porcupine County, I'm afraid," I said, and waited.

"Don't make no never mind. Go away."

"Mr. Pennington, please put down your rifle. Lean it against the doorjamb. It is making me uncomfortable."

In answer he gripped the stock tightly, but did not swing the muzzle in my direction.

"Mr. Pennington, you are committing assault."

"I ain't pointing it at you!"

"No, but you are brandishing the weapon in a threatening manner."

"Go away!"

"All I want to do is ask you a few questions," I said. "If you answer them, I will go away and take my deputy with me. If you do not answer them, we will go away, but then we will be back with the state police Emergency Services Unit. That's also called the SWAT team. I think you know that things will not end well."

The old man lowered his rifle and pointed it at the ground.

"Against the doorjamb, please," I said.

Slowly he complied, keeping his eye on me.

"What do you want to talk about?" he said.

"Billy Gibbs."

Pennington spat into the dust in front of the house. "That black bastard. He belongs in prison. You shouldna never let him go. He's gonna rape more white girls."

The old man either had not heard the news or was pretending. The former was plausible. Eccentrics who live as deep in the woods as the Penningtons do often don't get news until it's old, when they come out from under their rocks and go into town for food or booze. They may have radios but often don't listen to them much, nor do they own computers. The phone company doesn't try to run landlines to them. They often communicate with the outside world only by disposable cell phones — if they're within range of a cell tower. Coverage in Porcupine County is spotty.

"Mr. Pennington, Billy Gibbs was murdered the other day."

A look of astonishment enveloped his face.

"What happened?"

"Shot through the back from close range. They found his body out at St. Ignace." I did not mention either the strangling or the hanging.

"The back?" Pennington finally said. "He oughta watched the bullet coming."

"Mr. Pennington, where have you been the last seven days?"

"You don't think I did it?"

"Please answer my question."

"Right here," he said. "'Cept for going out to Eddie's Wednesday night."

That was the day before Gibbs' body had been discovered.

"Anyone see you there?"

"See me there? I was thrown out. Bastards cut me off."

I looked at my boots and tried not to crack a smile. "That'll be easy enough to check," I said. "You're not on my suspect list anymore, Mr. Pennington. For the moment, anyway. Thanks for the chat."

With that, each member of his family slowly emerged from the cabin and the woods and surveyed Annie and me. Nobody carried a weapon. Except for the tall woman they were all short of stature and slight of physique. They looked at us with vacant, possibly inbred eyes. The Upper Peninsula has a reputation for first cousins marrying each other, probably unfounded except that its schools' special education classes seem to be larger than those anywhere else. Or maybe that's a canard floated by unkind folks in Wisconsin and Minnesota.

As Annie and I drove away, she turned to me and said, "You seem pretty sure Pennington was telling the truth."

"We can check his alibi easily," I said. "And did you happen to see their feet?"

"I didn't notice," she said.

"Sheriff Novikovich said the only prints at the scene were made by size eleven boots. None of those Penningtons wore larger than size eight, and they were all in Nikes or New Balance running shoes."

"You have the eyes of an eagle," Annie said.

"Don't start," I said, although my deputy probably was not referring to my genetic makeup.

"So the Penningtons are really off the hook? We can take them off the list?"

"No, not at all. Remember Rule Number One in the sheriff handbook," I said. "Everybody's a suspect until we convict the person who did the crime."

"Mm. What's Rule Number Two?"

I was silent for a moment. "Working on it," I finally said.

Annie snorted.

"Oh, we have a whole bunch of rules," I said. "It's not easy to quantify them. Some of them are more important some of the time and just move around on the list."

Annie laughed. "You always have an answer."

"Some of the time," I said, and pointed the Expedition in the direction of the sheriff's department.

EIGHT

ONE SUSPECT SHOVED lower on the list, though not completely absent. At the office I called my Eddie's Bar canary, and he confirmed that all the Penningtons except for the woman had been drinking there the night in question. Their noisy conversation had had to do with "spics," "wetbacks" and the porous border on the Rio Grande, not African Americans or Jews. In fact, none of them had mentioned Billy Gibbs since the night he was found not guilty. That particular night after the trial, the old deputy said, they had used every pejorative term in the lexicon for African-Americans and had added some of their own.

The next morning Sheriff Novikovich called. Two days after the trial, Billy Gibbs had rented a two-room lakeside cabin at Freda, paying for the month in advance. Half a dozen of the residents said they had seen a tall black man either jogging or walking the beach alone at various times of the day, sometimes gazing down at the dark sand as if lost in thought.

"That explains the sand in his pant cuffs," Selena said. "The Houghton sheriff's department found nothing interesting in the cabin. Just a duffel with three days' change of clothes. No vehicle. We've sent out a BOLO for a tricked-out Ford F-150 Super Crew Cab, XLT chrome trim, ruby red metallic in color, with leather, Sirius radio and chrome step bar. All that ought to be pretty visible."

"Without a doubt. That truck says 'Steal Me.' "

"Wonder if it was," Selena said. "Steve, it's unclear

to me why Gibbs went to Freda, of all places. It's only an hour from Porcupine City. Not that far out of town, if you're trying to put some distance between it and yourself."

"Maybe it's because Freda is so remote and relatively unpopulated," I said. "You have to drive for miles over rough two-lane roads to get there. If you want to lay low and out of sight but keep fairly close to home, I can think of lots worse hideouts."

"Do you think he hid there just to collect his thoughts," Selena said, "or because he was afraid someone was gunning for him?"

"I do think he was scared," I said. "I would have been. Black man, white girl, rape trial."

"This isn't the South."

"No, it's not. But the Upper Peninsula has crazy haters, like everyplace else, and one of them could have had it in for Gibbs."

"Do you have any suspects?"

"Lots," I said. "But no evidence."

"Who are they?"

"The usual extremist folks, far right-wingers to far left-wing radical feminists. I all but eliminated one of them yesterday and today I'm going to eliminate another."

"Eliminate?" Selena said, mock alarm in her voice.

"From my list of top suspects, I mean."

She laughed. "Who's next?"

"The young woman's father," I said. "Gene Stenfors."

The Stenforses lived in a comfortable ranch home set into the woods off Norwich Road three-quarters of a mile south of M64, the broad two-lane highway that runs through the woods along Lake Superior between Porcupine City and Silverton thirteen miles to the west. A three-car unattached garage sat next to the house, its doors open, revealing a

75

late-model Dodge pickup, an almost new Ford Explorer, and a big snowmobile atop a trailer. Gene Stenfors had done well for himself as an independent insurance agent with customers all over the western Upper Peninsula and northern Wisconsin. For a Yooper, he was a rich man. Deena had led a comfortable life, at least materially.

A big golden retriever greeted me with happy yips as I emerged from the Expedition. Carla Stenfors cracked open the front door, peered out suspiciously, and quickly closed it. I strode up the sidewalk to the door and pressed the doorbell. No answer. I pressed it again, and heard the chimes tinkle.

I was about to pound on the doorjamb and shout "Sheriff's department!" when the door slowly opened and Gene Stenfors appeared. He was in bathrobe and slippers, gray, unshaven and hollow-cheeked. He looked thin, wan and depressed, quite unlike the imposing figure he cut in public.

He was polite, not hostile. "Sheriff Martinez?" he said.

"May I have a word with you, Mr. Stenfors?" I said.

He stood silent for a moment, considering the question.

"This is about the black man?"

"I'm afraid so."

"You'd better come in," he said, pulling open the door.

Carla Stenfors stood by the kitchen doorway, also in nightclothes and robe, hugging herself tightly. It was after ten in the morning and I wondered if these poor souls ever got dressed and went out. The shades were pulled and the house gloomy and untidy. This was an unhappy household, and it probably had been for months, ever since their daughter reported that she had been raped.

"Coffee, Sheriff?" Carla said. At least things were not so bad that she couldn't rise to the social occasion.

"I'd love some," I said. I always accept the offer while making house calls because the polite ritual of perking, pouring and serving tends to relax everybody. Of course I often have to make pit stops afterward.

Cups in hand, the couple sat on their living room sofa while I took a chair across the coffee table from them.

"First of all," I said, "this must have been a terrible time for you."

Tears sprang to Carla's eyes and the cup quivered in Gene's hand.

"We've lost our daughter," he said. "We failed her."

"How so?" I said. I had a pretty good idea, but wanted to hear their version.

"We didn't stand by her. We didn't support her. She didn't want to have anything to do with us during the trial. Now she says she doesn't ever want to see us again."

"Why do you feel you didn't support her?" I said.

"You know, Sheriff," Carla said, darting a glance at her husband.

I decided to be blunt. "Mr. Stenfors, your daughter told us you would hit her when you found out she had had sex with an African American. She told us you had struck her in the past for other reasons."

It was as if I had slugged Gene with the truth. He gasped and nearly spilled his coffee.

"She said that?"

"Yes. And I was told by a reliable witness that she once went to school with bruises on her face."

What was left of the air in him suddenly whooshed out.

"That's because I love her too much," he said.

Carla moved a few inches away from him on the sofa. The look on her face suggested that she also had been the recipient of a few similar expressions of his affection.

"I only wanted the best for her," he said. "We gave her everything. She repaid us with her . . . her behavior."

"What do you mean by her behavior?"

"Drinking. Associating with the wrong kind of people."

" 'Wrong kind of people'? How so?"

"People who are not like us."

"In what way?"

Gene bristled, having been forced into a corner.

"People who are not white. Most of them have no future." He glared at me, challenging me to contradict him.

There it was, out in the open. The Indian part of me wanted to meet the challenge of Stenfors' bigotry, but the sheriff part of me told me to shut up. Stenfors had a constitutional if not moral right to believe and say what he wanted to. I decided to return to the reason I was there.

"Mr. Stenfors," I said, "do you have a shotgun?"

"No," he said. "I don't hunt." That was almost certainly true. I had checked Department of Natural Resources records and he had never applied for any kind of game license. I could always get a warrant to search the house for weapons, but felt that unnecessary for an initial interview.

"Where were you last Wednesday night?"

"You don't think . . . ?" They always say that, especially the innocent, and always the guilty. But this thin and haggard man could not have lifted the body of Billy Gibbs into a noose on a hanging tree, not without help. "Here at home," he finally said. "With Carla. We watched television."

"What did you watch?"

" 'NCIS.' A rerun."

"What was the episode about?"

"The Jew—I mean, the Israeli agent killed her brother," Stenfors said. "I don't really remember."

That would also be easy enough to check. And Stenfors had responded immediately, without stopping to plumb his mind for a plausible lie.

I looked over at Carla Stenfors and raised an eyebrow. She nodded. I decided to believe both of them. At least for now.

"Thank you, Mr. and Mrs. Stenfors," I said, and stood up to leave.

As I turned, a large rubber shoe mat in the hallway behind the front door caught my attention. Among the footwear resting inside the mat were a well-used pair of Field & Stream boots. I strode over to it.

"May I look?" I said.

"Go ahead."

Size ten, about right for a man of Gene Stenfors' medium height. The boots at the tree in St. Ignace had been size eleven.

"Thank you again," I said as I opened the door. Both nodded without speaking.

Then I stopped on the front stoop and turned. Even though it was none of my business, I just had to say it. Cops should not be both cops and social workers, but sometimes I can't help crossing the line.

"Mr. Stenfors," I said, "if you can see your way to changing your mind, I think Deena can change hers. You could start by getting anger management counseling."

I did not wait for an answer.

One more call to make before packing it in for the day. This was to the farm of Elizabeth Waters in the southwestern reaches of the county, near Lake Gogebic.

Liz Waters was not a farmer but a former adjunct instructor in women's history who had bounced around a dozen Midwestern state universities, never earning a doctorate and achieving tenure but keeping her shaky career alive through influential friends, as do so many academic hobos. On her "retirement" from academic life — she finally had run out of places to go — she inherited a large pile from her industrialist father and bought a failed

79

cattle farm. It became her headquarters for a steady stream of radical feminist screeds against patriarchal male oppression. The Porcupine City Herald actually printed a few of them, mainly to counterpoint the Bible-thumping — mostly against abortion, undocumented immigration and "Barack Hussein Obama" — of a number of right-wingers whose letters to the editor soon proved predictable and tiresome even to their fellow evangelicals.

"Mzzzzz Waters," as Ginny archly called her, was a familiar figure at County Board meetings. Although the board rarely discussed an issue having remotely to do with feminism, she loudly and at length questioned every decision it made and demanded documentary evidence for every penny spent. At every meeting she used up every second of her legally allotted three minutes of citizen comment while the commissioners stared at the ceiling and twiddled their thumbs.

Once the board president made the mistake of idly wondering out loud why a female hired county official wouldn't be happy with a reduced salary because her husband had such a cushy income. Wouldn't that help the county's meager coffers? he asked. Liz Waters exploded from her chair in the audience and lunged at the president as arms reached out to restrain her. "Equal pay for equal work, you son of a bitch!" she yelled. Gil, who was representing the sheriff's department while I was away somewhere, had to frog-march her out the door and threaten arrest for disorderly conduct if she tried to get back in.

I was interested in her because she had been an original member of the Weather Underground when the clandestine student revolutionary group was formed in the 1960s at the University of Michigan. She had never been indicted in any of the violent events the Weathermen fomented, although it was later rumored that she helped make the bombs they planted in federal buildings. After the end of the war in Vietnam, the influence of the New Left petered out, and most of the Weathermen finally grew up and became more or less functioning adult members of society.

Not Liz Waters. She simply shifted her target of oppression from imperialism to patriarchy. "The only good male is a dead male," she liked to say, inverting the old libel against Indians. To her it didn't matter that Billy Gibbs was a member of an oppressed minority. He was male and therefore by definition guilty. Liz plastered the county with handbills advancing the cause of Deena Stenfors and advocating life imprisonment at hard labor for her alleged assailant. When the not guilty verdict was handed down, Liz climbed atop her table at Merle's Café and shouted that "the people must take matters into their own hands and impose the most extreme penalty on this evil man!" Even the closet bigots were shocked.

I doubted very much that she had had anything to do with Gibbs' death — some people just expend so much energy and anger in verbal assault that they have nothing left to act with — but it was my duty to check her out. That was not a task I relished.

"What the fuck do you want?" she snarled from her garden as I drove up, tendrils of her hair, wild and fiery red from endless bottles of toxic coloring over the decades, waving in the breeze. She defiantly thrust her hoe over her head like Che brandishing a Kalashnikov.

"You sure know how to say hello, don't you, Ms. Waters?" I said politely.

I often first-name citizens I know, just to keep things neighborly, but not in this case.

"State your business."

"Billy Gibbs."

"What about him?"

"Where were you last Wednesday night?"

"At a meeting in Eagle River."

"A meeting of what?"

"None of your business."

"I will need to check your alibi."

"You think I did it?"

"You tell me."

"I'm an old woman. How could I do anything?"

True that.

"All the same," I said, "you were heard to threaten Mr. Gibbs' life after his acquittal. And now he has been murdered."

"I was at a meeting of historians at the Eagle River Public Library. Ask Molly Peterson, the head librarian. She was present."

"Wait right there, please."

I took out my cell phone. Two bars, good enough. I called the Vilas County courthouse at Eagle River in Wisconsin, an hour and a half south of Porcupine City, and asked for the library number.

"Ms. Peterson? Sheriff Steve Martinez of Porcupine County. I'm calling to see if Elizabeth Waters was present at a meeting in the library last Wednesday. She was? You do? I will. Thank you. Bye."

I hung up and said, "Ms. Peterson said you were indeed there. She also asked me to tell you not to come back. Anyway, you're off the hook for now."

"For now? Are you kidding?"

"Until we find Billy Gibbs' killer, you're still a suspect."

Rule Number Two finally came to me. Make sure suspects think they're still suspects. Keeps them off balance.

Liz Waters really wasn't under suspicion any more, at least seriously, but I was feeling irritated enough not to let her think so. She has that effect on people.

I drove away, drumming my fingers on the steering wheel in frustration.

At Ginny's that night I said, "There go my three best suspects. I don't have any more. Except a few hundred living-room extremists either too chicken or too sensible to act on their beliefs."

"What about Deena's friends? And other people who thought she got a raw deal because she was a woman who cried out?"

"Yeah, there are some of those besides Liz Waters," I said. "But I can't think of anybody crazy enough to commit murder."

"They say you men are just good old boys sticking together, eh?" Ginny said, obliquely changing the subject.

"Pretty much."

"I think you do that sometimes," she said. "Not in this case, though."

"When have I ever done that?" I said indignantly.

"Just the other night," she said. "Remember, you and the deputies promised to sponsor Just Soup, and at the last minute all of you except Annie begged off and all the wives and girl friends had to do it."

Just Soup is a three-year-old third-Thursday-of-each-month tradition in which diverse groups of Porkies — the Friends of the Wolverines, the volunteer firemen, the Kiwanis, the Eagles, the VFW, the hospital, various churches and even the local model airplane club — host a free all-you-can-eat soup-bread-and-dessert evening at the Methodist church. Everyone in the county is invited, and many come. The underlying reason is to help feed the indigent without making it look like a handout, and demonstrate that at table everyone is equal. A few poor folks do attend — fewer than we would like — but volunteers drive loaves and tureens out to the countryside to serve many too ashamed or too infirm to attend. Such impromptu charity and fellowship is common all over the county. I never miss Just Soup, not just for the often interesting company but also because its volunteers serve first-rate homemade soups and breads. Billy Gibbs had done his turn stirring soup and serving tables when Czecko Trucking was the sponsor, and so had Deena Stenfors, as part of a high school senior class project.

"But we had too much on our plates!" I said, oblivious to my own irony. Ginny wasn't, and grinned broadly. "The Gibbs case had just broken and we had to get moving on it!"

"You are a terrible liar, Steve," Ginny said. "You just forgot. Remember, it was Wednesday morning when you called and said you were too tied up and couldn't possibly get it together. Annie and I saved your bacon."

"The pea-and-bacon soup *was* rather good that night," I said.

"Oh, shut up," she said, dropping her robe and cocking a saucy hip. "Come here."

That always shuts me up.

NINE

THE SECOND WEEK of December brought the snows. Late in November there had been a couple of dustings, two or so inches, but now it snowed every day, slow, heavy flakes drifting down all day from the sky and piling up on the flats. Often wet, wind-driven snow and sleet howled in off the lake, coating buildings, vehicles and people with ice and thundering like machinegun fire on slick tin roofs. County plows emerged from their garages and fought to keep the roads open, helped in their mission by citizens with pickups hired to clear private driveways. I had to pull my deputies from the hunt for Billy Gibbs' killer to deal with auto accidents and broken trees across roadways, and make well-being checks on snowed-in elderly citizens.

As the snow pack piled up and piled up through January, there was a shortage of liquid propane gas, whose price shot through the roof as the temperatures dropped below zero. Customers had to turn their thermostats low and rely on fireplaces and electric heaters to ride out the cold. The price of heating oil also rose. Firewood suddenly became scarce.

All over the frigid Upper Peninsula, bone-chilled folks huddled in layers and layers of wool and down. For the first time in decades, Lake Superior froze completely over from the Upper Peninsula north to Ontario and Sault Ste. Marie west to Duluth. By the middle of February the old-timers were declaring it the hardest winter they had ever endured, and the National Weather Service agreed that it was a once-in-a-generation event. Before it was over,

upwards of 30 feet of snow had fallen on the Upper
Peninsula, less than three feet short of the all-time record
set during the winter of 1978-1979.

On the coldest nights, when the temperature crept
toward twenty below, the jail hosted half a dozen homeless
people who couldn't even punch their way through the
snow, more than six feet deep on the flats, to find shelter
by breaking into hunting shacks in the forest. In the
mornings they fought through cutting winds across town
to the charity kitchen at St. Vincent de Paul. Despite its
dwindling reserves, the county tried to keep the indigent
alive, and Gil gratefully accepted donations for breakfasts
from Merle's.

The joke in the Upper Peninsula is that in winter
there is nothing to do but move snow, drink, and make
love. Plenty of the first and last went on, and plenty more
of the second. My deputies and I pleaded with barkeeps
not to overserve their patrons, but especially in the dead of
winter they have to make money, and people need to pass
the time. We spent inordinate amounts of time breaking up
fights and arranging jailhouse sleepovers.

The deep cold and snow hung on through the
middle of April. My counterparts in other counties also
had their hands full just helping citizens survive, let alone
fighting crime. Selena Novikovich declared that she was
going to resign and move to Florida if winter didn't go
away soon. Not until the third week of March was the
coast guard icebreaker at Sault Ste. Marie able to start
chipping away to clear a path for lake freighters to get
from the Soo locks to Lake Superior ports in the west.

The spring thaw had not yet begun to clear the
ground by the first week of May when Will Jackson, the
Porcupine City village president and chief of the volunteer
fire department, called. "Billy Gibbs' trailer is on fire!" he
said. "We need help!"

The place was still under seal. I had promised the

landlord that it would be released as soon as we either solved the case or suspended our investigation. I'd forgotten all about it.

"Mind the store!" I shouted to Gil as Chad, Annie and I dashed outside to the Expedition. On the way across town we picked up a couple of latecomer volunteer firemen and skidded and slipped the five miles out to Gibbs' old double-wide, Annie—who liked to race stock cars on her time off—expertly handling the wheel of the heavy SUV. Two miles out, we could see and smell the smoke rising from the trees.

When we pulled up at the driveway on U.S. 45 leading fifty yards in to the mobile home, we found the two Porcupine City Volunteer Fire Department pumpers sitting idle on the verge of the highway, their crews staring forlornly at the blaze. Small explosions of glass bottles and pressurized cans accompanied the flames' roaring symphony.

"Can't get in there without a plow," one of the firefighters said. "Drifts still seven or so feet on the road. Even if the county could get a plow in there, it'd take half an hour to clear. So we're just letting it burn. Nobody was in there anyway—it's been vacant since last fall."

The fire, now at its peak, blazed merrily, black smoke belching into the air as a stiff crosswind pumped oxygen into the blaze. It was a hot fire. Trailers burn like matchsticks, their combustible lightweight construction materials constantly feeding the inferno. Soon the aluminum roof melted and collapsed, sparks flying, and the lightweight steel framing in the walls warped and fell into the blaze.

Firefighters hate trailer blazes in the boonies. Usually there are no hydrants five miles out of town, and if no retention ponds lie nearby, there's nowhere to get water to fight the fire. Even when water is available, narrow hallways and tiny rooms hamper the crews as they try to rescue people and pets trapped within. Trailers burn quickly, and there's often no time to get inhabitants out. That's why proportionately three times as many people die in trailer conflagrations as they do in ordinary home fires.

"Where's the propane tank?" I asked.

"Upwind of the trailer," Will said. "The wind's keeping the flames away. I think it'll be okay." We could see the tank, sited a good ten feet from the mobile home. Sometimes a residential propane tank is drained when the occupants of a house are away for the winter and the contents returned to the supply company, but Gibbs' place had been sealed since his murder, and the gas was still there.

"Steve, I think the fire may have been set," Will said. "Usually trailer fires are triggered by cooking stoves, or faulty heating or electrical equipment, but the power has been off to this place for months. And, you know . . ." He left the thought unfinished, but I knew what he was talking about.

"We'll see if we can find out," I said.

Within the hour the fire had diminished to a smoky smolder with a few hotspots and a county plow had cleared the gravel driveway. The firefighters moved in with extinguishers, knocking down the remaining flames.

Part of one wall still stood, the wind having driven the combustion away from it. The rest was a jumble of burned flooring, twisted aluminum and warped steel.

Will and his crew poked through the wreckage hunting for clues.

"Steve, look at this," Will said. I kicked aside a charred kitchen chair and stepped up to the wall that still stood. The interior wallboard remaining on the framing clearly had been ripped off in chunks, the fasteners scattered on what was left of the floorboards.

"Somebody tore apart the place," I said. "Probably

looking for something."

"And torched it," Will said from what had been the kitchen. "Look, here's where it started." He held up the remains of a plastic gasoline can and the clockwork of a crude timer. "The fire spread from here."

"Now why would someone rip up and then burn the place?" I said. "I don't think there was anything worth stealing." Everything of value, including the audio equipment Gibbs' firearms and ammunition, had been impounded until the murder investigation was either concluded or suspended.

"Tracks over here!" Annie called from a few yards behind the cabin. Two sets of snowshoes had etched a fresh trail through the woods from the highway at a point fifty yards south of the driveway to Gibbs' place. Whoever made them did not want to be seen approaching the cabin. I was now almost certain that two people were involved in the events surrounding Billy Gibbs.

I fished out my cell phone and called Alex.

"Looks like it's time to get back to work on that investigation," he said.

Our old BOLO on Gibbs' tricked-out truck had not borne fruit. Nobody had seen it anywhere. It had disappeared. Maybe it had been hidden somewhere.

Back at the sheriff's department I called Selena in St. Ignace and told her what had happened.

"This case has been on ice too long," she said. "Literally."

"Only thing we have to go on is Gibbs' truck," I said. "If we can find it maybe we'll find something in it."

"There's always the possibility it was painted, or ended up in a chop shop and the parts have been scattered to the wind," Selena said. "Nobody's applied for a license plate with that VIN."

"Nobody seems to care anymore."

"About the truck?"

"About Billy Gibbs."

As winter had settled in, the grousing at Merle's and the bars had shifted from the Gibbs murder to snow and ice and survival. Casual bigotry gave way to bitching about dwindling stocks of propane and firewood. Everybody was thinking about something fresh. People tend to live in the present, not the past.

What's more, forty per cent of homicides in the United States never get solved. For every six killers convicted, four get away with the crime. Cases grow old and cold and end up frozen in the back of forgotten filing cabinets. A celebrated murder that reveals something about the society in which it happened might rate a magazine article or two, or a chapter in a dreary sociological study, but those also tend to disappear into the dusty shelves of history.

But, dammit, I cared.

I went to the big old-fashioned wooden filing cabinet in the corner of my office and hauled out the thick Gibbs case file. Maybe going over it one more time would suggest a new angle, a new approach. I spread the papers and photographs over my desk.

"Whatcha doing, boss?" Chad said.

I told him.

"Been thinking about that," he said, "ever since we got back from the fire. Annie and I want to get back on the case."

I rubbed my eyes and sighed.

"We've got so much to do now that I can't afford to put you on it," I said.

"We'll do it on our time off," Chad said.

"Why?"

"Steve, we don't like unfinished business any more than you do."

"But I'll need you to work overtime," I said, carefully avoiding the unhappy fact that we couldn't afford to pay for extra hours and just let them build up to be paid sometime in the future, if ever. The contract with the deputies' union forbade that practice, but sometimes you just have to do what you must.

"Doesn't matter," Chad said. "We'll find a way."

It was at that moment that I decided to press Chad into becoming undersheriff when Gil retired. I was getting on in years, too, and thought I might also retire at the end of my next four-year term. Chad Garrow clearly looked at law enforcement as a calling, not merely a job. He cared about Porcupine County and its people. He had the experience. People liked him, partly because, big as he is, he does not throw his weight around.

That is a good thing for more than one reason. Chad is a one-man disproof of the myth that large men are graceful on their feet. So clumsy and ham-handed is he that he's the last deputy I'd send to investigate a burglary in a china shop. Ginny hides the delicate dining chairs when he comes over for dinner. He weighs well over 300 pounds and is an important reason we changed from rump-sprung Ford Crown Victoria squad cars to beefed-up Expeditions.

Still, when the time comes, he'll make a first-rate sheriff for a host of reasons, all of them good.

"Shut the door, Chad."

All ears in the squad room perked up. I rarely closed my door. When I did, someone was either going to receive bad news or have a new one ripped. Usually it was the former. I do most of my ripping where people can't either hear me or call for help. And not often.

"Chad, you know Gil's retiring soon."

"Yes?"

"When that happens, I'd like you to be my

undersheriff. There'll be a bit of a raise, you'll get your own office, and you mostly won't have to go out of it in bad weather."

He blinked. "Thanks, Steve, but . . ."

"But?"

"I'd never . . ."

"You never thought about advancement? You would be happy just to be a deputy all your working life?"

"Well, yes, but not so soon." I could see that Chad had been blindsided by the offer.

"Comes a time in the life of every man, Chad, and this may be the one for you. You've been a deputy for ten years now and won lots of commendations, and, frankly, I think you've got the right stuff to become sheriff someday."

"But being undersheriff would mean being stuck in the office all day. I'd rather investigate than administrate." I looked at him. He was a bit of an unconscious poet, although his metaphors would win no prizes.

He reminded me of Alex Kolehmainen, who just a few years before had passed the state police lieutenant's exam just to establish his intellectual equality with his girl friend, Lieutenant Sue Hemb, who headed the troopers' forensic psychology department. Alex has repeatedly refused promotions to a lieutenancy so he can continue to go out in the clean cool air of the Upper Peninsula, as he puts it, and fight crime as a sergeant.

"Not necessarily," I said. "Gil may spend a lot of his time doing paperwork, but he often goes out and bosses crime scenes. The undersheriff is an executive officer, you know."

"Well . . . "

"Look, Chad, think on it a while before you make up your mind."

"How long do I got?"

I looked at the clock and plucked a time out of the

air. "Midnight."

"You want me to call you then?"

"Wait till the morning, please."

The phone at Chad's desk rescued us both.

"Go answer it," I said.

He did.

"It's Joe Koski at Merle's. Ralph Michael just walked in."

Ten minutes later I slid into the booth across from Michael. "Welcome back, Ralph," I said. "Looks like North Dakota agrees with you. Working on trucks there?"

In the months since the goodbye party that had ended unhappily at Billy Gibbs' place, the young mechanic had lost belly fat and put on muscle as well as a tan that had lingered over the winter. When Gibbs was found hanging from a tree at St. Ignace in December, we had asked the North Dakota state police to check Ralph's whereabouts and interview him. They found him on an oil rig outside Minot. He had been on the job site without letup since arriving the previous May. The trooper reported that Ralph, who had an airtight alibi, seemed genuinely surprised and dismayed when told about the murder, and said he had no idea why Billy was killed or who could have done it.

"Not trucks," Ralph said. "Roustabout. Pay's the same, and it gets you outdoors."

"What are you doing back in Porcupine City?"

"I kinda miss the place," he said. "I wanted to go ice fishing and took a couple weeks off."

"Wish I could do that," I said. "Too much going on."

"Yeah. I heard about the fire soon as I got here."

"Any ideas?"

"Not one." I believed him. Simple, open and uneducated men like Ralph Michael tend to wear their

93

thoughts on their faces rather than hide them behind layers of wariness.

"I wanted to talk to you about Billy," I said, "because you knew him about as well as anyone else here did. You worked with him, you drank with him, you were buddies. You even got in a fight with him once, if I recall right."

Ralph ducked his head and smiled shyly. "Yep."

"Did Billy tell you much about his life?"

"Some. He said life was mostly pretty good when he was a kid. He had no brothers or sisters. His dad was a postal clerk and his mom is a nurse. They lived in an apartment building his dad had bought and fixed up. He said he did okay in school but cared about athletics more. When he was a senior in high school his dad was killed in one of those random Chicago shootings and he decided to get away after graduation by going into the army."

I could tell that was a long speech for Ralph. He seemed almost winded.

"What do you remember most about Billy?"

Ralph was silent for a moment, then he said, "His truck."

"Fancy, wasn't it?"

"Yes. It was the thing Billy most loved. He took an awful lot of care of it. He changed the oil every thousand miles and was always fussing with the shocks and springs, trying to get it to ride better. The hood was always up. He washed it about every other day and even detailed the engine. He never left home without that truck. At lunchtime at work he would go out to it and wipe off the bird crap and polish out the spots."

"Obsessed, huh?"

"You could say that."

"You kept the truck for Billy while he was in jail, didn't you?"

"Yep."

"Notice anything odd about it?"

"No. It was just a cool truck."

"Ever look around inside?"

"Just a bit. Nothing to see, just leather seats and a great sound system. Billy wouldn't have liked it if anybody else went inside, so I had it locked in a neighbor's garage until after the trial. When I left for North Dakota, I left the truck keys with the guy who owned the garage. He liked Billy and said he wouldn't charge rent. Billy picked it up the same day he was freed."

"Did he ever say anything about the army?"

"He said he liked it, except when the shooting started."

"He say anything about being a black soldier in the army?"

"Not much. He said once in a while a white guy would have it in for him because he was black but it didn't sound like a problem for Billy. He dealt with it."

"Like he dealt with you," I said, grinning.

Ralph looked away. "I'm kind of ashamed of that."

"It's okay. We all say dumb things."

In for a penny, in for a pound. "Ralph, do you think Billy was murdered because he was black?"

He sat silent, looking into the distance, for a long moment. "I don't know. There are some people around here who don't like blacks and Jews and Indians and Mexicans, but most of them are all bullshit and no action. Assholes. Besides, most people liked Billy. He was a really nice guy. Even when people got plastered and came up to him and told him how proud they were to know him, he didn't get pissed. He just smiled and said 'thank you' and when they weren't looking he'd wiggle his eyebrows at me and roll his eyes."

I laughed. "Been there, done that more times than I care to count."

"You know Sarah Nesbit?" Ralph asked.

"Do I ever."

Sarah Nesbit is a no longer young but still attractive woman, a painter from somewhere in the East, who fancies herself the center of a Porcupine City salon made up of amateur artists, wannabe writers and other people she thinks are "interesting." In a town where most women dress in jeans and sweatshirts or fleeces, she is a colorful fashion plate, but not in the style of Judge Andrea Cunningham. Sarah revels in what she calls "found textile art" from people's attics and the St. Vinnie's rummage shop. She loves Southwestern Indian silver jewelry and bedecks herself with Navajo and Zuni necklaces and bracelets. She clanks when she walks. If you can't see her coming, you can hear her.

As a grande dame she is far from haughty and inapproachable. Children love her impromptu summer art classes on her front porch. She both volunteers at and donates to the local animal shelter. She has tried for years to get me to attend her Wednesday evening "soirees," but I'd rather not be anybody's interesting Indian, however gracious the hostess.

"Sarah try to get Billy at one of her parties?" I asked.

"All the time. He always said he couldn't make it. I kept telling him to just say no, that it wasn't his scene, but he didn't want to offend her. He liked her. Everybody does."

What else do you remember?"

"Billy was always flush. He owned that truck outright. No payments. He paid cash for it. He also picked up lots of bar tabs for other people."

Gibbs must have inherited something, I thought, but his mother was still alive. Unless his father had had the rare foresight to make a will providing for both wife and son, the mother would have inherited everything. That would be simple to check out.

Ralph suddenly looked up and said, "I just

remembered. Billy said he had something going on when he left the army. Something on the side. I never asked. But he sounded worried when he said it."

"Anything else?" I said.

"I miss Billy. If he were still alive we'd be going fishing today."

THE RIDDLE OF BILLY GIBBS

TEN

A FEW DAYS later we held what Alex, a lifelong fan of the Dick Tracy comic strip, always calls a "Crimestoppers Skull Session" in my office. Chad, Annie and Gil crowded in, Sheila sat behind me taking notes, and Alex darkened the doorway in his usual fashion.

"The Billy Gibbs case has been cold too long," I said.

"No pun intended, of course," Alex said.

We all looked at him.

"The winter! The winter!" Alex all but shouted. "Have none of you any sense of humor?"

We all shook our heads. This winter was just too harsh to laugh about.

I chose to ignore the trooper. "So what have we learned since last December?" I said.

Chad leaned forward. "I talked to Iris Krulich this morning. She's — was — the owner of Gibbs' trailer. She said he paid cash in advance for one full year, that he said he didn't want to bother with monthly checks. She said it was fully insured and once the insurance survey has been done she's going to clear the site and rebuild with manufactured housing instead of a mobile home.

"But she was miffed because just before renting to Billy she spent a lot of money on rehabbing the trailer. New roof, new interior insulation and walls all around, new kitchen appliances. Thousands of bucks. Now it's all gone.

"But something occurred to me. The new walls were the usual one-eighth-inch printed hardboard screwed into steel studs, and the lines of screw heads covered with long aluminum battens. If Billy had wanted to hide anything in the walls, it'd have been easy—just unclip the battens and unscrew a piece of hardboard."

"Whoever ripped apart those walls and set fire to the place wasn't so delicate," Annie said.

"Or didn't want to waste time," Gil said.

"It's one thing to search a house," I said, "but it's another thing to torch it afterward. Usually the person who tosses a place cleans it up if he doesn't want the search to be discovered, or leaves it a mess if he doesn't care. But setting fire to it suggests another motive. Anger, rage, maybe hate. In this case, possibly racial hate. I think that's probable but we don't know for sure."

"What could Billy have been hiding in the walls?" Chad said. "Money? Jewels? Bearer bonds?"

"From what we've learned, he had plenty of money," I said. "But nobody seems to know where it came from. When we interviewed his mother after his death, she said he sent money home to her regularly, in five-hundred-dollar checks. Bank records corroborated that. The deposits were all in cash or paychecks from Czecko Trucking. He always deposited his paychecks rather than cash them, as most people around here do. His bills were paid by automatic withdrawal. He didn't use an ATM much."

"He carried a pretty good roll of bills," Alex said. "It was still in his pocket when his body was found. Where did all that cash come from?"

"Maybe his truck," I said. "Maybe he was using it as a mattress. Ralph Michael said that he almost never let it out of his sight. And now nobody knows where it is. The VIN plate has never turned up. The truck could have been painted and sold south of the border, or parted out, or burned."

"Or hidden in a garage or barn somewhere," Annie said. "Maybe Billy knew something was going to happen and didn't want it found."

"If he stashed that truck, he probably rented a space somewhere," I said. "Paid for a long while in advance as he did the trailer, no questions asked."

"If we find that building," Chad said, "we find that truck, and maybe we also find the answer to the mystery."

"Or not," Gil said, ever the skeptic.

"One more thing," I said. "Ralph said Gibbs seemed to be nervous over something that happened in the army. 'Something on the side,' he said. He said he didn't know what. When we checked with Fort Lee the personnel archives people said Gibbs had an unblemished record. Nothing in it suggested otherwise. We ought to take another run at his military service."

For a while we all fell silent. "Okay," said Alex, "who's going to do what?"

"Annie," I said, "you take point on finding that truck, okay? Shake out the rental garages in Porcupine County, both the ones advertised and those that might have been rented under suspicious circumstances."

"Right," she said. "I'll also have to spend a lot of time out in the countryside looking for likely buildings."

"Call the sheriffs in all the counties between here and Mackinac," I said. "See if you can get them to spare a deputy or two for a while on this mission. I'm sure they're as busy as we are, but this is a big case, and they're not going to want to miss out on the credit for helping solve it."

I looked at Chad. "Would you kindly see if you can run down the money angle? Where it came from, where it went, how, and in what sums?"

Chad, a crackerjack phone investigator, nodded.

"Alex?" I said.

"As soon as I finish this stupid make-work project investigating all the sheriffs and police chiefs of the Yoop for conspiracy to commit felony police brutality," he said,

"I'll see what I can do."

State police headquarters in Lansing had tasked their finest investigator to lead what we all considered a harebrained scheme, one to get all the state's law enforcement agencies to improve their relations with the public. It was a six-week job and Alex couldn't devote any of his time to doing what he does best—catching criminals.

"As for me," I said, "I'll pursue the army lead Ralph Michael suggested."

"How are you gonna do that, boss?" Chad said.

"I know a guy."

Gil snorted. "Inasmuch as his troops are riding madly off in all directions, the widely respected veteran undersheriff of Porcupine County, the one who is going to retire this fall, will spend the rest of his professional life serving warrants and summonses because no one else is around to do it."

I sat up with a jolt. So absorbed had I been in the case of Billy Gibbs that I'd forgotten the conversation with Chad the previous day. I shot him a questioning look.

He shrugged and nodded. He was in.

"I know a guy," indeed. Most of my professional life I have been a networker, building relationships with those I run into, first in school and then on the job. The advice came early. "Make friends," my adoptive father, a veteran Methodist minister, had said when I was still an adolescent. "Make as many friends as you can. Make friends with smart people and ambitious people as well as just good ordinary people. Do them favors. Ask the plainest girl in your class to the prom. Carry groceries for the neighbor lady. It's not only the Christian thing to do, but also you could need these people someday. What goes around comes around, you know."

The acceptance came late. In high school I was painfully aware that I did not look like anyone else, that my mahogany skin, black hair and deep-set dark eyes set me apart from all the white kids. Proud aloofness was my way of dealing with my difference. I did not warm up to others and always allowed them to take the first steps of friendship, to meet me more than halfway. It took an unconscionably long time for me to learn that human relationships were two-way enterprises needing careful feeding and watering.

But I learned. By my sophomore year in college I'd become chummy with all sorts of people, including nerds and jocks, drudges and ne'er-do-wells. I'd met their parents, some of whom occupied influential posts in high places. "When you graduate, come see me," more than one of them said. But I was an Army ROTC student and of course had a military obligation to fulfill.

In the service I worked hard and kept my nose clean, and made sure my superiors knew it. I also buddied up to all the other second lieutenants in my MP company, and soon we all took care of each other in ways one rarely sees in civilian life. In the military a soldier is most loyal to the other men in his squad, then those in the larger platoon. Junior officers first care for their subordinates, then for each other. In an unexpected firefight my company had with a battalion of Iraqis we thought had surrendered, I saved the life of a fellow lieutenant and earned his deep and enduring loyalty.

It happened on the 26th of February, 1991. That was the third day of Operation Desert Storm, and my MP company was tasked with coordinating the surrender of scores of poorly trained and deeply frightened Iraqi conscripts demoralized by the lightning air and armored blitz the coalition had mounted against Saddam Hussein's occupying forces in Kuwait. "Shock and awe," the technique would be called in the next war in that part of the world, and in this instance it worked.

Not all the Iraqis had been defeated so easily. One

diehard group of about thirty soldiers advanced toward us under white flags, and as we prepared to take them into custody, they opened fire with rifles and rocket-propelled grenades. Although some of our MPs were killed and wounded in the onslaught, there were more of us than of them and we were better armed. In a ten-minute battle we blunted the assault and wiped out the enemy.

I spent the fight inside a Humvee, firing my Beretta with one hand out the right side door at suicidal Iraqis as they charged through the sand toward us, and with the other hand clamped down on the femoral artery in Lieutenant Kevin Barlow's thigh. It had been torn apart by a Kalashnikov bullet at the beginning of the battle and he was bleeding to death.

As soon as the shooting stopped I helped a corpsman wrap a compress around Kevin's leg and he was quickly evacuated to a field hospital in the rear as my unit advanced down the highway toward Iraq, this time taking nothing for granted as we accepted surrenders. We were probably rougher with the POWs than we needed to be, but there were no more suicide assaults against our company.

Later the next week I stopped at the main U.S. Army field hospital in Kuwait City to visit Kevin. He was sitting up in bed, crutches propped next to it, and looked awfully good for somebody who had been within inches of death.

"I owe you one," he said. "A big one." He embraced me, weeping. My own eyes were wet. We were now blood brothers, except our bond had been sealed in tears.

Now, more than two decades later, he was Colonel Kevin Barlow, commander of the Criminal Investigation Command School, Seventeenth MP Brigade, at Fort Leonard Wood. Time, I thought, to collect on that old favor. I picked up the phone.

Finding Kevin was easy. We had remained in touch

over the years, exchanging holiday greetings, and there had been personal items in the yearly newsletter our old battalion published every Christmas.

"First Lieutenant Stephen Martinez needs to speak with Colonel Barlow," I told the sergeant who answered the phone on the post. Upward through the ranks he transferred the call, through a chief warrant officer, a second lieutenant, a first lieutenant, a captain, a major and the lieutenant colonel who was the executive officer and seemed surprised the boss would deign to speak directly with a lowly junior instead of "pissing downhill through the ranks," as we often put it.

"Put him on! Right now!" I could hear Kevin bellowing from across the room on the exec's receiver.

"Steve! What can I do for you?" he said as soon as we were connected.

"I need a bit of a favor," I said.

"Anything for the sheriff of Porcupine County, Michigan," he said, and his words were heartfelt.

"Got a few minutes, Kevin? It's a long story."

"I'm all yours," he said. "Hold my calls," he told his first sergeant. "I'm going to be busy for a while."

For the next ten minutes I outlined the case of Billy Gibbs, from his discharge at Fort Lee and his arrival in Porcupine City to his death at the hands of person or persons unknown at St. Ignace, finishing with Ralph Michael's puzzled remark at the table in Merle's.

"This looks like a very interesting case," Kevin said. "I'll go through CID archives and see if there's anything there about Gibbs, and if there is, I'll be in touch in a day or so, maybe two."

He covered the receiver with his hand but I could hear him call out, "Major Waldron! Got a job for you!"

I smiled. Kevin was taking the case seriously enough not to entrust the inquiry to a warrant officer, the equivalent of a detective third grade in a major metro police department and the rank that does all the routine investigative shitwork. That might mean the colonel knew something I didn't.

Two days later the colonel lived up to his word.

"Steve?" he said, in a voice so quiet that I suspect he was keeping it low so he wouldn't be overheard at his office. "We've turned up some interesting information on your case."

"You have?" I said. "What is it?"

"It's confidential," he said. "Can't give you the details."

"Damn," I said.

"But."

"But what?"

"If you come down here, I think we can arrange something."

Colonel Barlow, I knew, was putting his career on the line. For me.

"When?"

"Tomorrow, if you like."

"Give me a couple of days to line up my ducks, and I'll be down."

"Best if you wear your sheriff's uniform and arrive in your official vehicle."

"Why?"

"Trust me."

ELEVEN

ORDINARILY I'D HAVE borrowed Ginny's thrifty little Prius for a long road trip to save on expenses, as I had in the past, but the colonel's suggestion meant I'd be driving one of the department's big Expeditions. Getting a majority of the county commissioners to reimburse my office for the 1,700-mile round trip from Porcupine County to Fort Leonard Wood in southeastern Missouri was going to be damnably difficult, but I had plenty of dirt on a couple of them — and they knew it. I wouldn't even have to threaten them, which would be illegal anyway, a form of police extortion. All I would need to do is lay my Lakota thousand-yard stare upon them. White men have attached so much emotional freight to what they think Indians plan to do that a cocked eyebrow scares them silly.

I packed my official sheriff's uniform — blue slacks with gold stripe, white shirt with four gold stars on the collar, and white garrison cap — but donned my everyday outfit, blue jeans and khaki work shirt with official sheriff's ball cap completing the ensemble. The Expedition is roomy and comfortable on the highway and ate up the 800 miles over twelve hours with no pain at all except at the gas pump. The drive down Interstates 39 and 55 through Wisconsin and Illinois to St. Louis is pretty, if you like vistas of cows and corn stretching to the horizon, and doesn't change much in Missouri. It would have been easy to fall asleep amid the rolling sea of farms, but I kept myself awake by tuning in to the news on National Public Radio as well as the Cubs-Cardinals twi-night game. I had long ago sworn off the Cubs — they broke my heart once too often — but still found myself listening to their games on the road. They helped the miles pass, even though they didn't rekindle my loyalty.

As an Indian who has never quite felt completely linked to the people among whom he dwells, simply because he is darker than them and comes from a vastly different history, I likewise have never managed to succeed in rooting for a professional baseball or football team. I've never understood the appeal of watching the antics of overpaid, undereducated and often uncivilized athletes in games that are forgotten as soon as they are over. Ginny, who has been a Detroit Lions fan ever since she was old enough to distinguish between a single-wing and a T formation, thinks I'm crazy as well as standoffish. She could be right and I know better than to argue with her. All the same, she always watches the Lions games with her girl friends because I'm too busy doing something else on Sundays.

On Friday nights, however, I do go to the Porky High athletic fields and root for the Gladiators, shrunken along with the diminished student body into an eight-man football team. On weekday evenings I'll go to the high school gym for the Lady Gladiators basketball games, and in the winter to the community center for age-group hockey games. It's true what the armchair sociologists say: rooting for local teams helps connect folks to their communities. Besides, I know most of the players and their parents, and underdogs have always appealed to me. Come to think of it, all of Porcupine County is an underdog, too.

At nearly 8 p.m., after the Cubs fell to the Cardinals in extra innings, I shook off my mild disappointment and parked the dusty Expedition in front of the Pulaski County Sheriff's Department in Waynesville, Missouri, gateway to Fort Leonard Wood.

"Sheriff Steve Martinez from Porcupine County, Michigan," I said at the dispatcher's counter. "Got business at the fort tomorrow. Any lodging for a visiting lawman?"

The dispatcher was not at all surprised. County budgets everywhere are pinched, and rather than spend money on a motel room, many LEOs — especially those from extraordinarily straitened departments like mine — will try to overnight in an empty cell in a county or city lockup. The Porcupine County Sheriff's Department was originally built with living quarters for the sheriff and his family, and while supplies are piled up in a couple of the empty rooms, we do maintain one bedroom as an impromptu two-bunk barracks for itinerant LEOs. That's also where I flop when staying overnight.

The dispatcher tossed me a key and pointed me down the hall.

"Cell A," he said. "That's the rubber room." Detox chambers will never be mistaken for five-star-hotel rooms, but the price is right. I lay down on the hard bunk and immediately slept the sleep of the just and impoverished.

The next morning. I shaved and dressed in the sheriff's Sunday best I had brought along, and in honor of my blinding sartorial elegance Sheriff Clay Potter of Pulaski County treated me to coffee and Danish in his office.

"Picking up a prisoner, Sheriff?" he said.

"Not exactly, Sheriff," I said. Many sheriffs are like surgeons, who punctiliously address each other as "Doctor" while scrubbing up for an operation. I have no idea why. A convention of county sheriffs constantly calling each other "Sheriff" instead of "Joe" or "Max" is always faintly comical.

"Mainly seeking information," I added. I didn't want to go further than that.

Potter understood.

"Good luck with that, Sheriff," he said. "Army's

tighter with info than a dog trying to shit a peach pit."

"Thanks, Sheriff," I said. "You come up and visit us in Upper Michigan soon."

"Might well do that, Sheriff," he said. "I hear you got humongous lake trout in your jurisdiction."

A few more such sheriffly exchanges, and I was off to the fort.

Fort Leonard Wood, named for a general whose name and fame everybody has forgotten except the army, is a huge military installation that sprawls over a goodly portion of the eastern Ozarks. It is not only a basic training center for infantrymen but also contains the Combat Engineers School, the Military Police Corps School and the Chemical, Biological, Radiological and Nuclear School. More than two decades before, I had begun and ended my army active duty at the fort.

At the covered main gate — it has always looked to me like a busy entry to a toll road — I showed my official ID to the bored young MP corporal guarding the portal. He checked his clipboard.

"One moment, Sheriff," he said, stepped back into his cubicle, and picked up the phone. I could not hear what he said except for "Yes, sir," as he hung up.

"Please pull ahead and move your vehicle into the right lane and park there," he said. "Colonel Barlow is sending an escort down. She will be with you shortly."

As soon as I parked he was at my window again, replaced at the gate by another MP.

"I'll wait with you, sir," he said, standing at ease.

"I don't plan to steal any ordnance," I said. "I used to be an MP myself, a couple of wars ago. Served with the colonel."

"Yes, sir, I know," the corporal said. "His office made that clear when I notified them you were here."

"I guess I must be somebody," I said. "Not because

I'm wearing these four stars on my collar. I'm only a county sheriff from the North Woods."

The corporal relaxed and smiled.

"The last time I saw four stars was when the Army Chief of Staff visited us about six months ago." I could hear the capital letters in his voice.

"Was that terrifying?" I said.

"Was it ever."

"Been there, too," I said. "What a nightmare."

At that moment the golden oak leaves of a major appeared beside the two-striper.

"I've come to collect the sheriff," she said. "Major Amy Waldron at your service, sir. I'll ride with you." She was short, smart, and stern, and probably the prettiest thing I had ever seen in camos. I did not, however, voice that opinion. I may have been a civilian but I was on an army base and the military took a sour view of innocent remarks that might possibly be construed as sexual harassment. Especially, I am sure, of a field-grade officer.

"They sent a major to fetch me?" I said. "I'd thought I'd rate only a private."

"Not according to Colonel Barlow, sir," she said, climbing into the Expedition's right front seat.

"I'm not in the army anymore," I said. "No need to call me sir. Besides, I was only a first lieutenant."

She relaxed and laid a brilliant smile upon me.

"Don't tell anybody I said this, Sheriff," she said, "but Colonel Barlow seems to think of you as a combination of Superman and Spiderman. Someday I would love to hear about whatever happened way back when."

"It was no big deal, really," I said.

"They always say that." She chuckled. "Turn right here. That's the Military Police Corps Regimental Museum."

We trundled past a long, low slab-sided building

that looked like a Home Depot. It wasn't there back in 1991 and didn't come along for a decade. Outside squatted a preserved Huey helicopter and a steel riverine patrol boat on blocks.

A few more blocks, and we passed what appeared to be strip mall. There, six heavily armed and black-clad soldiers looking like a SWAT team poured out of a wicked-looking armored vehicle and apparently broke into a smoking storefront. The whole thing looked very realistic to me.

"That's Stem Village, a mock town," the major said. "Named for an old commandant of the military police school. We train for everything today."

"Wasn't there when I was here," I said.

"Welcome to the modern army."

One more block, and she said, "Park here. We'll walk the rest of the way."

We strode from the lot to the Military Police School headquarters under a huge bronze sculpture of crossed flintlock pistols, the official insignia of the MPs.

We checked in at the front desk. "This way," the major said, parting a wave of camo-clad soldier-students just emerging from classes. Down the hall we swept through a door emblazoned "HQ US ARMY CRIMINAL INVESTIGATION COMMAND 17TH MP BRIGADE."

"Major Waldron and Sheriff Martinez for Colonel Barlow," she said at the desk.

"Go right in," the staff sergeant said. "The colonel's expecting you."

That impressed me. In my army days, junior officers were expected to wait in an anteroom long minutes, even hours, before the commanding officer was ready to see them.

Through the door as it opened I could see Kevin Barlow rising from behind his desk and sidling around it to greet his visitor with a huge smile on his face. That was very un-military, and I was moved.

"At ease," he told the major, who was standing at attention between us as he strode forward and grasped my hand in both of his.

"Steve, goddammit," he said. "Do you ever look good!"

"You, too, Kev," I said.

Except for two decades of creases and greying, he looked the same, a slim, bantam-sized man who seemed six inches taller just from his ramrod bearing. The major noticed that her superior officer gripped my hand a few seconds longer than he needed to. Her eyes misted slightly. I was moved myself. There is no greater bond than that between soldiers who together survive combat in close quarters.

The colonel broke the silence. "Thank you, Major," he said, and she saluted us both, turned, and left the office, closing the door behind her.

"We have so much to catch up on, Steve," Colonel Barlow said. "But I've got a brigade to run, a general to see and time is short. Sit down."

I sat in one of the two chairs in front of his desk and he took the other.

"Lifer juice?" he asked, pouring a cup of coffee. "We're opening a can of worms. What I'm going to tell you can't be repeated outside this office, okay? If your case ever should go to trial you can't use anything we talk about. Agreed?"

"Agreed," I said. "We'll find a way."

"Okay. This much is public knowledge. The United States forces are leaving behind about six billion dollars' worth of military materiel in Afghanistan as we pull out of that crapper. That's about one hundred seventy million pounds of vehicles, equipment and civilian gear such as toilets, air conditioners and nonclassified computers. It's way too expensive — or dangerous — to ship it all back to the United States. Some of it's being turned over to the Afghan armed forces, but most is either being cut up for scrap and given to local vendors or is being destroyed. Even washing machines and gym treadmills. They contain timers that could be used in bombs.

"One of the problems we have is that the Afghan army just isn't sophisticated enough to maintain a lot of this stuff. There's also a good chance that some rebels in that army will turn around and sell it to the Taliban. Another is that there's so much equipment. MRAPs, especially."

MRAPs, or Mine-Resistant Ambush Protected vehicles, are up-armored Humvees and personnel carriers that are resistant to improvised explosive devices on the roads.

"There are way too many of those vehicles in that theater," the colonel said. "Fort Fumble — I mean the Pentagon — in its infinite wisdom shipped many, many more MRAPs to Afghanistan than was necessary, and thousands of them have been sitting and rusting in motor pools waiting to be used. They never will be, at least by us."

"I'll be damned," I said. "The Defense Department has been offering a lot of surplus armored vehicles to civilian law enforcement in the 1033 program, but it's stuff that's already in the States, mostly used for training."

"Do you have any of it in Porcupine County?" Colonel Barlow said.

"Not really, except for a couple of M16 rifles we almost never have a need to use. We have accepted office supplies such as desks, computers, blankets, sleeping bags, digital cameras, tools and first aid kits. But I don't think rural sheriff's departments have any use for armored personnel carriers, although the state police SWAT teams might, once in a while. Even the Humvees are way too expensive to run and maintain. We'd use them only in

Fourth of July parades."

After September 11, 2001, the Department of Homeland Security encouraged police departments all over the country to accept free Humvees, Commando amphibious armored cars, M79 grenade launchers, helicopters and Bearcat armored trucks that cost three hundred and sixty thousand dollars each, all as part of the "global war on terrorism." But no truly rational cop wants a paramilitary law enforcement presence in his jurisdiction. The law is frightening enough without the use of Darth Vader weaponry. Besides, like surgeons with fancy new procedures, cops with high-tech military heavy weapons long to use them sooner or later. That leads to brute-force policing and sometimes ends up in social tragedies like the one that blew apart the town of Ferguson in Missouri.

"I see," the colonel said in a neutral voice. "Well, now for the stuff we don't want to get out."

"Yes?"

"You know there's corruption in every army," the colonel said. "Crooks in the ranks. Light-fingered supply sergeants in particular. It appears that your man's entire squad was not only peddling parts for MRAP Humvees but selling entire vehicles out of their garage at Bagram to some very shady Afghans. The CID investigators reported that they think the contraband was being resold down the line not only to the Taliban but also managed to reach the Assad gang in Syria *and* a shady group that much later was identified as ISIS."

"Isn't Iran in the way?" I said. "The Iranians support Assad and I'm sure would have let the equipment through to his forces in western Syria. But how would the stuff reach ISIS in eastern Syria and northern Iraq? Iran hates those guys as much as we do."

"CID thinks ISIS agents drove the stuff up through Turkmenistan," the colonel said, "then had it carried in ships across the Caspian Sea to Azerbaijan and finally rolled it down highways in eastern Turkey to Syria and Iraq. That's an old smuggler's route full of hands out for bribes.

"In any case, CID was getting ready to make arrests when the Pentagon handed down an edict to keep everything quiet and just ignore the thefts. No reason was given. Probably the army didn't want to be publicly embarrassed if word got out to the press that some of its own soldiers were crooked."

"Jesus," I said.

"Indeed," the colonel said. "Now, as for Staff Sergeant William Gibbs, the CID investigators said they thought that he was the banker for the entire Bagram garage operation. All the money from sales went to him and he held the dough."

"How much was involved?"

"The agents weren't certain, but they estimated between two and a half million and three million dollars. Possibly more."

I whistled. "That's a good chunk of dirty money," I said. "How did he get it out of Afghanistan?"

"That the CID doesn't know. If it was in American currency, he could have stuffed it into his barracks bag and carried that with him when he went home. Or he could have used a crooked Afghan banker to wire it to a bank offshore. Or he could have shipped it out on the back of a camel. There are hundreds of ways to smuggle money into the United States, but avoiding detection — or theft — is difficult."

"What else can you tell me about the investigation?"

"I can't show you the reports," the colonel said. "They're marked 'Confidential.' "

"Damn," I said. "Confidential" is the bottom rung on the official secrets ladder. Only "Secret" and "Top Secret" are higher.

"Seems like that's an improper way to classify information that would only be embarrassing if it got out," I said. "Selling army stuff is hardly a matter of national security. The generals are just trying to cover their asses."

"True," the colonel said. "Bureaucrats love to keep secrets just because they can. But I can do the next best thing. I can give you the names and Social Security numbers of all the men in Gibbs' squad. That's just 'For Official Use Only' information, marked 'Law Enforcement Sensitivity.' "

That means, I knew, that the material would be available to cops but not to snooping journalists armed with Freedom of Information Act requests.

"All have completed their enlistments and returned to civilian life," the colonel said. We don't know where they are, except for Gibbs, but it shouldn't be hard to find them."

"That ought to be enough to get started on," I said. "If Billy Gibbs was the bagman for that operation, it stands to reason that he may not have split the loot as promised, and one or more of those guys could have had it in for him."

"We're running out of time," the colonel said. "In a few minutes I've got to go see a general about something else. Here, I'll let you look at the names and numbers on the computer screen. Don't write any of them down—we don't want anything on paper. Do you still have that steel-trap memory?"

"Probably not," I said. "But I've got a pocket recorder."

"Great," said the colonel, spinning around the computer monitor on his desk so I could see the screen. "But kindly zap the memory as soon as you can."

A list of seven names, ranks, home towns and Social Security numbers greeted me. I whispered the entire list into my recorder.

"GIBBS, William F., SSgt, Chicago IL," followed by Social Security number and Ordnance Corps unit.

"AHERN, Michael G., SSgt, Holland MI," followed by the same.

"TANCREDI, Joseph E., Sgt, Muskegon MI," and the rest.

"BANKS, Keyshawn NMI, Cpl, Flint MI . . ." "No Middle Initial" in military fashion.

"Al-HABIB, Suleyman Abdul, Pfc, Dearborn MI . . ."

"CACOYANNIS, Ioannis NMI, Pfc, South Bend IN . . ."

"PERTTU, Arvo NMI, Pvt, Engadine MI . . ."

"Got 'em all, Kev," I said after ninety seconds of whispering into the recorder. "That's interesting. Everybody's either from lower Michigan or close to it."

"No surprise, Steve. All but Perttu and Gibbs were from a Michigan National Guard transportation unit based in Detroit. They were assigned to an Ordnance maintenance company when they were deployed to Afghanistan."

"What about that Arabic name?" I asked.

"Third generation Iraqi-American," the colonel said. "There are lots of Arabs in the Dearborn area, some forty thousand of them. They're mostly Lebanese descended from auto workers who immigrated in the 1950s."

"Perttu?"

"He's on the list, but the investigators said there's doubt that he was actively involved in the scheme. Not bright enough, they said. Nineteen years old. Barely passed the IQ test. The kind of soldier who never gets promoted. Now I've got to go. Can't keep a general waiting."

He stood and picked up the phone. "Send Major Waldron in."

The major materialized quickly, as if she had been waiting behind the door. Maybe she was.

"Escort the sheriff to the gate," the colonel said

THE RIDDLE OF BILLY GIBBS

suddenly, in a loud and annoyed voice that I was sure could be heard through the door and across the hall, "and make sure he gets out of Dodge." With that, Colonel Barlow shot me a sly wink.

"Yes sir!" Major Waldron said.

"Keep in touch," the colonel said in a whisper, tapping my forearm, and disappeared through another door.

As we exited the colonel's office, Major Waldron grasped me by the elbow. Her grip was gentle but firm.

"What's that all about?" I asked. "That 'get out of Dodge' stuff?"

"Tell you when we get to your vehicle," she said. "Meanwhile, I've got to put on my stern official escort face. Excuse me for that."

She steered me down the hallway and out the door, her grip unyielding, glaring a hole through oncoming ranks of soldiers so that they immediately made way for a pissed-off major marching a hapless country sheriff.

In the car, doors shut, I turned to Major Waldron.

"What the hell?" I said.

"You, Sheriff, are now officially persona non grata at Fort Leonard Wood. You wheedled your way into an interview with the CID commanding officer and tried to browbeat sensitive information out of him. He refused and cited national security concerns. You were impolite and swore at him. You are very lucky he did not call in a MP squad and bounce you into the stockade. Out of the goodness of his heart and his desire to maintain relations with law enforcement everywhere, he decided to let you go on the provision you agree never to come back. That is the story we are putting out if anyone asks."

"Then why give me such a VIP welcome in the first place?" I said.

"Gilding the lily," the major said. "We wanted to make sure everybody noticed your arrival as well as your departure. Just prettying up the cloak of deniability. Everybody now thinks that you were here, you demanded the impossible, and you were sent packing."

"I'll be damned," I said. "How much do you know about all this?"

"All of it, I think," the major said. "Colonel Barlow had me research the CID investigation of Sergeant Gibbs and his squad. I've been his aide for a long time. I guess I know him better than even his wife. Hell, I know his wife, too, and so does my husband, who's a lieutenant colonel. Off base and out of uniform we're quite chummy.

"The one thing I don't know is what you did for him, why he thinks you're such a hero."

As she gazed stonily out the window, the picture of an outraged officer escorting a disagreeable visitor off the base, I told her.

Just before she got out of the Expedition at the gate she turned to me and said softly, "I'm not going to salute you, *Lieutenant.* Too many eyes about. But you deserve one."

With that she alighted, turned and stalked into the guardroom building, the perfect example of military high dudgeon, no doubt ordering the MPs to shoot me on sight if I ever again should sully Fort Leonard Wood with my presence.

As I departed through the gate a pair of attack helicopters clattered low overhead, as if obeying Colonel Barlow and making sure I got out of town.

TWELVE

ON THE LONG drive back to Porcupine City I marveled at
Kevin Barlow's creativity. If in a future trial someone
should challenge our trail of evidence and demand a full
accounting, the colonel could easily deflect the request
with denials and evasive references to national security.
But I should not have been surprised. Nobody rises
through the military chain of command to a colonelcy
without learning a few tricks. I was sure that the old fox
would soon exchange his silver eagles for a brigadier
general's star.

    After crossing the Mississippi at St. Louis, I called
Sheriff Selena Novikovich at St. Ignace and told her that I
had turned up some information at Fort Leonard Wood,
but couldn't give her the details over an unsecured phone.
I'd do that from my office in the morning.

    "Meanwhile, there's a person of interest in your
jurisdiction worth locating," I said. "Arvo Perttu.
Discharged from the Army Ordnance Corps a year and a
half ago, still a private. Home town Engadine."

    Engadine is a tiny unincorporated community in the
western reaches of Mackinac County, a crossroads so small
and sparsely populated that it shares a zip code with
several other bumps in the middle of nowhere. It used to
be a stop on the Soo Line railroad, which hasn't sent even a
mixed freight train down that rusty old track, now owned
by the Canadian National, in at least ten years.

    "Think he's our guy?" Selena said.

"I doubt it. But he might know something. Wait till I get back and give you the details before picking him up."

"If we can find him. Eighteen months is a long time."

"Somehow I don't think you'll have much trouble."

"Okay. Bye. And, Steve?"

"Yes?"

"I have a feeling in my bones we're going to catch this killer."

"Hope you're right."

We hung up. I was beginning to feel the same way. Like me, Sheriff Selena Novikovich often follows her hunches, vague ideas formed by long experience in dealing with the caprices of criminal minds. Hunches develop largely in the unconscious and pop into the forefront of one's thoughts when triggered by new clues. Hunches that lead to success are few and far between, but sometimes they pan out.

Next I called Alex and gave him the same information I'd told Selena.

"Look in your in box tomorrow morning," I said. "I'll fax you all the details. But keep them under lock and key. This stuff's classified and if it falls into the wrong hands my ass will be burned and so will that of a very good friend."

"I hear you," the detective sergeant said.

Then I phoned Gil. "On the way home," I said. "New information. I'll arrive about two in the morning and will bivouac in my office. Get everybody into my office at eight a.m. and we'll discuss things."

" 'Bivouac?' " Gil said. "Are we back in the army again?"

"For a little while it felt that way," I said. "Complete to being thrown off the base with my tail between my legs."

I said that last for the benefit of eavesdroppers who

might be tapping cell phone conversations along Interstate 55 in Illinois. Those snoops might be working for the National Security Agency. It has been known to happen.

It had been a long day. I was bone tired and really should have begged a bunk at a sheriff's department somewhere in Wisconsin, but I kept driving through the night, my tires humming a monotonous tune on the blacktop. I stayed awake by counting mile markers and listening to truckers on the CB band, amusing myself by calculating the seconds as I slowly passed eighteen-wheelers before their drivers suddenly gasped as the big SUV with the star on its doors slowly appeared off their port beams. "Smokey on the prowl!" they called into their mikes.

At precisely eight a.m., unshaven and bleary-eyed after five hours of sleep, I called Selena from my office, first clicking on the encryption software to generate a code that scrambles phone transmissions. All Upper Michigan law enforcement agencies use the server that contains the software, thanks to judicious grant-writing with the federal government. I told her the whole story of my adventure at Fort Leonard Wood.

Then I did a Google search of the names of the seven soldiers without expecting to get any fruitful quick hits, and indeed got none, except for long rosters of White Page addresses for the same names. A rapid scan of LEIN, the online Michigan Law Enforcement Information Network, yielded nothing immediate except lists of names that would need careful and time-consuming winnowing down. I'd ask Chad and Alex to sift all that data later.

Finally I walked into the jail's kitchen-slash-conference room. Alex had already arrived. So had Gil, Chad and Annie. Sheila sat by, notebook at the ready. Garner Armstrong leaned against the refrigerator. Joe Koski listened from the dispatcher's desk next door. And there was an interloper at the table.

It was Jack Adamson, a retired FBI agent with whom I had investigated big cases in the past. Jack, who liked Porcupine County so much in his travels up here from Detroit, where he had been special agent in charge, had retired here. He lived in a comfortable cabin out on Norwich Road, and I ran into him often at events official and unofficial. Jack, who had neither spouse nor heir, was generous in his donations to Porcupine County institutions and always tried to make them anonymously, like Ginny.

"Why are you here?" I said.

"That museum piece over there invited me," he said, pointing to Gil. "He said you could use some help."

"You weren't supposed to say that," Gil said in his usual growl. "And who you calling a museum piece, you old bastard?"

"I'll deal with you later," I told Gil, who just grunted. Then I turned to Jack.

"I'd deputize you," I said, "but the county can't afford even a part-timer."

"I'm a retired high federal government civil servant," Jack said, "with a pension befitting such. I don't need your money. I'll do it for a dollar a year. Or the equivalent in coffee."

"Our coffee's not worth it," Gil said.

"I'll deputize you," I said to Jack. "Raise your right hand."

He did, and I did. I said the words, then opened my desk drawer, took out a badge in a leather wallet, and slid it over to him.

"Maybe you'd best go plainclothes," I said, "and haul out the star only when appropriate."

"You don't want me to shave and wear a suit and tie, as in the old days?" Jack said. Like everyone else in the Upper Peninsula that cool spring day, he was wearing a flannel shirt, jeans and hiking shoes. He also sported a flourishing white Santa Claus beard I thought was a rebellion against the rigid FBI dress code he had had to obey when he was an active agent.

"People would think you're a banker or undertaker," I said.

"Or a mobster," Jack said, completing the old joke about the few men who wore business suits in the Upper Peninsula.

"Come as you are," said Gil. "Just be sure your underwear's clean."

Chad, Annie and Sheila all giggled.

"Let's get to work," I said, and for the second time that morning described my adventure at Fort Leonard Wood, finishing with "What I've told you cannot leave this room."

After a moment of silence Jack said, "I can probably help you with the confidential stuff. I still do some consulting for the Bureau and have kept my security clearance. Want me to look into that?"

"I sure do," I said, "but take care, please. We don't want to jeopardize any prosecution that might emerge from this case."

"Or ourselves," Garner said.

"If that should happen," Jack said, "I can kick a few shins." Adamson was legendary in the FBI for his *lese majeste* with the lofty Washington hierarchy. He had been high in the headquarters pecking order himself, until he offended someone a bridge too far and was banished to Detroit. I was sure he had done or said something that would ordinarily have resulted in a summary firing but knew too much about the person he had crossed. I had no doubt he could do what he promised.

"All right," I said. "Let's everyone else report in. Annie?"

"Got started yesterday on the hunt for Gibbs' truck and first I called the sheriffs in all thirteen Upper Michigan counties and asked for help but all of them said they were shorthanded and I said who isn't and they said they'd give it a go anyway and get back to me in a few days."

That run-on sentence, delivered in a single breath, winded Annie, and she nodded to me, panting.

"Needle in a haystack, isn't it?" I said.

"Yes. We started with want ads going back a couple of months, and Craigslist, and found a few offers to rent that didn't pan out. Trouble is that most of these rentals are made by word of mouth. That's hard to pin down."

"Anything from the field?" I knew Annie had spent time driving around the county looking for locked barns and garages.

"There are three garages and one barn whose owners refused to open them up," she said. "They're just being assholes. I doubt the truck's in any of those."

Only if she believed it might be could she get warrants, and assholishness didn't constitute probable cause.

"Let's hope you don't stumble on a cat lab," Alex said. "Then we'll all have to work that one and lose time on the murder case."

Methcathinone labs are endemic in Upper Michigan. The inexpensive and highly addictive drug is easily and cheaply made, often in vans that move from place to place, but the byproducts are potentially so toxic that hazmat crews have to be called in for the cleanup after a bust. As soon as we shut one down and jail the makers, another lab opens up somewhere. They are a country sheriff's biggest headache, next to the caterwauling citizens who complain because it takes so long for the law to put the offenders in prison. The complainers have no idea how stringent the rules of evidence are, or how many man-hours of work it takes law enforcement to locate and prosecute the criminals.

The problem has been growing worse as wage-earning folks depart Porcupine County, often selling their houses for a pittance to outsiders looking less expensive places to live — and many of the newcomers use them for cat labs. Some of the younger perps peddle cheap heroin, and we're busting more and more addicts, some of them hookers barely out of high school.

"Chad?" I said.

"Zilch," he said. "I've found no trails to follow. If Gibbs salted three million bucks away in a Swiss or offshore bank or his mother's mattress, there are no numbers to check."

"Was Mrs. Gibbs' mattress checked?"

"Literally. A Chicago detective went over and re-interviewed Mrs. Gibbs. She willingly let him look around her apartment for cash stashes, including all the mattresses. She said she hadn't seen her son much since he got out of the army, except when he was jailed before the trial. She was believable, the detective said."

"I've got a strong feeling that if we find that truck we'll find something," Alex said.

"Maybe the CID report on that Bagram Airfield case will have some leads," Jack said. "I think I can get hold of it. May take a few days."

"Okay," I said. "Let's meet again in two days and compare notes."

Just then my iPhone buzzed. It was Selena Novikovich in St. Ignace.

"Secure the line, please," she said. "I just spent the last couple of hours with the subject you told me about."

The subject — out of habit Selena avoided using his name, even though our cell phone connection was encrypted — was Arvo Perttu. She had driven out to the hamlet of Engadine and found the young ex-soldier splitting firewood behind the modest three-room house where he had grown up.

As Selena drove into the driveway, she was struck by how astonishingly tidy everything looked. Many if not most backwoods homesteads in the Upper Peninsula appeared Dogpatchlike, covered by high grass and rusting old cars and trucks scattered willy-nilly, paint peeling from dried clapboards on the houses, their asphalt roofs patched with tin, broken fences barely holding back the encroaching forest. Not this one. Every bit of its broad yard had been mowed, the split-rail hickory fence kept straight and true. The small house was built of square-hewn logs probably a hundred years old, and its exterior left unfinished to bleach in the sun, but the window and door casings were freshly painted in forest green. Spring crocuses already were shoving their heads up from manicured beds along the front of the house. A dozen cords of high-stacked firewood marched in straight military ranks across one side of the property. Not a shred of refuse marred the scene.

Arvo Perttu was tall, black-haired, khaki-skinned and lean, still a sprout, Selena thought, but a good-looking one with an open and innocent face and a ready smile. His parents had died and left the place to him. Now he made his living "making wood," as Yoopers say, splitting it and selling it out of his yard, delivering it in a faded but well-maintained Chevy pickup to customers around two counties. Independent loggers sold him rough, ten-foot-long hickory, birch and oak logs the sawmills had rejected, and he used a chainsaw and a gas-driven log splitter. Even with the power tools, making wood was a hard, dangerous job that could be performed only between the spring thaw and the first snows of winter.

Most years the living was meager, but in this one the previous harsh winter and the promise of another to come was likely to keep the business booming from spring to fall. Many people in the U.P. would rely on firewood to stay warm because the price of liquid propane had shot out of sight in January. There was such a huge demand for LP gas that suppliers nearly ran out of it and rationed what they had.

The previous winter Arvo had sometimes earned a little money changing tires, washing cars and cleaning up in a local garage.

"The mechanics don't trust him," the owner of the nearby filling station where Arvo sometimes worked told Selena on her way to the young man's house. "They say he's just not bright enough to change a spark plug all by himself."

She thought Arvo was smarter than that — his truck, chainsaw and splitter also seemed to be well kept and in excellent condition — but she could see upon meeting him that he appeared to be slow-witted enough to be described with the polite label "mentally challenged."

When she wants to, Selena Novikovich can gently mother rather than frighten a subject into talking, and Arvo was the perfect childlike witness for such an approach.

"Honey," she said. casually perching on a leftover stump, "folks tell me you're a Finndian."

"Yeah, my grandma was Ojibwa," he said, proudly pointing to the carved cedar totem, a porcupine in a circle, on the front door. "She made that."

At the turn of the nineteenth into the twentieth century, some Finnish immigrants of both sexes, mainly male, married reservation Ojibwa and set up housekeeping in the then virgin forests of the Upper Peninsula. Both groups combined their skills, Finnish lumbering, farming and log cabin construction with Ojibwa forest survival and woodcraft. They were both oppressed peoples who had to deal with the prejudices of the Irish, Cornish and Croatians who dominated the area for decades. "No dogs, Indians or Finlanders allowed," tavern signs used to say well into the middle of the 20th century.

Today their descendants take considerable pride in being Upper Peninsula Finndians, as do the French-British-First Citizens *métis* of Quebec and the Maritimes, and tell their stories at both Finnish and Indian festivals.

Selena stepped to the door and caressed the cedar figurine. "That's very nice, Arvo," she said, genuine respect in her voice. "By the way, I hear you got out of the army a little while ago. How was it? How was the food?"

"It was all right," Arvo said slowly and carefully, as if plucking his words out of a deep box. "Food was okay."

"Only okay?"

"Well, okay is okay."

That, Selena thought, wasn't such a stupid response. Maybe it had only an existential meaning, but it was certainly defensible. Was there more to this young man than first appeared?

"What about your buddies?"

"They were okay."

"Okay" did seem to be the limits of Arvo's experience. Selena knew she was going to have to be more specific with her questions if she were to get anything substantial out of the young man. She wondered how the army could ever have accepted Arvo Perttu into its ranks. Some sloppy sergeant must have made a careless mistake while grading intelligence tests.

But Arvo was strong and healthy, the kind of young man who willingly worked at hard labor all day, slept soundly all night, and was ready for more in the morning. His demeanor seemed unfailingly pleasant, even when he suddenly asked Selena, "Why are you here?"

She was ready for the question. "It's about your time in the army," she said. "Not really about you, but about your buddies."

"They weren't my buddies," Arvo said, the shadow of a cloud suddenly crossing his face.

"Why?" Selena said.

"They made me do all the shit work, like washing and sweeping out Humvees and dumping oil drums. They wouldn't let me work with tools and stuff. They didn't want me to go out for a beer with them."

"That must have been awful."

"It was okay."

Despite herself Selena felt her heart going out to the childlike young man. She wanted to hug him. But she was a law enforcement officer and had a job to do.

"Arvo, I heard your buddies — I mean, the others in your squad — got into some trouble with the military police. Is that so?"

He was silent for so long that Selena finally said, "Arvo?"

He turned to the sheriff with a stricken expression. "I didn't tell the MPs anything," he said with more emotion than he had displayed all during the encounter. "The other guys said they'd kill me if I did."

"You're not in the army anymore, Arvo," Selena said. "You can talk to me."

"Where are the other guys?"

"Far away. Far away where they can't hurt you." Selena hoped that was true. She hated making promises she couldn't keep. But sometimes she had to.

"Arvo," she said in a gentle voice, "what happened?"

"The other guys were selling army stuff to Afghans," he said.

"What was the army stuff?"

"Parts. Engines. Wheels. Whole trucks."

"Did you see it happen?"

"Yes."

"How did it happen?"

"An Afghan would come in and give an envelope to Staff Sergeant Gibbs. Then he would leave and a little while later Private First Class Cacoyannis or Private First

Class al-Habib would drive the stuff off the base and come back without it."

Selena thought Arvo seemed to be painfully conscious of the difference between him and those with stripes on their sleeves, hence referred to the others in his squad by their ranks.

"The PFCs delivered the stuff to the Afghan buyers?" Selena said.

"I guess so. I didn't see it happen."

"How did that make you feel?"

"Not okay."

"Why?"

"It was American stuff. It belonged to America."

"What did Staff Sergeant Gibbs do with the money?"

Arvo hesitated, then said, "I don't know. I never saw it again."

"He didn't give you any?"

"No."

"Why?"

"He said it was better for me not to know."

"How did you feel about that?"

"Okay, I guess."

"What about the others?"

"I heard him tell them they would get theirs later, after they got back home. He said it was safer that way."

"What did you think of Staff Sergeant Gibbs?"

"He was nice to me. He never yelled at me when I fucked up, like the others did."

"What did you think about the others?"

"Corporal Banks was nice to me, too. He helped me figure things out."

"Why do you think Gibbs and Banks were nice to you?"

"I don't know. I'm a white boy and they were colored men."

"Did they know you were Finndian?" Selena said.

"Yes. They asked what my mom and dad were and I told them."

"What about Private First Class al-Habib?"

"He never talked to me. He didn't talk to anybody. He was kind of like me. Nobody liked us."

"Why do you think that was?"

"The other white guys said Private First Class al-Habib was a sand nigger."

"Sand nigger?"

"That's what they called Ay-rabs. Ragheads, too."

"What did they call you?"

"Private."

"Anything else?"

"I heard them say 'half-breed' a couple of times."

"Did they call Gibbs and Banks anything behind their backs?"

"Yes. Coal niggers. Sergeant Tancredi, Staff Sergeant Ahern and Private First Class Cacoyannis called them that. I don't think they liked colored people at all."

"Hmm," said Selena. "Well, Arvo, thank you for answering my questions. That was helpful."

She turned to go, then spun back around.

"Arvo?"

"Yes, ma'am?"

"Could I see your boots?"

"My boots?"

"Yes."

"Okay." He sat on a stump, removed both, and handed them to Selena.

Timberlands. Size fourteen wide. Not our man.

"Are you thinking what I'm thinking?" Selena said on the phone.

"Yup. If racism might be involved in this case, we'd better take a close look at Ahern, Tancredi and Cacoyannis first, then al-Habib and Banks," I said. "But it would help to have further confirmation that the first three are racist. That's just one soldier's view, you know. And, well, he's a little short of a full deck."

"Steve, I think Arvo Perttu, whatever his intelligence may be, is as honest as the day is long. And he has a good memory. He didn't stop to think about how to answer my questions but spoke up right away. Except for once when I asked what Gibbs did with the money. I doubt he knew. He may be a simple witness, but I think he's a reliable one."

"Simple and reliable. The best kind."

THIRTEEN

ALMOST IMMEDIATELY WE eliminated one of the suspects. Alex did a deeper search for Keyshawn Banks in LEIN, and came up with a list of half a dozen people in Michigan with that name who had been involved in misdemeanors and felonies ranging from blowing a stop sign to first-degree murder. Just one of them lived in Flint, and his date of birth and Social Security number were the same as that of the former army corporal.

This Keyshawn Banks had been shot to death just two weeks after Billy Gibbs' corpse turned up outside St. Ignace. There was no record on Google of a news story about the case. That did not surprise me. Most urban homicides of black men never make the media. Even to this day they're considered "cheap murders" without news value, unlike homicides of pretty blonde white women, that staple of cable television.

Banks had just walked out of a restaurant in a black neighborhood in Flint with his girl friend and was stepping out of under the sidewalk canopy into the street when he was struck squarely between the shoulder blades by a high-velocity rifle bullet. Several witnesses heard the shot and saw Banks collapse on the street, but no one saw his assailant.

"Wasn't a drive-by," Alex said on the phone. "Those almost always involve handguns or automatic weapons. The Flint detectives measured the trajectory and their best guess is that the shooter fired from atop a second-story roof a couple of blocks away. The coroner said he died instantly. Bullet tore the heart apart before exiting and embedding itself in the window frame of a store next to the restaurant. There was enough left of the slug to be identified as a seven-point-sixty-two-millimeter NATO military round. If the rifle is ever found, the striations on the slug probably can be matched to the lands and scratches in the barrel."

"Must be a million rifles chambered for that cartridge," I said. The 7.62mm had fed the old M14 infantry rifle that was the U.S. military standard until about 1970, and plenty of those were in civilian hands. A few M14s were still being used in the army and the marines as sniper rifles.

"Other than the bullet, the Flint cops had nothing to go on, and after the usual running in place, the homicide went into the cold case file. It was probably a murder. There's a tiny possibility that it could just have been random, the guy in the wrong place at the wrong time."

"Do you think so?" I said.

"Of course not, and neither do the Flint detectives, after I told them about the connection with Billy Gibbs. They've reopened the investigation and will share with us whatever they find if they ever find anything."

"What do we know about Banks?"

"Not a lot. Honorable discharge after three years in the army. As soon as he got out he worked part-time at a body shop and also went part-time to tech school studying computer hardware and programming. His girl friend told the detectives after the shooting that he had said he wanted to make something of himself. She also told them Banks spoke often about a windfall he said was soon to come his way, but never said what it was."

"Ah," I said. Another sign that we were on the right track. "What else?"

"Good student in high school and community college," Alex said, "but his grades weren't impressive enough to get him a scholarship anywhere. He wasn't an athlete. When he was sixteen he was swept up with several of his friends on suspicion of burglarizing a liquor store, but all of them were released for lack of evidence. Otherwise he had a completely clean record."

"Nothing to make him stick out, eh?"

"Except for one thing. A month before Gibbs was arrested in that sex case, the two of them went fishing together near Traverse City, according to Banks' girl friend. They had definitely kept in touch after the army. The girl friend said Banks had told her that Gibbs had been his best buddy in Afghanistan and they might be going into business together soon."

"What sort of business?"

"Opening a truck repair center."

"That makes sense with the computer stuff," I said. "These days trucks have all sorts of electronic controls, GPS receivers and engine computers. I think those two were ambitious. Gibbs implied to me that he was waiting to see how things went in Porcupine County before he decided what to do and where to go, but that was almost two years ago when he and Ralph Michael spent a sleepover in the jail. Of course time changes plans. Did Banks tell his girl friend where he and Gibbs might set up shop?'

"The Flint investigation report doesn't say," Alex said. "I'll suggest to the cops there that they explore that question on re-interview. Might lead somewhere."

"I will bet," I said, "that neither Gibbs nor Banks was thinking about opening a truck center in the Upper Peninsula. Not really because of racism but because the U.P. is a lousy place for new businesses these days. Population is dwindling, and the economy is in the toilet. It's almost impossible to get financing for new ventures. People propose all kinds of business schemes and get our hopes up, and then they just peter out for lack of money."

"But what if you have your own financing?" Alex

said. "Somewhere between two and three million dollars sounds like a very comfortable stake."

"Now there's that to think about," I said.

As for Suleyman al-Habib, the Iraqi-American in Gibbs' squad, Jack Adamson quickly took his measure. Two days after my conversations with Selena Novikovich and Alex Kolehmainen, the retired FBI agent came by my office, knocked on the door and said, "Got things to tell you."

"Sit down. Shoot."

"I'll begin at the beginning," Jack said.

"Fine," I said. Although it can be taken to extremes, a careful narrative that follows a time line rather than a bland report of highlights often helps make clear how events are connected.

"I got hold of the CID report on the Bagram case," Jack said. "Never mind how."

"My lips are sealed," I said.

"First thing I found was that al-Habib did not return to Dearborn after leaving the army. There are no reports of sightings since his departure from Fort Lee. He seems to have dropped off the face of the earth. And you know how hard that is to do nowadays."

Jack was right. Even paying cash and keeping to back roads doesn't always enable one to travel incognito. There are always networks of security cameras and government hackers skilled enough to get into them. Middle Eastern faces are also easily recognizable in rural America, and the dark suspicions of country folk in this media-whipped age of terrorism often result in frantic phone calls to the local gendarmes, who will make notes of them just in case and sometimes go out and question the suspect just to be sure. Such records are kept and can be accessed by law enforcement everywhere.

"What did the CID say about him?" I said.

"Basically what Arvo Perttu said, but in

considerably more detail," Jack said. "Gibbs was the bagman and the others the muscle. Perttu was squeezed out, as he said. Interesting thing is that al-Habib seems to have been the go-between in those shady deals. He was fluent in Arabic, passable in Pashto and knew quite a bit of Persian. He'd find and bring in the traders, help Gibbs strike a deal, and then see that the equipment was delivered to the right hands off base. He seemed to be the Number Two in the whole scheme, or so the CID said."

"We ought to check out al-Habib's history in Dearborn," I said.

Jack sighed and gazed at the ceiling. "Sheriff," he said. He never called me "Sheriff" unless he was vexed with me. "Sheriff, I wasn't born in a hayloft. What do you think I spent all day yesterday doing?"

"Sorry, Jack, just thinking out loud. Go ahead."

"Third generation Iraqi-American, as Colonel Barlow said. The CID report says his paternal grandparents emigrated from Baghdad in the nineteen-thirties to work in a Ford auto factory. His father worked there, too. The son's mother is Lebanese. She came over from Beirut after World War II and met his father at the Dearborn assembly plant.

"For three summers Suleyman worked at River Rouge, learning how trucks were built. He did well in high school, especially in languages. He just soaked them up. He was clearly bound for college, but went into the army first because he said he wanted to prove to the rest of the country that Arabs and Muslims were loyal Americans. He was quite the idealist, and that shouldn't be surprising.

"His family is Sunni and attends a progressive Dearborn mosque, one that allows women to lead prayers and even accepts gays and lesbians. As a freshman in high school Suleyman joined a mosque group that advocated friendly relations with Jews and Israelis, and even took a two-week brotherhood trip to Jerusalem with them."

"The army knew all this?" I said.

"Of course. Muslim military recruits are often the subjects of security investigations. I've done a couple of them myself." As a retired FBI agent, Jack often does a little part-time work checking out the bona fides of applicants for sensitive government jobs, and those in the army are some of them.

"With that kind of background," I said, "you'd think the army would have made him an interpreter."

"Given his work history, it was logical for him to join the Michigan National Guard transportation corps. When he was deployed it was also logical for the army to assign him to Ordnance at Bagram with the others from his Guard unit."

"Anything else?"

"One of the CID investigators said he thought al-Habib might have been coerced by Taliban or al Qaeda into proposing to his squad the scheme to sell equipment to civilians."

"What kind of coercion?"

"Threatening his family back home, maybe. And once the plot was under way, threatening to expose his role to the army."

"But he was an idealist," I said. "Any evidence for that stuff?"

"Only speculation on the part of the CID investigator. Suleyman could have turned. It happens. But the investigation was shut down before CID could follow that angle."

"What about Tancredi, Ahern and Cacoyannis? What did the CID have to say about them?"

"Nothing good," Jack said. "All three were competent soldiers during the work day but after hours were bad drunks, insulting Afghan civilians and military, generally being unpleasant assholes. Others in their platoon and company said they were glad they didn't have

THE RIDDLE OF BILLY GIBBS

to work next to them. And they were white supremacists."

I sat up. "How'd CID know that?"

"It tossed their foot lockers and barracks bags when they weren't looking," Jack said. "Neo-Nazi literature turned up in all of them. Mail from home."

"Nobody looks to see what's in the incoming mail?" I asked.

"Even the lowliest soldier has his privacy," Jack said.

Then it hit me, and I clapped a palm to my head. "Billy Gibbs probably came up to Porcupine County to hide," I said, "and chose to stay in jail rather than go free on bail because he feared that the publicity would tip off those soldiers to his location, and they might come gunning for their share of the money."

"And if they're racists," said Jack, "they might have another motive besides money. Revenge for being taken advantage of by a smart black man. Two black men, maybe."

"Looks like those three are our best suspects now," I said. "I guess we can put al-Habib aside, at least for now."

"We have to."

"What do you mean, we have to?" I said.

"It wasn't the Pentagon that ordered the suspension of the CID investigation. It was Langley. The CIA leaned on the Department of Defense, and shit ran downhill."

"Now you tell me. How'd you find that out?"

"Yesterday a young guy appeared at my door. He was CIA, and he said he had driven all the way from Washington just to tell me in person — no, *order* me — to drop my inquiries into al-Habib and all the rest. 'National security,' he said."

Jack's voice dripped with contempt. There is no love lost between the Central Intelligence Agency and the Federal Bureau of Investigation. Both government agencies are jealous of their turf and each believes the other encroaches on theirs. It is easier to pass an elephant through the eye of a needle than it is to get them to share information.

"But he didn't drive all the way from Washington. Probably flew into Duluth in a CIA Learjet and drove here. His car was a rental. It had a Hertz sticker and Minnesota plates."

"And that means?" I said.

"It just means his tradecraft wasn't very good. There was also no reason to lie, to claim he'd driven more than a thousand miles. Probably that just means the CIA assigned a very junior officer, one still wet behind the ears, to the case. His manner was blunt-force and in-your-face. Experienced agents tend to be quiet and subtle. But his credentials were genuine."

"How'd he find out that you were looking into the case?" I said.

"I asked, but he wouldn't respond," Jack said, "I think there was a flag on the case file that tipped off the Company if anybody outside CID peeked at it on a computer."

"There was no block on it?"

"Not at the time I looked. But there is now. I was a bad boy and checked again."

"All that explains why al-Habib disappeared," I said.

"He was probably picked up in a black Lincoln with shaded windows at the front gate of Fort Lee and driven directly to the Farm."

The Farm is the secret CIA training school for clandestine agents at Camp Peary near Williamsburg, Virginia.

"Wouldn't be surprised," I said. "Al-Habib had the perfect background for a covert agent inside al Qaeda or the Taliban, who may have thought his crookedness would make him easy to turn. And it also probably gave the CIA leverage to recruit him. Everybody wins."

"Except us, of course," Jack said.

I sat up. "Do you think that whole Bagram scheme was a CIA setup? Just to establish al-Habib's bona fides with the bad guys? Even if it meant selling American hardware to them? Hardware that might be used to kill Americans down the road?"

"Wouldn't put it past the Company," Jack said. "They do stuff like that all the time. They're masters of shady situational ethics. But in this case I think that they didn't recruit al-Habib until the CID had done the spadework. They just picked low-hanging fruit. That's my feeling, anyway."

FOURTEEN

THREE DOWN. THREE to go. Narrowing down a list of suspects is a mark of dogged police work, emphasis on dogged. It often takes months and even years of scratching and sniffing before a new lead emerges. Civilians never seem to understand that cases are not solved in fifty minutes, the way they are on television cop shows.

Chad soon announced that he had run into a brick wall trying to find the numbers of bank accounts Gibbs might have opened in the Caribbean and in Switzerland to stash the gains from the Bagram scheme. The former soldier had left absolutely no electronic tracks.

Annie had also come up with nothing in her fruitless search for Gibbs' truck, nor had her counterparts in other jurisdictions across the Upper Peninsula. The few warrants they had taken to recalcitrant property owners had turned up nothing of interest except a cat lab in Baraga County that was quickly shut down, and a traveling two-girl brothel in a small RV bus that had stopped inside a barn in Mackinac County, Selena's bailiwick. Inside the barn, one of the county's commissioners was caught quite literally with his pants down, and with relish Selena schooled him in the ethics of behavior before releasing him without charges. That benevolence, I was sure, would eventually benefit the following year's budget of the Mackinac County Sheriff's Department.

The first break came just before the Fourth of July, when Sheriff Mark Coyle called from Houghton County.

143

"I think we may have found Gibbs' truck," he said. "Some sport divers bumped into a pickup thirty feet below the surface of the water in an old quarry near Torch Lake. It's a red Ford crew cab. We're sending vehicles over there right now to winch it out."

"I'm on my way!" I said. "Annie! Chad! With me!"

The three of us hopped into Annie's Expedition and we laid rubber, blue lights flashing and siren wailing, all the way to Torch Lake, an hour to the east.

Twice we had to call Mark for directions over the bumpy gravel tracks of the deep woods near Torch Lake, and when we arrived at the sandstone quarry, two battle-tank-sized bulldozers from the Houghton County road commission had backed up to a sheer dropoff overlooking a dark pool below. The 'dozer operators were beginning to unreel three-inch-thick twisted steel cable from their winches and drop massive hooks to two waiting scuba-equipped deputies in the water below.

"I hope two 'dozers are enough," Mark said without preamble as we walked up. "That's a near vertical lift of more than twenty feet from the surface of the water, and the pickup's thirty feet down. We thought about hiring a heavy-duty wrecker truck with a derrick, but that would have strained the budget. These county guys aren't doing anything, anyway."

"Fuck you," said one of the bulldozer drivers cheerfully.

The other said, "Gonna have to get more cable from the county barn. Gonna have to belay our machines to a couple of those trees over there. We might not have the weight to lift that truck even together." He pointed to a stand of old-growth white pines that somehow had escaped the loggers a century ago. Their trunks easily spanned four feet. They looked immovable.

Stable fly season had begun a day or so before, and heavy spring rains had sprouted a bumper crop of mosquitoes, so many that the air thrummed with them. As we waited for more cable to arrive, the mounted forces of two counties retreated to the relative safety of their vehicle cabs, slamming the doors quickly to thwart squadrons of fierce biting flies that sounded as if an aircraft carrier's entire air group was warming up its engines.

"Where's the bug spray?" Annie said.

"Looks like Freddie forgot to put a can in the glove box," Chad said. Freddie Fitzpatrick was not always trustworthy with his upkeep of the department's vehicles, although he would often take his sweet time washing them just so he could stay outside in the sun instead of in his dark cell.

"I'll cut him a new one," Annie said.

"No, you won't," I said. "I will."

"Be our guest," Annie and Chad both said.

"Spray's not going to keep stable flies away," I said, an unhappy fact we all knew. Nothing does. These vicious nanovelociraptors creep inside collars and cuffs and bite. White socks draw them to ankles en masse.

"Shit," Annie said, and she spoke for two Upper Peninsula sheriff's departments as well as the Houghton County road commission. "At least they're not blackflies."

Those creatures, tiny sesame-seed-sized burrowing machines, creep inside collars and cuffs and raise angry welts. They swarm in the billions in warm weather. It was a little early for them.

"Did you know that blackflies cause river blindness in Africa and Central America?" Chad said conversationally.

"Oh, shut up," both Annie and I said.

Within the hour a truck laden with two rolls of steel cable arrived from Houghton and soon the bulldozer operators had hooked one end to their machines and wrapped the other around a huge pine. They were ready, and we all piled out of our vehicles to watch. Annie, who always took more care equipping her gear belt than the rest of us did, wore a head net and cursed less than the rest of us did.

Slowly the 'dozer operators lowered the two heavy cables toward the water. When the steel reached the surface, the divers grasped one of the hooks and guided it thirty feet into the murk, feeling around in the dark for towing cleats on either side of the truck frame. When the first cable was finally snubbed tightly the divers rose to the surface for the second cable and hook. After the longest fifteen minutes any of us had ever experienced in the bug-infested North Woods, the second cable was secured.

"Ready!" one diver called from below. "Start the winches!"

Slowly the operators spooled the cables upwards, both careful that the strain on each was equal. It wouldn't do to have one of them break or drag one of the trees out by its roots. But these guys were old pros and knew exactly what they were doing.

Inch by inch, foot by foot as the winches creaked and groaned, the cables rose, water streaming from their oily steel and spreading a sheen on the surface below. We could hear the pines creak and their tops sway as the winches ground. Twice the operators stopped the reels to check the tension on the cables at both ends of their bulldozers. The massive machines quivered and rocked slightly under the load, but their tracks did not move an inch.

After ten minutes we could see the shadowy outline of the truck's rear bumper appear a couple of feet below the surface of the water, and in another sixty seconds we spotted a red tailgate.

"It's Gibbs' truck!" Chad, Annie and I said simultaneously. Ruby red, Super Cab, chrome step bar. The license plate cinched it.

As the truck slowly ascended, water streaming from

every orifice, we could see that all the windows had been shot out. Dozens of bullet holes pocked every surface. The roof and hood had been violently dented, probably by a tire iron. The tires had been slashed.

"Somebody had it in for that truck," Sheriff Coyle observed unnecessarily.

"Probably the same somebody who had it in for Billy Gibbs," I said.

Slowly the dozers winched the truck over the stony lip of the quarry onto level ground. A deputy took a quick look through the windows without touching anything.

"Nobody inside," he said.

Another deputy had videotaped the lifting of the truck from the water and slowly walked around it with the camera, carefully documenting the visible damage.

By this time, Alex Kolehmainen had arrived from Wakefield and stood gazing open-mouthed at the devastated truck.

"Sheriffs," he said, "I suggest we haul this thing to the state police post at Marquette. The forensics lab there can go over it better than we can here."

"No argument," I said. Sheriff Coyle nodded in assent.

A flatbed tow truck soon arrived from Houghton and the remnants of the Ford winched aboard. Chad, Annie and I followed the tow, Sheriff Coyle and his deputies in their own Expedition close behind. Alex took the lead in his Tahoe. As the little police convoy made its way down and around Keweenaw Bay past Baraga and L'Anse, people stopped and stared at the shot-up red pickup. Finally, an hour later, we pulled into the state police garage at Marquette and the Ford was slowly lowered from the tow truck.

At Alex's direction a couple of technicians set up lights around the pickup. Another stood by with a video camera to record the proceedings.

When everything was ready, Alex nodded to us, stepped over to the pickup and opened the driver side door. What we saw made us raise our eyebrows. The interior of the truck had been utterly demolished. The door panels had been wrenched off and tossed on the floor, the headliner slashed into ribbons, the leather seats crisscrossed with deep knife wounds. The radio, CD player and other electronics hung in tatters from the dash.

"If anything was hidden in there," Alex said, "it's not there now."

"Look on the insides of the panels," I said. "Something might have been written on them. Names, numbers."

Over the next hour the technicians carefully combed the wreckage, laying every detachable item on a long table and photographing it. As they did so, they assembled the pieces in a loose jigsaw puzzle according to their placement inside the truck. In a while all four corners of the truck were jacked up a foot while the techs rolled around underneath on creepers, searching for nooks and crannies that might have been missed when the truck was first searched and destroyed before being given the deep-six.

Four hours later we still knew nothing. Not a single clue had turned up. Nothing had been taken from the truck that we could discern. All its equipment was there, although in terrible condition.

"How long do you think it was in that quarry?" I asked Alex.

"Judging by the sediment and the slight rusting, at least over the winter," he said.

"Could it have been dumped about the time Gibbs was killed?"

"Most probably. We can do some testing and try to pinpoint the exact time."

"There's one conclusion I think we can safely

draw," I said.

"What's that?"

"The same person who murdered Gibbs probably murdered this truck. Look at the similarities. Gibbs was killed in extreme anger, his trailer was stripped and torched in a frenzy, and this poor Ford was ripped apart, shot up and drowned just as savagely."

"Why would the killer do that to a *truck*?" Chad asked.

"Because he didn't find what he was looking for. If he had, he'd just have taken it and dumped the truck into that pond without tearing and shooting it up. Same with Gibbs' trailer. I think this fellow is badly in need of anger management counseling."

Fleetingly I thought of Gene Stenfors and quickly sent him back down the suspect list. He was physically incapable of inflicting such destruction. Revenge for what had happened to his daughter would have been his only motive, and that was almost certainly not enough to lead to a destructive search for hidden treasure.

Just before suppertime Joe called from the dispatcher's desk. "Tim Alderson here to see you," he said.

"Send him in," I said. Tim is a good fellow but he was the last person I wanted to see today. He is one of the six county commissioners and a reliable ally. He is sometimes able to persuade the other commissioners to loosen their death grips on the purse strings for the sheriff's department. When he comes by to talk to me in person, however, he never brings good news.

"Do you for?" I said.

"Steve," he said slowly, sliding his considerable bulk into the chair across the desk from mine, "the county board is unhappy."

"Including you?"

"Well . . ." He hated being the bearer of bad news,

too, especially when it was news he agreed with.

"I'm a big boy," I said. "You can tell me."

"The board is upset that the department is spending so much time on the Gibbs case," Tim said. "Can't you let the state police handle that?"

"Why?"

"There's a huge backlog of summonses and warrants at the county building," he said. "The judges are going nuts because they can't get anything done unless the paperwork is delivered. The village council is pissed, too. Ordinances aren't being enforced."

Porcupine City used to have its own police department, with several officers and a chief. After World War II, as officers retired or moved on to other jurisdictions, the department was gradually phased out because of lack of funds. Since the 1970s, when the last village cop retired, the village has contracted with the sheriff's department to enforce its laws. Now and then Gil sends out deputies to tell people to fix their roofs, mow their lawns, rake their leaves and tidy up their garbage, and to make sure zoning ordinances are observed. This is nickel-and-dime stuff that the village initially addresses by sending out stern letters, but citizens are more apt to obey warnings from uniformed officers than they are paper nastygrams.

"Tim," I said, "what you say is true. But you know that my department is grossly understaffed and has been for years. We are down to four corrections officers and four road patrol officers as well as Gil and myself—just half the manpower we had a decade ago. This is not nearly enough. The corrections officers can't go out on patrol because overseeing the inmates is a full-time job. The road officers have to patrol the entire county while at the same time investigating crimes. And now you're telling me we can't investigate the murder of a prominent citizen of Porcupine County?"

"Well," Tim said, waving his palms in placation, "that murder happened in Mackinac County, didn't it? Way over on the other side of the Yoop?"

"Possibly it did. But Billy Gibbs was a Porky and he may have been murdered because he was a black man, because he was acquitted in a controversial Porcupine County case involving rape and a white woman. I cannot ignore that."

"Steve, the case is old and getting older," Tim said. "The board wants us to forget it and move on. Gibbs was only — "

He didn't finish the sentence. Tim's notion, I thought, was just another example of the sad state of race relations in the United States. White Americans tend to believe that in the long run, justice for a single black man hardly justifies the inconvenience of a couple of thousand people in an entire county. But I thought that to let the case of Billy Gibbs wither and die on the vine of memory simply was another short-sighted postponement of a terrible reckoning that needed to be faced.

"Steve, aren't you getting a little obsessed?" Tim said. I looked him in the eye.

"Tim, if caring about justice is obsession, then I guess I am."

I leaned back in the chair and took a deep breath. "Tell the county board we'll start on that court backlog right away. Tell the village to send over a new list of the most important things that need taking care of. I'll put a couple of deputies on them."

"Thanks, Steve," Tim said. He was vastly relieved that I saw things his way, or appeared to. He stood up, nodded, and left.

Gil's face quickly appeared in my office door. He had heard the entire exchange. Before he could open his mouth to protest, I said, "Chad's stumped at the moment and Annie no longer has a truck to look for. Put them on court and village duty for the next two days, and then we'll take things from there."

"Okay," Gil said. Not "yes, sir" or "right away, sir," as an old first sergeant would respond to the company commander. "Okay" not only meant he was fine with the order but also that he approved of it, and would see that it was done and done well. He knew I was buying time for what was most important to me. To us all at the Porcupine County Sheriff's Department, for that matter.

"Steve," Sheila trilled from the squad room, "Mel Atwater just called. Big storm's coming up tonight. Weather Bureau says it'll be a nor'easter, a hard blow, fifteen- to seventeen-foot waves, fifty-knot gusts. Small craft warnings are out. Mel's radioing all the boats that have left the harbor in the last couple of days and haven't come back."

The veteran harbormaster was a mother hen for all skippers who kept their craft in Porcupine City Harbor, and we entrusted him with the upkeep of the Boston Whaler that we used for rescue operations and sometimes criminal investigations.

Before I could ask, Sheila said, "Mel says the Whaler is gassed and ready to go, but he's pulling it up on a trailer and staking it down." That made sense. Powerful waves could wash up through the channel from the lake to the marina and toss small craft around like matchsticks, although the harbor was protected on three sides by earthen berms. Big boats could ride things out, but I knew that Mel would have called the owners of small outboard-propelled craft to come and pull theirs onto dry land.

I sighed. "Just what we need," I said. "Another weather extreme."

The previous winter not only had been one of the coldest and snowiest in memory, but also for the first time in a quarter of a century Lake Superior had frozen over from the American shore all the way to the Canadian. The ice had broken up many weeks past the normal time, slowing the opening of the shipping season. Floes and bergs had remained afloat offshore well past Memorial Day rather than disappearing at the beginning of April, and on the third day of June I had awakened to a vast ice field floating a few feet away from my cabin. Heavy goose-drownder spring rainstorms had repeatedly flooded swamps and inshore wetlands. The level of Lake Superior was a full foot above the previous year's mark and was rapidly approaching an all-time high. Man-made global warming was probably the culprit, the climate scientists said, although there were plenty of naysayers about that, especially in the rural Upper Peninsula. But everyone agreed that the weather was changing, and not for the better.

FIFTEEN

WITH A START I realized I had been neglecting Ginny. I had not stopped by her house except for a brief hello once or twice ever since Billy Gibbs' trailer burned down two weeks earlier. I had not spent a lot of time with her over the winter, either, thanks to long hours fighting the social consequences of snow and frigid temperatures and bunking at the jail rather than going home. We'd missed three consecutive Sunday-morning breakfasts at Merle's, a tradition that helps keep many Porkies rooted in their home town and linked to their neighbors. Our relationship had become one of hurried cell-phone calls ending with "Love you, goodbye." It was a long time since we had last shared her four-poster upstairs, and I was missing it badly.

She turned from the stove when I opened the back door. "Look what the cat dragged in," she said in reasonably friendly fashion, although I thought I heard an edge to her voice. "Coffee?"

"Please," I said, although it was late and I'd been drinking coffee all day. I didn't want to turn away any invitation, no matter how small.

Ginny didn't move in for a kiss, but leaned against the refrigerator and contemplated the haggard, unshaven, unkempt and probably smelly lawman in her kitchen. "Are we still seeing each other?" she said, only half in humor. "Because it seems to me that hasn't happened much lately."

"No, it hasn't," I said, "but that's hardly my fault."

When this happens she always makes me feel defensive. She doesn't mean to, but she does. Because, dammit, even though I don't want to admit it, she's right.

"I know, long hours," Ginny said. "And because you care."

She understood.

"The county doesn't seem to," I said, my expression forlorn.

She sat down and put her hand on mine. She always does that when I'm feeling sorry for myself.

"Ginny," I said, "maybe I'm a lousy sheriff."

"That I don't believe, not for a second. Why do you say that?"

"The county board seems to think so. It's pissed because we haven't been doing our jobs, even though we're shorthanded. We haven't been serving papers and we haven't been enforcing village ordinances. We've been chasing around all over Upper Michigan looking for a killer instead.

"What's more, I had thought the county was a tinderbox waiting to explode after the Billy Gibbs verdict. It wasn't. It may have rumbled and belched and farted, but it didn't blow. I didn't keep the lid on. The citizens did, all by themselves. But now everyone just wants the case to go away so they can put their blinders back on, as always happens in matters of race. Am I still misjudging them?"

"Opinions are not acts," Ginny said. "They can be ugly and they can be hurtful, but they're not illegal."

"You're telling me."

"Sometimes I think you mistake the one for the other," Ginny said. Now she covered my hand with both of hers.

"All right. But it still takes only one citizen of Porcupine County to murder another."

"Are you sure that happened?"

"I don't know. I just don't know. It just might have

been one of Gibbs' fellow soldiers."

"Explain, please," she said. I hadn't yet told her about the results of my trip to Fort Leonard Wood, about the CID investigation of Gibbs' squad, about Jack Adamson's inquiries and the CIA squelching of them, about the murder of Keyshawn Banks and the disappearance of Suleyman al-Habib, about the hate literature found in the personal possessions of Staff Sergeant Ahern, Sergeant Tancredi and Private First Class Cacoyannis, about what we'd found after the trailer fire and what we'd found when Gibbs' truck was raised from the quarry. So I did, in as much detail as I could remember.

"Gibbs may have been murdered because he was a black man who slept with a white woman in Porcupine County and beat the sexual assault rap. Or he may have been murdered because he ran off with dirty money in Afghanistan and cut out his army co-conspirators — and maybe because he was a black man, too, and some of the others had it in for black people. The killing of Keyshawn Banks reinforces that theory. We don't know why he was killed, let alone by whom, but coming so soon after the Gibbs murder can't be a coincidence."

"Money and racial animus," Ginny said. "Two strong motives."

"Stronger when taken together," I said. "The race angle is easy to figure out. The money angle, not so much. If we can find out where it is, we might find the killer."

"Could the killer already have the money?"

"Yes, but I doubt it. If he had found it in Gibbs' truck, wouldn't he just have dumped the truck without sodomizing it?"

"Maybe not if fervent racial hate was a factor," Ginny said. "Rage makes people do terrible and irrational things."

"Of course. But that truck was so torn apart that I don't think whoever dumped it found anything. I think he kept looking until there was nowhere left to look, then he shot it up and pushed it into the quarry."

"You said Chad couldn't find an electronic trail for the money."

"That's right. He even had the Afghan cops in Kabul looking at bank records."

"That's surprising. I thought there was no love lost between Afghans and Americans."

"No, but cops are cops, and they tend to want to help each other look for criminals. Anyway, sometimes soldiers opened accounts in Kabul and some of them presumably used them to launder money. Nothing turned up. It appears Gibbs didn't spirit the money out of Afghanistan by wire."

"Could he have physically smuggled cash out of the country?" Ginny said.

"It's possible, but it wouldn't have been easy. Trunks and barracks bags are often opened and examined on the way. Also, would you ship a couple of million dollars home in a package? He might have needed a confederate, maybe a fellow soldier rotating home, and who's to stop one of those from just keeping the money?"

Ginny hauled out a World Atlas from the book-choked shelves in the pantry and opened it. What she said next did not surprise me, because she is both highly educated and well informed. More so than I am.

"What about driving the cash from Kabul to Karachi on the Gulf of Oman in Pakistan by way of Kandahar?" she asked. "That's only a thousand miles. Maybe the money could have been laundered in Karachi, or sent in a box aboard a cargo ship to the United States."

"We thought of that," I said. "But NATO doesn't use the southern Kandahar to Kabul route for military convoys. Too many Taliban and warlords. Rather, it has been using a couple of highway routes from Karachi east to northern Pakistan and into Afghanistan through the

Khyber Pass."

"If Gibbs had wanted to use a courier to send the money by road, he'd have risked it being snatched by bandits, or maybe the courier would just keep it," Ginny said. "Couldn't he have dressed as a civilian and used the Kandahar route to carry a suitcase full of cash to Karachi? Two days down and two days back. Could he have taken a few days' furlough for that? Or gone AWOL?"

"Yes. His squad probably could have covered his absence for a while, four or five days maybe."

"Did the CID report say anything about that?" Ginny said.

"I never saw it," I said, "but I think if it did Jack Adamson would have mentioned it. Now he's been warned away from the case and we can't check on it. In any event, whatever actually happened, it's almost certain that the money got here somehow, and Gibbs was spending it."

"So the question now is where the rest of it is," Ginny said.

"And who's looking for it? Besides us."

I gazed over the table at Ginny. Unloading on her not only helped me to see things more clearly but also reminded me how very much I depended on her love and counsel.

"Darling," I said. "I'm not going to be a stranger anymore."

"Oh, you will be, sometimes," she said, smiling sweetly and a little sadly. "You're a sheriff. You can't help it. But maybe you can help *me* with something."

"What's that?" I said.

"Campers on my beach. They set up a tent this afternoon. They won't leave."

"No problem," I said. Once or twice a month the department receives a complaint about trespassing on private beaches, and usually a deputy goes out to handle

158

things. But here I was, quite conveniently.

I strode the sandy path from Ginny's cabin twenty yards to the beach and came upon a two-person nylon backpacker's tent in the middle of the sand halfway between the tree line and the water fifty feet away. A young man and a young woman sat on a nearby log sunning themselves.

"Sheriff's department, Porcupine County," I announced, and they turned to look at me. "How you doin'?"

"Okay," the young man said. "Is something wrong?"

He was mildly tanned, wearing floppy blue swim trunks, and I could see that his backpack was one of L.L. Bean's better models. His companion, clad in a black bikini of fairly modest cut that almost succeeded in covering her shapely buttocks, also appeared to be of respectable origins, so far as I could tell.

"Well," I said, keeping my voice casual, "the owner of this property does not want you to camp on it. You will have to pack up and move on."

"But, sir, I believe we have a right to be on the beach. Isn't it a federal law?" The young man spoke politely and sincerely, and I decided to answer in kind.

"I'm afraid that's a common misconception," I said. "There is no federal law about beach rights. There *is* a Michigan state law. It is based upon a legal case called Glass versus Goeckel, and in its infinite wisdom the Michigan Supreme Court in 2005 handed down a ruling. It says that property owners own the beach down to the water's edge, but that the legal doctrine of public trust allows people to walk on the land between the water's edge and the ordinary high water mark."

I kept my voice calm and pedantic, like a professor addressing a seminar from his notes. Always make your subject think you know more about the law than he does.

Sometimes you actually do.

"But doesn't that mean we can be here?" the young man said.

"It means you can *walk* along the beach. The ruling never said anything about sunbathing, picnicking or camping, only walking. That means you have to keep moving. You can camp here only with the permission of the property owner, and she doesn't want to give that."

"Why not?"

"She doesn't know you. And you didn't ask permission."

The couple looked at each other and stood up.

"Okay," she said. "We'll go."

"*Where* can we camp?" the young man said.

"You ought to be able to find a property owner down the way who'll say okay," I said. "Just keep walking until you find one. Knock on doors."

"What if nobody's home?" the young woman said. "Would we be bothering anyone then? There are a lot of summer places where folks haven't yet arrived."

"Legally," I said, "you would be trespassing." I applied a faint but distinct emphasis to "legally."

She got the message. "Thank you, sir," she said, helping her companion roll up the tent. "See you around." They prepared to leave, backpacks over trunks and bikini, getting ready to trudge in the firm damp sand a few feet from water's edge.

I started to add a word of caution, but they stopped before I could speak.

"Exactly what is the ordinary high water mark?" the young woman said. She was intelligent and curious. I was impressed.

"That the Michigan Supreme Court didn't define very well," I said. "In these parts we try to use common sense. The beach is only about fifty feet wide here. In a storm the water will wash up to the tree line. That could be called the high water mark on this particular beach. In other places it's not so clear. If you walk on the wet sand along the water's edge, which you will anyway because it's easier, you'll be fine."

"Thank you," the young woman said, turning to leave.

"Oh, one more thing," I said in what I thought was a pretty good imitation of Lieutenant Columbo. "You don't want to camp anywhere near anybody's beach tonight."

"Why not?" they both said.

"A helluva storm's coming in by midnight tonight. See those dark clouds to the north? Super high waves, super high winds. The kind of thing we usually see in November."

"*Now* you tell us?" the young woman demanded.

"One thing at a time," I said. "More efficient that way."

The truth was that I was having a little fun at their expense, partly to forget the tension with Ginny, partly because the young people were so clearly non-Yoopers, well-to-do yuppie puppies from Chicago or someplace like that. Not that I had it in for visitors, but sometimes I felt a little snarky, especially when things were difficult.

"If I were you," I said, "I'd spend tonight and maybe tomorrow night under a strong roof. This oncoming storm is forecast to hang around for a couple of days. Luckily there's a motel just a quarter of a mile west down the highway. The rates are very reasonable, and they'll let you cook at one of the picnic tables outside. If you want to go there, I'm sure the lady who owns this beach property will let you walk through it to the road. It's just a hundred or so yards away."

"Thanks, Sheriff," they said in unison. "We had no idea a storm was coming."

Most visiting hikers and campers in the Upper Peninsula have the sense to check the weather forecast before arriving, but this pair clearly hadn't.

Dutifully they asked Ginny at her back door if they could pass through, and she assented.

"Mission accomplished," I told her.

"Thank you again," she said. "Dinner?"

"Yes. I've missed you."

The only thing better than forgiving, the saying goes, is being forgiven.

The residents of Porcupine City, just a mile or two away from Lake Superior, spent the night mostly unaware of the inhuman force of the fifty-four-knot gale that whistled, howled, whooped, dipped down and slashed through town. Nor'easters are always noisy, and inland this one was merely noisier than usual. Everywhere it sounded as if a freight train was coming through, its locomotives having lost their mufflers. Some people lost power, some lost a few trees and bushes, some lost branches, some lost shingles from their roofs and quite a few lost sleep, but when morning came things looked mostly normal from their point of view.

Along the shore of Lake Superior it was a different story. The waves — at one point mini-tsunamis seventeen feet high — slammed into tree lines and scoured out enormous tangles of roots, toppling birches and beeches, and carried away tons and tons of sand. People lost beloved sand beaches. Some whose houses and cabins had been built close to the shore line discovered that only a few feet of sandy bluff remained between their homes and the lake. Old-timers said the storm — a November blow in late July — was the most violent and damaging in their memory, just as relentless as the one that sank the 730-foot-long lake freighter *Edmund Fitzgerald* off Whitefish Bay and drowned twenty-nine sailors in the eastern reaches of the lake in 1975.

Almost every hour all night I slipped out of Ginny's

four-poster to call Joe Koski at the sheriff's department to check on events. He kept in steady touch with the coast guard, the Army Corps of Engineers, other law enforcement departments, and park rangers. Miracle of miracles, no reports of injuries, let alone deaths, rolled in. We didn't have to call out the search-and-rescue squad, whose members were standing by at their homes, ready for action.

Ginny's house sat well inland from the beach, protected from storms by several yards of thick woods, and though all night we could hear the heavy pounding of the surf, counterpointed by the crash and splinter of massive logs tossed ashore like pick-up-sticks, her property escaped damage.

The storm mostly had blown itself out shortly before dawn. The forecast two-day tempest thankfully had been compressed into one. At six a.m. I left Ginny's house with bacon and eggs still warming my belly and drove to my lakeshore log cabin five miles west on the highway, worried sick about what I was going to find.

The cabin itself had weathered the storm well, thanks to its location on an escarpment of bedrock several feet above the lake and its protection on the lakeside by a low concrete sea wall and several layers of gabions, huge steel-mesh baskets filled with rocks, that the previous owner had installed forty years before I bought the place. The lakeside windows somehow survived stinging spray from the crashing surf not twenty feet away. So did the asphalt shingle roof.

The beach, however, was an unholy mess. Thousands of cubic yards of sand on either side of the cabin had disappeared, replaced by drift logs, some of them two or three feet thick and twenty feet long, scattered helter-skelter along the beach. The waves had scoured out roots of stout birches and pines, and toppled them into the water. My shoreline was a good ten feet farther inland than it had been. I was going to have to hire someone to reinforce it with many tons of rock riprap. That meant going to the bank, hat in hand, for a loan.

That also meant begging permission from federal and state bureaucracy to save my land. In these parts the Lake Superior shoreline is largely wetland, and protecting it against storms requires permits from both the DNR and the U.S. Army Corps of Engineers. The state usually moves quickly in the permits process, but the federal government takes its sweet time. I hoped the job could get done before the November gale season tore away even more land. For a good two hours, as I surveyed the damage, the matter of Billy Gibbs slipped entirely from my mind.

At midmorning, on my way to the sheriff's department, I called Jack Adamson and Alex Kolehmainen, and asked them if they could drop by for a short conference. Both agreed.

"Now then," I said, when we had put away the first cup of jailhouse coffee, "let's talk about where we go from here in the Gibbs case."

"I've got to be careful," Jack said, "not to leave footprints."

"Me, too," I said. "My little visit to Fort Leonard Wood might have shown up on CIA radar. Quite possibly CID's pulling up of one of its own cases on the computers didn't raise a flag, but we can't assume that."

"Not me," Alex said. "The CIA hasn't put me up against a wall yet, and, besides, it has no jurisdiction in the United States, does it?"

"Maybe not legally," Jack said, "but it can step on your dick any old time it wants to. Those guys have big shoes."

"All the same," Alex said, "those three unpleasant fellows from Gibbs' squad are in Michigan, or at least they came from here. They are now civilians and therefore subject to the tender mercies of the Michigan State Police if they are in-state and the indignant bluster of the Porcupine County Sheriff's Department if they are in-county. Who could gainsay our efforts to find out what they are up to today? And it's doubtful the CIA would spot our trail if we're careful."

"Don't be so sure," Jack said. "They've got eyes everywhere. Even out here in the middle of nowhere."

"They didn't slip a bug in your underpants?" Alex said.

"No, but they did my cars," Jack said. "That young guy who came out to warn me off crept out in the dead of night and slapped GPS bugs on both my Accord and my Explorer. I watched him do it on infrared video. Not very skillful, was he?"

Even in retirement Jack, having plenty of enemies he had put into federal prison for long stretches, had mounted motion-detecting cameras on the four corners of his property as well as his garage and front door, and wired them to a recorder in the house. Not even a chipmunk could cross the property without his knowledge.

"The bugs still there?"

"Of course," Jack said. "I'm driving the vehicles into town to shop and go fishing, but when I'm wearing my investigative hat, I borrow Zoey's pickup."

Zoey Rasmussen is a well-to-do widow from northern Illinois who lives across the way and a few hundred yards south of Jack's place on Norwich Road. She keeps llamas and horses, some of them hers, most of them boarded, in a large meadow with a stable and helps teenagers learn to ride. Like Jack, she came up to Porcupine County on business once upon a time, liked what she saw, and eventually bought her place. In her early sixties she's still a good-looking woman and Jack wasted no time making friends. Now Jack and Zoey are more or less keeping company, as the old folks still say.

"I'd loan you one of the department's vehicles," I said, "if we had one to loan." We have two Expeditions, a stupidly overpowered late-model Mustang the DEA had given us for our long-defunct D.A.R.E. program, and a five-year-old federal-grant Dodge Charger nobody liked because its trunk was too small to hold the usual country lawman's equipage. For odd jobs we also have a fifteen-year-old rustbucket Chevy pickup, a hand-me-down from the U.S. Forest Service's law enforcement arm, but it's so ancient and battered we usually forget to put it on our official equipment list. We were hoping the village would contribute to the matching federal funds we had to come up with in order to get another Expedition. It would have been easier to accept a Pentagon gift of an armored personnel carrier, but of course we couldn't afford the gas to run it.

"We'd loan you one from the state police garage, too," Alex said. "But we don't have enough wheels to go around, either."

"No problem," Jack said. "Zoey likes me. I pay for the gas."

"I will refrain from making a crude and suggestive remark," Alex said.

"That must take incredible forbearance," Jack said.

"Oh, shut up, the both of you," I said. "Now, how're we going to do this?"

"I'll look into the whereabouts of Ahern, Cacoyannis, and Tancredi," Alex said. "The army at Fort Lee will have their forwarding addresses of record at the time of their discharge. Should be easy enough to get."

"Will the CIA be watching?" I said.

"Doubt it," Alex said. "They didn't recruit those guys, only al-Habib. What interest could the Company have in them?"

"All the same, watch your ass," Jack said.

"Meanwhile, I'll go consult the Southern Poverty Law Center about that hate material the CID found in their lockers, and see what those assholes are up to these days."

"Let's be careful out there," I said.

"Yes, Sergeant Esterhaus," Jack and Alex said simultaneously. Every cop in the world knows that tag line from "Hill Street Blues." And takes it seriously.

In the late afternoon, when Annie and Chad rolled in from the village hall and county courthouse, respectively, I asked them how their day had gone.

"Not bad," Annie said.

"The dark side of police work," Chad said morosely.

"Spill it," I said.

Annie, a friendly and open person who likes to get out to schmooze with the public, had been in her element. She flipped open her notebook.

"The village gave me a long list of infractions to deal with. Couple of construction sites without building permits. I shut them down and the site bosses headed for village hall to get the permits. They said they just forgot. Bullshit, of course."

Sometimes, but not too often, a parsimonious contractor will start a job hoping the authorities won't notice so that he can save on the fees and hassle for the building permits. They often get away with it when the job is in the woods out of sight. That was, I knew, going to happen on the lake shore as panicky landowners begged contractors to ignore the permit process and bolster their battered properties right away. Neither the DNR nor the Corps of Engineers had much in the way of machinery to enforce their rules. Often the fines they did levy when they managed to discover infractions were so small the contractors considered them part of the cost of doing business.

"A citizen had complained that a neighbor was operating an unlicensed restaurant off her front porch," Annie said. "Turned out to be three small children peddling lemonade and cookies for the last couple of weeks, to earn money for summer camp. They were good, too."

"The children?" I said.

"No, the cookies. The lemonade was a little sour."

"Did you bring me any evidence of the crime?" I said.

"I knew you would ask," Annie said, handing me a napkin-wrapped chocolate chip cookie as big as my fist.

"Thank you," I said, taking a bite. Indeed it was good. "Go on."

"There were the usual eyesore complaints, a fallen-down garage and a loose pile of gravel, livestock on property not zoned for it, that sort of thing. Everybody cooperated and promised to clean up, and nobody gave me lip.

"There was only one real problem. A really crazy cat lady."

"Who was that?"

"Angie Johansson out at the end of Simpson Street. She's got to be past ninety. I think we're going to have to do a well-being. Her place smells to high heaven of cat pee. It's falling apart. She's a hoarder. And she refused to come out of the house and talk to me."

One of the most unpleasant tasks of a rural county sheriff is looking after the health of very old recluses whose slide into dementia includes the complete collapse of their living conditions. Often they subsist on dog food, snared rabbits and questionable water from nearby creeks. Often they suffer from hoarding disorder, squalor piled atop squalor. Their pets run loose and reproduce wildly.

They often have no family to make decisions for them. In these cases we have to coordinate official visits from the health department, the mental health clinic and the county legal office, then find places for the recluses to go, often to adult foster homes and sometimes Medicaid beds in nursing homes. They never go willingly, and afterward we are left with a massive cleanup job. Sometimes the places are so hopeless they are seized for back taxes and are either auctioned or simply burned down as the fire department stands by.

"Okay, get the procedure started," I said. "It'll take a while to get everything lined up. Maybe even a month."

Annie left my office and I turned to Chad. "Yes?" I said.

"Same old same old," he said. In Porcupine County, serving papers from the court is one of the most necessary—and boring—tasks of a deputy. Usually the recipients are expecting them and are resigned to being ground down by the wheels of justice. Only on television shows do rural folk mulishly greet the polite proffer of a civil summons by brandishing a shotgun. If the papers involve a criminal warrant, however, the deputy will take along a backup officer or two "to facilitate an orderly transition into custody," as official police lingo has it. But that rarely happens.

There was no real action for Chad today, and it made him antsy. He wanted real police work, and he wasn't getting it.

"Just one more day," I said.

"Then what?" Chad said.

"Then you're mine," Gil said from his office door, his voice a mix of gravel and small metal parts. "We will commence your higher education."

Which, of course, was learning the ropes of the undersheriff's office, most of which had to do with routine administration—scheduling, budgets, and the like. I knew Chad was not looking forward to pushing paper, but he had assented. I knew the possibility of running for sheriff when I eventually stepped down was attractive to him, and he knew he had to pay the price.

Besides, the undersheriff occasionally was able to get out of the office to field-general a big crime scene, and the prospect of that kind of excitement — however infrequent it might be — was enough to get Chad to take the bait.

"All right," Chad said, with only the faintest touch of resignation.

SIXTEEN

THERE WAS ONE more woman in my life to placate, and she
was the sheriff of Mackinac County. I felt chauvinistic
thinking of Selena Novikovich first as female and second
as a law enforcement officer, but I couldn't help it.
Knowledge is intellectual but attitudes are inborn. I'd
grown up believing that women needed to be taken care of
and it was hard to shake that article of faith, even though
today it just seems faintly ridiculous. But I also thought
that Selena would understand if I apologized. We were
much the same age and she'd grown up with the same
mythology.

As it was I apologized only for not keeping in better
touch over the last several days.

"That's okay, Steve," she said. "We both have too
much to do."

My kind of . . . um, sheriff.

Quickly I filled her in on the discovery of Billy
Gibbs' truck and its deplorable condition, as well as what
we'd learned about his fellow army squad members and
the CIA involvement with one of them.

"Hmm," she said. "I think I'll go out and ask Arvo
Perttu a few more questions. I don't think he was
consciously holding anything back, but maybe I can
approach things from a different angle and jog some more
marbles out of his head. Maybe some important details are
stuck in his brain somewhere."

"I don't envy you," I said. It's one thing to

interrogate bad guys, but coaxing salient information out of the mentally challenged is not easy. They are often so unaware of the relationships between people and events that they don't make connections until much later, if at all.

A week went by while Alex rummaged around lower Michigan, investigating the surviving three members of Billy Gibbs' army squad. He did so without the knowledge of the upper hierarchy of the state police. Alex's immediate boss at Wakefield has known and trusted the trooper for many years, and when the sergeant says he has to go somewhere, the captain always assents. After all, Alex has never embarrassed him with his superiors in Lansing, and results usually trump procedural irregularities.

Not that Alex cuts any corners, at least none that ever have been successfully challenged in court. Like any cop worth the badge, he knows exactly how far he can go in negotiating the vast murky underbelly of the law. I have never had cause to question his methods, although over the years a few of them have turned out to be novel enough to be surprising. When he had something to announce, I never asked how he got his information. That would come out sooner than later.

"Got some stuff," Alex said on the phone late one morning with his usual lack of preamble. "Call a meeting of the minds. One o'clock okay?"

Chad and Annie both were on duty and in the office, and I'd seen Jack come out of Merle's with his lady love. I called him on his cell. He said he'd be there.

At one p.m. I gaveled the meeting to order with the butt of my .357. I didn't have a genuine gavel, and the hickory grip made a nice official sound on the oak of my desk.

"Spill it, Alex," I said.

"Very well. Let's start with former Private First Class Ioannis Cacoyannis," he said. "Twenty-four years old, hometown South Bend, Indiana."

He wrote the name on the chalkboard hanging on my office wall.

"Interesting name," I said. "Greek, of course."

"Ee-oh-ann-is?" Annie asked.

"Yaw-ah-nees," Alex said. "I looked it up with Google. Anyway, he was born in a small town called Kalavryta on the Peloponnesus in western Greece. In 1995, when he was two years old, his parents emigrated to the United States and opened a restaurant in South Bend. They had been successful restaurateurs in Greece and their new place became quite popular. Neighbors say Mama and Papa were proud of their Greek heritage. For a long time they didn't bother to translate their menus into English. They didn't need to. They were drawing Greek immigrants from all over Northern Indiana."

"Probably explains why the guy's first name wasn't changed to 'John,' " I said.

"Right," Alex said. "Now about Kalavryta. It has an interesting history."

"Is that relevant to our investigation?" Gil said, surprisingly mildly. Cranky and impatient as he could be, he always kept an open mind.

"Maybe," Alex said.

"Go on," I said.

Alex flipped open his notebook and said, "During World War II—on December 13, 1943, to be exact—the Germans rounded up all male residents of Kalavryta who were over fourteen years old, led them to a field, and machine-gunned to death somewhere between six hundred and a thousand of them in retribution for the deaths of eighty-one German soldiers at the hands of Greek partisans. Then the Nazis burned down the entire town. Only thirteen of the men survived. They hid under piles of bodies and were missed by soldiers finishing off the survivors. One of them was Georgios Spilopoulos, the

173

maternal grandfather of Ioannis Cacoyannis."

"Holy cow," Chad said for all of us.

"How did you find out all that?" I asked.

"Had dinner one night at the restaurant," Alex said, "and got into a conversation with the owner, Takis Cacoyannis. Ioannis' father. He had had a little too much *ouzo* and was feeling morose."

"Did you ask him about his son?" I said.

"Oh, no. I didn't need to. There was a picture of him in his army uniform on the wall of the restaurant. I said, 'You must be proud of him,' and the room suddenly turned cold. His father just looked away. His mother had icicles in her eyes."

There was a pause while Alex, a born ham actor, let the suspense build.

"Then what?" Gil said.

"My little songbirds told me that young Ioannis was quite the Hitler Youth in high school. As the CID told you, Jack, he gets a lot of hate literature, mostly neo-Nazi stuff, in the mail. Once a week he drives down to Wakarusa, a small town twenty-one miles southeast of South Bend, and goes to meetings of the American National Socialist Movement. There are about a dozen members. They sing the 'Horst Wessel Lied,' stomp around the room in brown shirts and swastikas, curse Jews and blacks, and generally make unpleasant idiots of themselves. But in private. They don't go out in public to demonstrate, even on Halloween."

"Why not?" I said.

"They're scared of getting beaten up," Alex said. "They're candy-asses. They need to wear jackboots to get a hard on. Excuse me, Annie."

"Excused," she said with a wry but relaxed smile. "The metaphor is apropos."

"Now for the best part. Ioannis Cacoyannis still lives at home with his mother. He almost never goes out, except to those meetings. He does not travel outside that twenty-one-mile radius of South Bend. The only place he ever seems to go is to work five days a week at a Chevrolet dealership five blocks from his house in South Bend. He's a certified automotive technician, as they call greasemonkeys these days."

"What about the father?" Chad said.

"Mother and Daddy are separated, though they still run the restaurant together."

"Isn't it odd that someone with that family history could become a neo-Nazi?" I said.

"Not necessarily," Alex said. "It's a form of psychological rebellion. Ioannis was an abused child. His father regularly beat the shit out of him, and his mother just as regularly told him he deserved it. I talked to Lieutenant Hemb about him, and she said she wasn't surprised. There's some kind of shrink term for hating your parents so much because of the childhood trauma they inflicted upon you that you embrace the historical horrors the family suffered."

"How did you find all that out?" I said.

"Dogged police work." Alex flashed a wide grin around the room. Everyone chuckled, but with an undertone of admiration. I could think of no one else in law enforcement who knew so many sources and could get his hands on so much information. Alex was a master at digging up old juvenile cases that should have been long suppressed, usually by pumping the memories of the investigators involved.

"You think Ioannis could be Billy Gibbs' killer?" Annie said.

"Doubt it very much," Alex said, shaking his head slowly. "This guy is all talk and no ballgame. He's afraid of his own shadow. He might follow a leader into one scheme or another, but when push comes to shove he just hides in the fort he's built of army blankets in his bedroom in his mother's house. This fellow has no backbone to speak of."

"Really?" Chad said.

"Metaphorically speaking," Alex said. "Right up your alley."

We all laughed. Chad's police reports often take flight into quasi-literary fancy.

"Could he have cooked up something with former Sergeants Tancredi and Ahern? Do they keep in touch?"

"Oh, yes. Cell phone records show they speak with one another two or three times a month."

"About what?" Gil said.

"I have no idea," Alex said. "I'm not a magician."

That just meant that Alex had not pulled sufficient strings at the National Security Agency to obtain transcripts of eavesdropped conversations. It was doubtful, anyway, that the NSA's electronic surveillance spooks had targeted three insignificant ex-soldiers with honorable discharges. No reason to do so.

"Well, what do you know about those other two guys?" Gil said.

"Michael Ahern. From Holland, Michigan. Now twenty-eight years old. Staff sergeant, eight years in the army. Two tours in Afghanistan. Child of a single mother — daddy disappeared before he was born — but no other anomalies in his childhood that I could turn up. Mother was gainfully employed as an elementary school secretary for decades. Graduated in the upper quarter of his class at West Catholic High in Grand Rapids, where he commuted from Holland. He had two years at Kalamazoo College, where he did fine, but dropped out for financial reasons and went to work as an auto mechanic at a Toyota dealership in Holland.

"At about the same time, he joined the National Guard and drove to Detroit regularly to do his reserve duty. His service record there was very good and he was promoted regularly. Like all the others, he was discharged honorably. The CID didn't have enough on them for the army to do otherwise."

"Where is he now?" I asked.

"Grand Rapids," Alex said. "He's a salesman at a big used car emporium there. He's come up in the world. Sort of."

"All this tells us nothing," Gil said. "Don't you have anything better?"

"I was getting around to that," Alex said. I was not surprised. Alex always leaves the climax for last. Gil, who is impatient to a fault, was annoyed as always.

"Go on," I said.

"Michael Ahern is a neo-Nazi like Cacoyannis," Alex said. "He gets all kinds of hate literature in the mail and online as well. But he is not an official member of any group, white supremacist or otherwise. He does not go to meetings or demonstrate on the sidewalk. Rather, he runs a web site that's worth checking out. Here's the URL."

I tapped it into my computer and in a second the home page popped up. A variation of the infamous Nazi *Parteiadler* — a bold stylized eagle gripping a circled swastika — sat atop the words "In Defense of White Christian America." Inside the circle a cross replaced the swastika. The "sun cross" goes back to prehistoric times, and is a common symbol used by neo-Nazi groups who don't want to frighten people with the real thing.

Underneath was a photograph of a young man in black jacket and black necktie staring into the distance, a high sun on his prominent cheekbones and blonde hair. On his left arm was a red brassard with a black sun cross in a white circle. He looked like a recruiting poster for the Waffen-SS. Under the photo was the caption "Alois Wagner, webmaster."

"That's Ahern," Alex said. "He goes by a *nom de guerre* in that world."

I scrolled down to the first paragraph. In portentous

177

prose it proclaimed the dangers pure Americans—all white and chiefly Northern European—faced from the relentless influx of black- and brown-skinned immigrants. Race mixing, the screed said, threatened the healthy genes of the founding fathers. It went on to warn against Jews in business, in the government, down the block and even next door. They needed to be deported along with Negroids and Mongoloids if the United States was to be saved.

In that section most of the language, unlike the usual neo-Nazi web sites, was not bombastic and spittle-spattered, but calm and measured, offering plenty of purported facts and apparently careful reasoning. Ahern was either a pretty good writer, had lifted the stuff from elsewhere, or had employed a skilled editor. In either case he knew how to capture and hold an audience.

Colorful, well-drawn maps accompanied a historic time line showing what it said was the migration of proto-Aryans from antiquity into the modern age, settling in the Scandinavian countries and northern Germany.

Several pages were devoted to the rise of the National Socialist German Workers Party, the history it depicted accurate enough but slanted to favor the rise of Adolf Hitler and his minions. They segued into a section called "My Modern Struggle," a dubious autobiography that seemed to be three-quarters direct quotes from *Mein Kampf*—and in the original German, untranslated.

"The guy thinks he's Hitler reincarnated," Chad observed unnecessarily.

Despite the quiet tone of his beginning, Ahern soon descended into vituperation about "the Jew government," "the Jew media," and "the Jew virus," outlining a bizarre conspiracy to take over the world. He finished with a plea for donations and a promise to keep them secret.

Nowhere on the site did the name "Michael Ahern" appear. He had carefully kept that out, either from a lack of courage or an abundance of self-preservation.

"What a shithead," Gil said, echoing what we all felt.

"Is he married?" Annie said.

"Divorced three times."

"Grounds?"

"No-fault. That's often the reason given when a sane party wants to get shut of the insane party. Sue thinks Ahern is probably mentally ill," Alex said.

"Aren't they all?" I said.

"Nothing we can do about him, though," Alex said, "except keep an eye on him. The Holland cops know all about him."

"All talk and no walk?" I said.

"Apparently," Alex said. "Personally, they say, he's very charming and glib. 'Alois Wagner' is the go-to guy for quite a few clueless local broadcasters looking for commentary whenever members of hate groups are caught doing illegal things. I can't believe they let him spew his stuff on radio or television, but they do. They're always looking for shock value. And they get it from him."

"Think he's our man?" Gil said.

"Probably not. For the last eight months or so he hasn't moved outside the southern Michigan area. All his credit card charges have been local. Traffic cams haven't spotted his license plate except in or around Holland."

"If he's clever," Annie said, "he could have stolen a car and used cash, couldn't he?"

"Yes," Alex said, "but I doubt it. Guys like this talk a good conspiracy but make lousy conspirators."

We all sat silent for a moment, then I said, "What about Joseph Tancredi?"

"Ah, saved the best for last," Alex said.

Gil issued a loud raspberry. The rest of us laughed.

"Let me begin at the beginning. Okay?"

Gil glowered.

"First of all," Alex said, "Tancredi's the only one of that bunch with a real police record. Twice he's been busted for assault. The first one was a bar fight and the other guy refused to press charges. The second was in a dustup during a civil rights demonstration in Detroit. Apparently he pushed a black guy who was marching. The guy pushed back, Tancredi threw a punch, and then the pair was pulled apart. The black guy won't back down and so Tancredi's going to trial in a couple of months. He's out on his own recognizance."

"Sounds like a hothead," I said.

"Long juvenile record," Alex said. "I reached out to the officers who dealt with him in high school and they said he was a mean bully who fixated on people of color. Shoved black kids in the hallway, spat on their sandwiches in the lunchroom, taunted them at football games, that sort of thing. He got punched out once or twice for his pains, but the school administration managed to shove everything under the rug. It was terrified of racial confrontations becoming public.

"The funny thing is that Tancredi comes from a comfortable middle-class background. Mommy's a third grade teacher in the Muskegon public schools and Daddy's a low-rent criminal lawyer there. Of course Daddy protected his son. Every time he got into trouble Daddy made sure he was well lawyered up. The cops were never able to nail him on anything, even the time in his senior year when he beat hell out of a black classmate who hit on his girl friend. The guy was in the hospital for three days. Tancredi is a big guy, six-four and two-fifty, and quick to use his fists."

I sat up. "This sounds promising," I said. "That's a hate crime."

"The cops thought so," Alex said. "But the lawyer Daddy hired — someone from his own law firm — managed to persuade the judge that it was just male-against-male jealousy. Got him a short term of supervision."

"Muskegon's not far from Holland," I said. "About thirty-five miles. Was Tancredi acquainted with Ahern or Cacoyannis before the army?"

"With Ahern, yes. Tancredi is just a year younger. No sign he knew Cacoyannis before they served together in the National Guard at Detroit. After high school Tancredi and Ahern got together at white supremacist survivalist camps in the countryside. Sort of like Boy Scouts with SS daggers. They joined the National Guard together and still keep in touch by phone. Tancredi didn't do well in high school and had drifted from job to job before enlisting."

"The army never knew about Tancredi's juvenile record, did it?" Chad said. "Sealed, wasn't it?"

"By law, yes. Daddy made sure of that," Alex said. "The cops said he pointedly told them those records — and their investigations — should stay buried and that he'd make a lot of trouble if anything came to the National Guard's attention. The cops were only too glad to tell me off the record all about Tancredi's past."

"Like the others," I said, "he was given a honorable discharge. Emphasis on 'was given.' From what we've learned, he certainly didn't earn it. What's he doing now?"

"Lives in Gary, Indiana," Alex said. "Fuel truck driver. Hauls gasoline in eighteen-wheelers from refineries in nearby Whiting to central and northern Wisconsin. And — wait for it! — *the Up-per Pe-nin-su-la of Mich-i-gan.* Including Porcupine County. Been doing it for more than a year."

Our collective gasp must have been heard all the way to Merle's. Chad pounded his desk. Annie quivered in glee. Gil sat bolt upright. And Jack, who had during the entire meeting sat silent, eyes closed and arms folded, let out a heartfelt *"whoooooo!"*

"We've got motive," I said. "Now we've got

opportunity. Means shouldn't be so difficult. Most of all, we're now close to probable cause."

That would enable us to get search warrants and build a solid circumstantial case against Tancredi—if he were our man, and I was growing ever more confident that he was.

"What now?" said Chad. "Bug his truck?"

"Not necessary," Jack said. "Most trucking companies install GPS transmitters on all tractors in their fleets so the home offices know where their rigs are at all times. It would be easy to zero on one of them and follow it all over hell and gone while sitting in a comfortable corner office with a view."

"Typically, gasoline deliveries follow the same schedule week in and week out," Alex said. "There's a real routine to it. Trips are planned carefully in order to save fuel getting from place to place. Once we've figured out the routine by watching a couple of times, we wouldn't need to tap into a bug's transmission all the way up from the refinery."

"Couldn't we just talk to the trucking company?" Annie said. "Find out the routine that way?"

"Too much risk of somebody tipping off Tancredi," Jack said.

"But when he gets to Porcupine County," Chad said, "we could then track the bug and see if he takes any side trips."

"Trouble with that," Jack said, "is that the trucking company would know, too. They wouldn't want an employee deviating from routine and wasting fuel. If Tancredi took any side trips, he'd probably park his truck overnight somewhere, maybe at a motel he's used several times, before heading back to Whiting the next day or the one after that, or maybe taking a day's rest before going home. To get around he could borrow a car or pickup, maybe from a friend. In any case we'd need to keep eyes on him. Our own eyes."

"All righty," I said. "Let us gather around the campfire and conspire."

SEVENTEEN

"WE'VE GOT ENOUGH now for a pretty good working theory," I told Ginny as we settled into the soft top-grain leather sofa in front of her fireplace, wineglasses in hand. For the first time in months I felt contented. Things were going well with both my job and my lady.

"Here's how we think it's gone down. These seven soldiers were in a squad whose members conspired to sell surplus army vehicles to all comers at the air base at Bagram as the American involvement in Afghanistan wound down. Two were African-American. One is Iraqi-American. Four are European-American, if you want to put it that way. Of those four, one is mentally challenged and the other three are virulent neo-Nazis.

"Billy Gibbs was the brains and the bagman. He collected and held maybe three million dollars in payment for the contraband. Keyshawn Banks, a fellow African-American, probably was his best friend and helped set up and carry out the scheme. Suleyman al-Habib, the Iraqi-American, served as the go-between with Arab buyers, and we think the CIA is now using him as a covert agent in that region. We think the three amateur Nazis — Michael Ahern, Ioannis Cacoyannis and Joseph Tancredi — played comparatively minor roles, perhaps as gofers and laborers. One white soldier, Arvo Perttu, wasn't bright enough to participate and was pushed out.

"When their unit was rotated home, Gibbs apparently still held the money. He came up to Porcupine

County to get out of sight, and it was far enough away from central and southern Michigan so that he wouldn't easily run into his former squad mates. Banks got a job in a Flint body shop and went to school to further his knowledge. Those two very likely were planning to open some kind of truck repair center with the loot. Al-Habib was now out of the picture working for the CIA. Ahern, Cacoyannis and Tancredi all got jobs of one kind or another and kept in touch, still feeding their white supremacist delusions.

"Maybe in the beginning at Bagram there was some kind of agreement to divide the money, but why should two ambitious black guys want to share with a bunch of no-account racists who hated their guts?"

"One moment," said Ginny, who had been listening, one leg tucked under a knee, on a corner of the sofa. "We need another log."

She got up and expertly inserted a chunk of oak into just the right place on the fire. Unlike many Yoopers, she wants nothing to do with trendy and expensive cast-iron Vermont stoves. Maybe wooden log fireplaces are inefficient as hell, most of the heat wasted up the chimney rather than radiating into the room, but she loves to watch the merry dance of flames from hardwood on a stone hearth. She also loves to make wood and swings a double-bitted axe expertly in her back yard, piling a winter's worth of logs into two or three cords in a few weekends. I love to watch her doing these things, and I also love that she is modern — and sensible — enough to keep her house warm in deepest winter with a furnace that burns natural gas from the pipeline that runs along the highway.

I refreshed our glasses of merlot and examined its deep purple-red color as I returned to the topic at hand.

"We don't know what exactly has happened or is happening among those three Hitlerites," I said, "but our evidence suggests that Cacoyannis is too chicken-hearted to do anything, that Ahern is all talk and no action, and that Tancredi, who has a history of violence, is the one to watch.

"First of all, his job as a gasoline tanker driver brings him up to Porcupine County regularly. We don't know for sure — we have not yet subpoenaed the trucking company records — but we think he was here when Gibbs was killed, when Gibbs' house was burned, and when Gibbs' truck was destroyed.

"We think Tancredi is driven by three things: greed, anger, and racial hate. He was angry with the two black men for keeping the proceeds from their scheme, and that drove him to murder them both. Of course we don't have anything but circumstantial evidence that he killed either man, but the chain of reasoning fits.

"So is the idea that he killed Gibbs in a paroxysm of rage fueled by racial animosity. And he burned that trailer and just slaughtered that truck for the same reason and because he couldn't find the money inside either of them."

"So *where's* the money?" Ginny said.

"That we don't know," I said. "We're missing something."

"You'll find it, Steve," she said.

The fire had burned low and it was getting late. "Let's turn in," Ginny said, yawning, the familiar signal that she was weary and wanted to go right to sleep.

That was fine with me. All night I spooned her and we both slept through to dawn without awakening.

The next morning Ginny announced that she was driving to Wausau in central Wisconsin for a historians' meeting and that she would be back late, probably after midnight.

"Now you be careful," I said. "Maybe you should spend the night there and drive back in the morning."

The impulse to protect my lady love comes from my old-fashioned upbringing, and I can't help it. Every time

186

Ginny goes out after dark, a piece of me worries. No matter that she is more than capable behind the wheel, has handled plenty of suicidal deer on the highway, and knows more than a few self-defense moves. I just don't like her going out at night alone. She pats me on the cheek and calls me "atavistic."

Ginny silently rolled her eyes, gave me a damp *mwah*, and I was off to work.

"Selena's on the phone," Sheila trilled as soon as I plunked myself into the swivel chair.

"Put her on," I said.

"Steve?" said the sheriff of Mackinac County.

"What does your husband say when you go out by yourself at night?" I said without thinking.

"*Excuse* me?"

"Oh, never mind. None of my business. I shouldn't have asked."

"Worrying about Ginny, are we?" Selena sounded amused.

"Never mind, I said."

"Does it ever occur to you," Selena said, "that Ginny worries about *you* when you go out alone at night?"

"Why would she? I'm a lawman."

"Exactly."

"Yes, well, what are you calling about?" I said. This conversation was getting out of hand.

"Steve, you are a piece of work," Selena said, laughing. "Anyway, I talked to Arvo Perttu again yesterday."

The sheriff of Mackinac County had rolled up the driveway and stepped out of her cruiser as the young Finndian walked out of his house to meet her. There were now large gaps among the cords of firewood that lined the fences around the yard, and a huge pile of freshly made oak and hickory squatted by Perttu's gas-powered log splitter, awaiting stacking. The place was still trim and squared away, and business seemed good.

"Selena!" Arvo called.

"Arvo!"

For the last few months the sheriff had made a point of stopping in Engadine and casually chatting with folks. True, an election year was coming up, but Selena had always thought that part of good sheriff work was shooting the breeze with citizens, asking questions and listening to their concerns. Sometimes crimes even got solved that way.

She had run into Arvo Perttu several times and had exchanged pleasantries, once over coffee at a nearby cafe after she had encountered him dropping off a free load of firewood at the home of a widow she knew was indigent. Selena had thanked him for his charity, and as time went on she slowly won his trust, and soon he was calling her by her first name instead of her title. She liked the young man. He may not have been an intellectual wizard, but he was a hard worker who not only produced things of value but shared them with needy folks. To Selena that was the most important mark of a person of consequence, a trait far more valuable than education, wealth or social prominence.

"Arvo," she said, "maybe you can help me with something."

"Sure," he said. "What do you need?"

"We're still investigating the case of Billy Gibbs," she said, "and frankly, we're stumped. Maybe you can remember something more than what we talked about last time. Anything might help."

"Well, let's see . . . " The young man sat down on a stump and stared off into the woods, reaching back into the dimmest recesses of his memory, trying to pull out something that might help the sheriff.

"One time," he said, "I went into Staff Sergeant Gibbs' office and saw some ladies' things on his desk. Rings, bracelets, a couple of pairs of earrings, and a necklace."

Perttu closed his eyes and rubbed them vigorously, as if trying to pull images from the back of his mind. "They were yellow. Like they were made of gold. They looked like they came from shops in Kabul."

"What did Staff Sergeant Gibbs say?"

"He said he was sending them home to his mother for Christmas. He put them in his desk drawer right away. Later he gave me a package with his mother's name and address on it and asked me to carry it to the post office at the PX and mail it. He wanted the package insured for a thousand dollars. He told me to be very careful and not lose it."

"That was very nice, wasn't it," Selena said, "that the staff sergeant was so generous with his mama?"

"Yeah. Now I remember that later on I mailed maybe four or five more packages for Staff Sergeant Gibbs to his mother."

"Did he want them insured every time?"

Perttu was silent for a moment while he tried to remember. "I think so," he said finally. "Yes. Yes, he did. A thousand dollars every time."

"Were the packages heavy?"

"Yeah, a little. But no, not real heavy."

"Did you have to fill out little slips of paper saying what was in the packages?" That would have been necessary if they were to be insured.

"Yeah, yeah," Perttu said.

"What did you put down?"

" 'Gifts.' Just 'gifts.' Staff Sergeant Gibbs said to do that."

"Did the others also mail packages for him?"

"I don't remember. No, I don't think so."

189

THE RIDDLE OF BILLY GIBBS

"Why do you think the staff sergeant trusted you?"

"He was a nice guy," Perttu said. "It made me feel good to do things for him."

And, Selena thought, because Billy Gibbs didn't trust the others, or wanted to keep them in the dark.

"Arvo, honey," Selena said in her best motherly tone, "all of this is very helpful. Thank you so much. Is there anything else you can remember about Staff Sergeant Gibbs? Did he and Corporal Banks get along well?"

Somehow the juxtaposition of the names of the two soldiers loosened another nugget of memory from the granite matrix of Perttu's brain.

"Oh, yeah," he said. "Off duty they worked on motorcycles together."

"Did you see them do that?"

"No, but I heard them."

"Heard them?"

"They made lots of noise. They used an empty one-car garage near our place that was part of the big buildings at Bagram. I don't think they wanted people to see what they were doing."

"Why? Were the motorcycles stolen?" Selena said.

"I don't think so," Perttu said. "You could buy them cheap in Kabul. Lots of army mechanics fixed them up for fun."

"What kind of noise did they make?"

"Motorcycle noise. Revving. Roaring."

"I mean the noise Staff Sergeant Gibbs and Corporal Banks made when they worked on the bikes in the garage."

Perttu sat silent for a few moments as if the source of the sound had occurred to him for the first time and he was trying to make sense of it.

"Banging," he said. "Hammering."

"That's an odd noise to make working on bikes, isn't it, Arvo?"

"Banks was a body shop man at home. Maybe he was fixing fenders. Must have been a lot of them."

"Did you actually ever see any of the bikes?"

Perttu thought for a little while. "No."

"What do you think they were really doing?"

"I don't know."

A stricken expression came over the young man's face, as if he had realized that something not very good probably had been going on in that garage but he had never considered what it might be. Suddenly Selena regretted having pushed his simple but fragile buttons, but she also knew that doing so had yielded two possibly important clues.

She took his hands in both of hers. "Arvo," she said, "thank you so much. You have been very, very helpful, and I am proud of you."

She would have hugged him, and almost did, but at the last moment decided that that would have been inappropriate and un-sheriff-like.

Before Selena could get into her cruiser, Perttu strode over and stood by the open door.

"How are Staff Sergeant Gibbs and Corporal Banks, anyway?" he said. "I ain't seen them in a coon's age."

Selena stared at Perttu in astonishment. "You didn't *know*?" she said.

"Know what?"

The sheriff racked her memory about the day she had first encountered the young man. No, Gibbs' death had not been mentioned, nor had that of Banks. She had simply assumed that Perttu knew. Everyone else in the Upper Peninsula seemed to. But the young man lived such an isolated life, both physically and mentally, that the news had never arrived in his head.

"That both Gibbs and Banks are dead," she said. "They were murdered."

Now it was Perttu's turn to stare. For a long

moment he said nothing while the news slowly dripped into his consciousness.

"They're . . . *dead?*" Confusion and pain contorted his face. "That's bad."

"I'm afraid so," Selena said.

"Was it because of Afghanistan?" Perttu said.

That impressed Selena. Despite his uncluttered mind, or maybe because of it, Perttu was still able to make simple connections, to understand cause and effect. That was probably how he managed to live alone and without assistance in the woods.

"We think so," Selena said. "I mean, the police do. But we're not sure. That's why I'm here talking to you, and why I came the first time."

"I thought maybe it was because they had been arrested and were going to jail for what they did in the army," Perttu said.

The young man was clearly shaken and Selena led him back to the stump where he had sat while they talked.

"I'm sorry they're dead," he said. "They were nice to me."

"Arvo," Selena said, "it's my fault you didn't know. I just thought you did. I promise that from now on I'll make sure you know everything."

He looked up at her, gratitude chasing grief from his eyes.

"Thank you," he said.

And, despite herself, Selena embraced him.

"Well!" I said. "This is indeed very, very helpful. I'd give *you* a hug if I could."

"That would hardly be proper," Selena said, with a barely suppressed chuckle, "let alone professional. But I won't charge you with harassment."

"We're on to something here," I said. "I'm not sure quite what."

"Do you think Gibbs was converting his loot into gold jewelry and sending it home?" Selena said.

"Some of it, maybe," I said. "A few thousand bucks at the most. Not three million. That would be way too much jewelry and way too many packages. The army would have noticed. The Afghans, too. Let me run this past my clandestine banking expert and I'll get back to you."

"Do that, Steve," Selena said. "I'll think about that hug. If it's okay with Ginny . . ."

She broke the connection and I laughed. My counterpart in Mackinac County may be a sworn law officer but she is also a flesh and blood woman, the kind who makes a good friend and has a sense of humor besides. I didn't feel quite so awkward and clueless about male-female relationships anymore.

"Chad!" I called into the squad room. He came out of Gil's office, where the undersheriff had been explaining the intricacies of the department's books.

"Yes, boss?"

I told him what Selena had told me. He listened with mounting interest.

"Let me consult my oracles and soothsayers," he said, "and I will cast the chicken bones."

"The what?" I said.

"Never mind," he said, and went to his desk in the squad room, where he picked up the phone and began consulting his oracles and soothsayers. I was sure most of them were legitimate financial professionals, but I was equally sure that some of them flew under the radar. Chad has his sources and is a demon researcher besides.

"Steve?" Chad said at my door a couple of hours later.

"Sit," I said. "Whatcha got?"

"Enough to get us somewhere," he said.

"Speak."

And Chad spoke, for a full twenty minutes. He

193

began with the fragile financial system in one of the world's most corrupt countries. In recent years Afghanistan almost had been blacklisted from the world's banking system for its wide-open money laundering, an industry that served terrorists as well as Americans, Europeans and Afghani poppy growers.

"This isn't just laundering," Chad said. "It's industrial-strength power washing. Billions and billions of dollars in criminal cash is converted through Afghan banks into instruments that can't be traced. This money completely bypasses the computer networks set up to follow financial transfers of cash throughout the rest of the world.

"Much of it is just smuggled out of the country in the form of currency, piles and piles of it. That's easy to do if you're a heavy hitter and are able to grease the palms of the right Afghans. There are special rooms at Kabul International Airport where VIPs check through suitcases and trunks full of folding money without going through official cash-counting machines that are supposed to stop the flood. Many of the smugglers then fly to Dubai International Airport and exchange the cash in shops that specialize in gold bullion. For those in a hurry, there are rows and rows of vending machines that dispense pure gold bars.

"But Billy Gibbs was small potatoes. Three million dollars isn't anywhere near enough to gain access to those VIP rooms. It would have been difficult for him to get that cash out of Afghanistan by conventional methods. Trusting it to couriers would have been both expensive and risky. Mailing or shipping currency wasn't an option. He couldn't let it out of sight if he wanted to meet up with it when he got home. So he might have had to smurf it out in a different form."

"Smurf?"

"Smurfing is breaking large deposits into ones small

enough to fly under the radar, say in sums of fifty thousand bucks or so. Nobody would notice. That's why Arvo Perttunen's story makes me think Gibbs was buying gold jewelry to mail home in small amounts. He could lose one or two shipments, but the rest would get through."

I did some numbers on my desk pad and shook my head. "Three million dollars divided into fifty-thousand-dollar chunks equals sixty shipments — way too many for army postal clerks not to notice," I said. "He must have found another way."

"Right," Chad said. "But what?"

"And where?" I said.

EIGHTEEN

WE LAID TENTATIVE plans for the next step. When Tancredi left Whiting on his next delivery trip, Jack would be waiting near the Michigan-Wisconsin border, where he would pick up the gasoline truck's GPS signal on his laptop. We were not yet sure what route Tancredi would take, but when we had figured that out, Jack would follow him in Zoey's old pickup, and keep his eyes on the eighteen-wheeler all day and, if necessary, all night. The old G-man had had decades of experience staying undetected during tails and stakeouts, and I was confident his quarry wouldn't rumble him.

In the meantime Chad and I still tried to figure out how Gibbs had smuggled home the bulk of his treasure. We couldn't ask the army to check its postal records to see how many packages he had mailed back to Chicago. That would trip hairtriggers at the CIA and bring the full fury of the agency down on us. Nor, for the same reason, could we approach Colonel Kevin Barlow at Fort Leonard Wood.

For hours Chad and I threw out ideas and quickly shot them down. I revisited the conversation I had had with Ginny about how the money could have gone by road, by ship, or by plane, and each scheme sounded less plausible the second time around.

"Five bucks get you ten that Gibbs converted all the cash into gold, mostly in bullion," Chad said. "That's easy to do in the gold shops of Kabul. A few hundred thou here, a few hundred thou there, and nobody notices."

196

"All right, then, let's say that's what he did," I said. "Now the question is: How did he get the gold to the United States?"

For a while we sat in meditation, drumming our fingers on my desk in unison, raising such a symphony that Sheila came in and told us to please be quiet so she could get some work done.

Then Chad's eyebrows rose. "Arvo Perttu said there was a lot of hammering and banging going on in that closed garage at Bagram. That's not the kind of noise you make fixing a motorcycle. Keyshawn Banks was a body shop man, and Gibbs had that kind of experience, too. Maybe they were hammering gold into motorcycle fender linings, then shipping the motorcycles home? No, that's not plausible. Three million dollars' worth of gold weighs something like a hundred fifty or two hundred pounds, depending on its purity. How many motorcycle fenders does that make? Let's say five pounds of eighteen-karat gold lining the inside of each fender . . . and that's thirty fenders, two per motorcycle. Who sends home fifteen motorcycles? Or even seven or eight, if they split the bikes between them? Of course, shipping home privately owned motorcycles isn't illegal, but that number would have been noticed immediately. There would have been close inspection. Too much risk."

"If they were fashioning gold into objects to ship home," I said, "what else could they have made that would pass muster?"

"I don't know," Chad said. "If they used wooden crates to ship the objects, the results would have been very heavy and probably trip metal detectors. Foot lockers, which every soldier sends home, would make more sense, but then the weight of the contents would also invite attention. The weight would have to be spread over too many foot lockers not to be noticed."

Annie, who had been listening at her desk close to

197

my office door, suddenly stood and strode in.

"You remember the old story of the Russian peasant who went home from the collective farm every day with a wheelbarrow?" she said.

"No," Chad said.

"Tell us," I said. I remembered the story vaguely.

"Every day for many years the peasant left the farm with his tools piled in a wheelbarrow," Annie said. "Pretty soon he seemed to be awfully wealthy for a peasant, and a secret policeman watched him carefully. Every evening the cop examined the tools in the peasant's wheelbarrow but couldn't find any contraband.

"This went on for years, and soon both the peasant and the secret policeman were retired. The peasant was living very comfortably, but not the policeman. One day in a tavern the cop said to the peasant, 'It's been a long time and it doesn't matter anymore, but I *know* you were stealing from the farm. *What* were you stealing?"

"Wheelbarrows."

"Your point?" Chad said.

"What if the foot lockers themselves were made of gold?" Annie said. "I mean, if Gibbs and Banks hammered the gold into trunk frames and covered them with some sort of epoxy paint? Yes, the frames would be softer than steel, but the hardboard panels could keep the lockers stiff enough to stand up through a shipment or two.

"The lockers would be heavier than steel-framed trunks, but a clever cookie could fill them in a way that likely would escape notice. If I were doing it, I'd fill the trunk with sheets of Styrofoam and then put a couple of layers of something innocent, like paperback books or Afghani rugs, on top. All told, the trunk wouldn't be any heavier than the others, and anybody opening the top of the trunk wouldn't see anything unusual."

"Annie, you should have been a master criminal," Chad said, admiration in his voice.

198

"If that idea pans out, Deputy Corbett," I said, "there will be a raise in your future."

"No, there won't," Gil said from his office. Nothing discussed in mine escapes him. "We can't afford it."

"Be that as it may," I said, "it won't be difficult to find out if Gibbs and Banks sent home two or three foot lockers each. They're probably still at their parents' homes. You know how young people use Mommy and Daddy's house to store their crap until Mommy and Daddy have had enough and order the kids to clean it out or it all goes to Goodwill."

Alex called an old chum at the Flint Police Department and asked him to obtain a search warrant, just in case, then go to the home of Banks' parents and ask if he could look at any trunks or crates that belonged to their son. We doubted that they would refuse. After all, the law still was hunting the killer or killers of their son.

I enlisted a couple of buddies in the Chicago PD on the same mission, but didn't have confidence that Gibbs' mother wouldn't balk at the request, especially if she were aware that her grandson had done something fishy in Afghanistan and if she had concealed that knowledge during the interviews after her son was murdered. Whether that was true or not I didn't know, but I asked the Chicago cops to give it a go anyway.

The Flint police had no difficulty getting Banks' parents to agree to a search. In fact, when they asked the lead detective exactly what the cops were looking for, she said simply, "Foot lockers that your son might have sent or brought home from Afghanistan. Suitcases. Trunks. Crates or any other kind of shipping container."

Immediately the mother led the police to their garage, where Banks had stored his foot lockers. There were two. The detectives dragged them out and opened them. Empty. One of the detectives pulled out a pocket knife and rapped one end against the nylon covering the metal frame. The dull clunk sounded like steel, but none of the detectives had any idea what rapping on precious metal should sound like.

"May we cut back the covering?" the lead detective asked Mrs. Banks. She nodded.

With the pocket knife the detective cut slashes near the corners of the locker and pulled back the fabric. Carefully she scraped away the paint covering the metal. A shiny gray scratch greeted her. She scraped three more locations with the same result. Then she shook her head, opened the second locker, and repeated the slashing and scraping.

"Not gold," she said, and immediately regretted her words, for both Mr. and Mrs. Banks gasped.

"Gold?" said the mother. "What . . ."

The detective stood up and decided to take a chance. "Mr. and Mrs. Banks, the state police think smuggled gold might have had something to do with the murder of your son. They don't know exactly how, who or why. But they think they're getting closer to the truth. We must ask you not to tell anyone what has happened here today. We have to keep it secret so that the killer doesn't find out what we know. Can you do that?"

Both parents nodded, determination in their eyes, and the detective relaxed.

"Just a minute," Mr. Banks said. "Keyshawn brought home three trunks."

"Three foot lockers like these two?"

"Yes. About two weeks after he got home, he put one of them in his car and said he was driving it north to give to a friend."

"Did he give a name to the friend?"

"Billy Gibbs," Mr. Banks said. "Yes, the brother who was murdered in the U.P. just before our Keyshawn was killed. They served together in Afghanistan, you know."

The detectives knew that other Flint police had visited the Bankses after both events, and the couple had been forthcoming with what they knew about their son and his friend, and had assented to a search. The two empty foot lockers had been found, examined and dismissed as irrelevant to the case.

"Did your son say anything else about the locker he took north?" the lead detective said.

"No. He said just one thing before he left."

"What was that?"

"He said, and I quote, 'Gonna have some good news soon.' "

In Chicago, Billy Gibbs' mother wasn't so cooperative. "You already done searched the house!" she said. "I've already told you what I know. Go away!"

"But we're still trying to find your son's killer," the detective said.

"You're never gonna find him," she said. "You're trying to drag Billy's name through the mud."

"Why would we want to do that?"

The mother said nothing and just glared at the two detectives on her stoop. The first one decided immediately that Mrs. Gibbs knew something she hadn't told the law after her son was shot to death. But the cop wasn't going to tell her that resistance might constitute interference in a murder investigation. He wanted to see what he could find first. He had only our theory, not probable cause. A theory isn't enough to secure a warrant, so he decided to try a little honey.

"It's your right to refuse us entry," he said. "But if you allow us to look around again, we just might find something that leads to the arrest of the person or persons who killed your son. Wouldn't you want that for him?"

For a long moment she stood silent, probably

weighing protecting her son's reputation against justice for his killer. She was still a mother who had lost her only son. Then she decided.

"Okay," she said. "Come inside."

The detectives nodded and did so.

"You be careful," Mrs. Gibbs said. "Don't make a mess. Put everything back the way you found it, okay?"

"We promise."

Mrs. Gibbs sat in a chair at her dining table and glowered silently as the two detectives methodically mounted their search, opening closet doors and bureau drawers, patting everything with gloved hands. With a small file one detective made minute random scrapes on silver forks and spoons but were satisfied with just examining the proof marks on bottoms of sterling silver serving bowls and plates. The lawmen carefully returned everything to their drawers.

They weren't just being polite and considerate. If evidence of a crime was found, it would have to be photographed and videotaped *in situ*, and it wouldn't do for a jury to see on a screen that the cops had tossed a place in destructive fashion, as often happens in low-budget movies.

Room by room the officers went, finding nothing of interest. In the second-floor hallway, however, there was an attic hatch with a disappearing ladder. Quickly the lead detective found the electric switch that opened the hatch and lowered the ladder. Both cops scrambled up.

The attic, like every other in all the houses in town, was filled willy-nilly with all kinds of stuff — old furniture, cardboard boxes, blankets and clothes, the detritus of people unable to throw anything out because it might be useful to somebody some day in some year too far off to contemplate. This was a kind of hidden hoarding, but not a pathological one like those seen on television reality shows. All families did it. The stuff was out of sight, out of mind, and remained so until it was time to move.

The two detectives started at the north side of the attic and worked their way south through the disorganized clutter, carefully lifting away cardboard boxes and blankets layer by layer and returning them to their original places as they progressed foot by foot through clouds of dust. This was, they realized, going to take hours, maybe even all day.

Then the lead detective coughed and said to his partner, "There's a pretty heavy layer of dust over most of this stuff. It's been there for years. Let's look for a spot that doesn't have much, maybe a year or so."

"Right," said the partner, turning off the overhead lamps. Both cops bounced their flashlight beams at shallow angles across the tops of the piles. Thick mantles of dust particles diffused the beams more than thinner layers. Row by row, stack by stack, pile by pile the beams streamed.

"Hold on," said the lead detective. "This looks promising. Not much smutch there."

Several layers of blankets and quilts stored inside plastic dry-cleaner bags sat atop a layer of sagging cardboard boxes several feet from the south end of the attic. Carefully the detectives removed each layer and set it aside.

"Aha!" said the lead detective. "Foot locker!"

A single gray trunk, four feet long by two feet wide and eighteen inches deep, stenciled "SSGT WILLIAM F. GIBBS" and followed by the name of his army unit, squatted in the shallow dust on the floor.

"Not locked," said the partner.

"Open it."

The lid swung up, the hardboard cover flopping loosely at one end because part of the metal framework of the trunk was missing, broken off, its raw edge covered with a dab of paint the same color as the rest.

The lead detective scraped away at the framework with his penknife. A deep golden glint met the beam of his flashlight.

"Mrs. Gibbs opened up after that," I told my own crew of conspirators in the kitchen of the jail the next day. "She admitted that her son had sent home gold jewelry. She says she didn't know that there was gold in the frames of the locker, but that he had brought home four foot lockers and taken away three of them. He left the fourth in the attic and came home several times 'to get stuff out of it,' as she put it."

"Has the mother been charged?" Annie said.

"No," I said. "But the cops have told her to stay in town until further notice. She knows she's being watched."

"If Tancredi is the killer," Chad said, "do you think he knew how all this went down?"

"No," Jack said. "He would have burgled both houses looking for the trunks. No reports he ever did that. I doubt that he knew how Gibbs got the gold home, only that he did. And he's still looking."

"So are we," Chad said.

"Hey!" I said, in one of those little epiphanies that beams Jesus light into the dark holes of every difficult case in a law enforcement officer's life — if he's lucky. If they pan out, they're called successful hunches. "Gibbs' truck!"

"There wasn't any yellow in them thar bullet holes," Alex said. "He didn't hammer sheets of gold into Ford fenders. Or engine hoods. Or bumpers."

"Did your guys check out the frame?" I said. "Test the metal?"

"I don't think so," said the trooper. "No reason to — then. But there is now."

"Where's that truck?"

"Still at the state police garage. Sitting in a corner covered by a tarp while the case drags on. It's still evidence."

"Let's go!"

I usually hate it when law enforcement officers flick on
their blue-and-white lights and sirens just to shoulder
aside traffic and get to the lunch counter faster, and have
told my deputies that unnecessary flashers and noise will
bring down my wrath. Fireworks should be left for true
emergencies. Ours certainly wasn't an emergency — Gibbs'
truck was going nowhere — but developments in the case
were coming so thick and fast that we unconsciously had
been swept up in the excitement. And so our eager little
convoy of two police vehicles containing five law
officers — Chad, Annie and I in one and Alex and Jack in
the other — sped from Porcupine City to Marquette in
record time.

The state police technicians had already yanked the
tarp off Gibbs' truck and set up lights around the
perimeter when we arrived at the post garage in a cloud of
dust, like a posse on ponies.

"What now, boss?" the lead technician said.

"Strip it down to the frame," Alex said.

"Shall we video the procedure?" the tech said.

"By all means," the trooper said.

As the sheet metal of the fenders and hood were
unbolted and placed aside, the techs scratched the metal
inside and out with sharp tools, looking for the yellow
gleam of gold. We knew they wouldn't find it there, as the
jagged and rusty bullet holes already had proven, but the
techs wanted to follow careful procedure just in case they
had missed something in the earlier examination months
before. Three hours of painstaking work passed before the
inner skeleton of the truck stood before us.

"Typical fully boxed ladder frame of the Ford
pickup," the lead tech said. "Looks normal to me. The side
rails are essentially hollow steel tubes with a rectangular

cross-section. Real strong and resists twisting."

"Hollow?" Alex said. "Not solid through its thickness?"

"Yep."

Alex looked at me, then at Jack. Chad and Annie were already nodding like eager bobblehead dolls.

"You got a drill that can get through that steel?" Alex said.

"We got drills that can get through mountains," the lead tech said. "Diamond tipped."

"Go ahead."

The tech rolled up a heavy half-inch electric drill mounted on wheels and jacked it up to a spot just outside the center of the frame. He looked up at Alex.

"Shall I?" he said.

"Be my guest," the trooper said.

"Cover your ears," the tech said, handing us all protective earmuffs.

Quickly the drill chewed through the antirust coating on the frame and bit into the steel with a scream we could hear inside the muffs. Sparks flew. Several times the tech backed off the drill, sprayed water onto the frame to cool it, and resumed drilling. Tiny shards of shiny gray steel dripped onto the garage floor.

"Look!" Annie shouted.

Flecks of golden metal glowed among the gray dust.

"Bingo," Alex said quietly.

NINETEEN

OVER THE NEXT two days the techs would carefully
disassemble the entire truck frame, torching it apart in
several places and melting down the precious metal inside.
It was eighteen karats in purity, about seventy-five per
cent gold, the rest other metals to give it strength. That day
we didn't know for sure how much was in that truck, but a
tech on the teardown job estimated that once the gold had
been melted down and separated from the dross,
something like a hundred forty to a hundred fifty pounds
of full twenty-four karat metal would be harvested. At
prevailing prices that would bring about two million to
two and three-quarters million dollars.

"Now why would anyone hide gold inside the
frame of a truck?" Chad had said on the way back from
Marquette. "There are so many better hiding places!"

"Like what?" Annie said. "Your mattress?"

"Old mine shafts, pansy beds in the backyard,
between two courses of brick in a new garage, et cetera, et
cetera. Who could possibly think of a hollow Ford frame
rail? Besides, the gold would be so hard to get at. You'd
have to take apart the whole truck. All that's so far-fetched.
Who would think?"

"There ya go," Annie said. "You answered your
own question."

I couldn't help laughing.

"Gibbs kept some of the gold in that trunk frame at
his mother's house," I said. "The Chicago PD said it was

worth about a hundred fifty thousand bucks. If half the frame is gone, that means the whole locker originally was worth three hundred thou, something like that. Gibbs probably would break off a chunk from the frame every time he went down to visit Grandma, melting down the gold into ingots, and selling them to gold dealers for cash, keeping each exchange small enough so as not to attract attention, and using a new dealer each time. He maybe put some of the cash in the bank and carried some around as ready money. No wonder he always seemed so flush."

"Where's the trunk now?" Chad said.

"Evidence room at CPD headquarters," I said. "I hope it doesn't disappear."

"They're that bad, eh?" Annie said.

"It's a huge department," I said. "It's bound to have a bent cop or two now and again." Jewelry, cash and drug evidence often disappears in the long months before cases come to trial.

While we waited for the complete results from Marquette, we decided to start moving against Joseph Tancredi. Jack Adamson immediately volunteered to drive to Indiana and coordinate things, including a search of Tancredi's apartment in East Chicago near the Whiting refinery after the ex-soldier had left for work. Rather than lie in wait on the Wisconsin-Michigan border, Jack would take up the tail at the beginning as Tancredi drove north on his delivery route.

"We'll get warrants faster with my FBI credentials," he said. "I can also lead the search of the apartment so that the local cops don't mess things up."

"There is a definite advantage to bigfootedness, isn't there?" I said.

"You bet," Alex said.

One edge a federal agent's badge gives him is instant cooperation from local law enforcement officers, who might slow things down with state troopers and out-of-jurisdiction deputies and municipal officers while checking out the bona fides of those who claimed to be a step or two up the status ladder. G-men may be disliked, but they are respected — and feared. Nobody gets in their way. I was grateful we in Porcupine County had our own two-legged battering ram in coat and tie. Well, Pendletons and jeans these days, but still.

It took Jack all of ten minutes to persuade a local Indiana judge to issue two warrants — one to search Tancredi's apartment and the other to obtain GPS codes from the trucking company. The next morning Jack and two uniformed patrolmen watched from an unmarked East Chicago P.D. cruiser on the street as Tancredi emerged from the building, got into his car and drove to the refinery. They waited until the car had disappeared around the corner, then strode to the apartment building's front door.

Jack could have rung up the live-in custodian, showed him the warrant, and had him open Tancredi's apartment door. But the veteran G-man believes the fewer casual witnesses there are, the less chance his quarry will realize he is being investigated. People do talk. At the door Jack pulled out a leather case containing a full set of professional lock picks.

"That's illegal," said one of the uniforms. "Those are burglar tools!"

Jack gave him his best shut-up-and-watch-how-it's-done glare. "National security," he said, the federal agent's standard justification for doing anything, legal or not. That usually works.

Within ten seconds they were inside.

"Don't touch anything," Jack told the patrolmen. "Just stand there and keep an eye out the front window in case the subject comes back. Sometimes they remember they've forgotten their lunch."

Jack first swept all three rooms of the small apartment with his eyes and an electronic bug hunter, looking for hidden cameras or recording devices, and found none. With gloved hands he opened drawers and examined their contents, first taking pictures with his iPhone and using the results to return the objects carefully to their original places. In a closet he found a twelve-gauge Savage over-and-under shotgun. In a nearby drawer he found a nearly new 9mm Beretta stamped "M9." It had once been military issue, and the serial number on the frame had survived. Jack photographed the number and immediately e-mailed the picture to me, first calling ahead to let me know it was coming.

As soon as the photo appeared on my computer screen more than 400 miles north in Porcupine City, I scrabbled in my desk drawer looking for the notebook I had carried during my search of Gibbs' double-wide trailer after he had been charged with sexual assault. Quickly I found the pad and compared the numbers. Then I called Jack back.

"It's a match," I said. "That Beretta belonged to Gibbs. We can't use it as evidence because the original warrant I used to examine his trailer didn't allow me to search for it. But that shotgun was probably used to shoot him in the back, although we'll never prove it."

Although I didn't point out the obvious to the veteran agent, I told myself silently, *We now know that Tancredi had been in Gibbs' trailer. Just one more piece of evidence that we can use at trial, and we'll have enough for an arrest.*

"I'm still tossing the place," Jack said, although "tossing" was hardly the word to describe his careful and meticulous examination.

"Okay," I said. "Stay in touch."

An hour later Jack called back. "Steve, check your email," he said.

I did so. Four photographs had arrived. One was a full-on shot of a pair of hunting boots. Another was a closeup of the leather tongue in one of them. "FIELD & STREAM," it said. "11 M." The third photo was of the sole. I'd have to wait until the boots arrived at the Michigan state police lab to be absolutely sure, but I knew — just knew — that the sole would match the bootprints Selena Novikovich had collected at the hanging tree near St. Ignace.

The fourth photo was of a sporterized surplus M14 rifle, one whose wooden military grips had been replaced by a lightweight plastic stock. A scope — six-power by the look of it — sat atop the receiver. There was a brief note underneath the photograph: "Sending this to Flint PD forensics." There the bullet that killed Banks would be compared with one fired by the rifle in the police laboratory.

I called Jack. "Good work, G-man," I said. "Looks like we've got enough."

"Maybe more than enough," he said. "There are grains of what look to me very much like black sand stuck in the stitching of the sole. Lab'll be able to tell what it is and possibly where it came from."

Chad and Annie had crowded into my office to look at the incriminating photographs.

"Why don't we just grab him up now?" Annie said. "Even to this youthful and inexperienced law enforcement mind it looks as if there's evidence enough to send Joseph Tancredi to prison for the rest of his natural life."

I turned back to the phone. "Good luck on the tail, Jack," I said, and hung up.

"From the beginning, Annie," I said, "it has seemed to me that Billy Gibbs' killer may have had help. Gibbs was not a small man, but tall and athletic and muscular, with military training, the kind who was always alert to everything going on around him. It would not have been easy to get the drop on him. Or to carry away his body from wherever he was killed.

"There was a single moccasin print near the tree where Gibbs was strung up. It could have been put there quite a while before that event happened and by someone who had nothing to do with it, but it could also have belonged to an accomplice. You see?"

"I do," said the young woman, not at all abashed. "I'd forgotten."

"Devil's in the details," I said.

That reminded me to call Selena right away to tell her what we'd found. And, afterward, to call Ginny and suggest lunch at Merle's.

"I'll buy," I said.

There was a small but surprised gasp from the other end. At restaurants we always go Dutch to preserve the financial dignity of the impoverished lawman.

"You must have had some good news," Ginny said.

"You could call it that," I said.

Jack Adamson was still on the job down in northern Indiana. Shortly after noon he breezed into the dispatcher's office at the trucking company in Whiting that supplied the local refineries with gasoline haulage.

"FBI," he said. "I have a warrant for all your trucks' on-the-road GPS codes."

Sophisticated electronic snooping devices can zero in, identify and map code transmissions on the road, but Jack didn't have one, nor was there time to get one. He needed to know the precise code emitted by Tancredi's eighteen-wheel tanker in order to follow it on his laptop screen. Besides, the tanker had already merged into a wide river of hundreds of trucker transmissions heading north in and around Chicago and toward Milwaukee.

He didn't want to ask for Tancredi's code by either the driver's name or destination, as we had originally planned. The dispatcher might defiantly tip off the target after Jack left. That would be interfering with a federal investigation, a felony, but threats of retribution do not always work. Sometimes people just wanted to be assholes. This one in particular.

"That could be a bogus warrant," the dispatcher said, contemptuously tossing it on his desk. "And that could be a fake badge. Gotta check out this shit with the court first." He made no move to pick up the phone, but turned back to his clipboard.

Having dealt with many assholes during his long career, Jack had a ready answer.

"That is your right," he said without raising his voice. "But you are delaying an official investigation involving national security, and that is always a mistake."

The dispatcher looked up at Jack. "So what you gonna do?" he said. "Bust me?"

Jack just gave him a tight smile and his federal-agent version of the Lakota thousand-yard stare.

For ten long seconds they silently locked eyes. Then the dispatcher caved.

"The codes are on these two sheets," he said, turning the clipboard toward Jack. "They're arranged by truck number and destination. Let me go make copies of them."

"Okay," Jack said, but followed the dispatcher into the next room and watched as he ran the sheets through the office copier. The sheets did not contain the drivers' names, and Jack knew that those would be on another set of documents. But he did not want to demand them. He did not want the dispatcher thinking he might be after a particular driver. Maybe the FBI was just interested in patterns, not people. That would make the dispatcher less apt to send out a warning call to his troops. If he was enough of an asshole to do that, the drivers wouldn't think they were being singled out, especially if their deliveries weren't bogus.

"Thank you," Jack said. "I don't think I need to tell you to keep this whole thing under your hat. If all goes well, nothing will happen, and we'll all be able to go home to our families tonight."

The dispatcher nodded. He understood the implicit threat.

With that Jack walked out to his car — actually Zoey Rasmussen's old Dodge pickup — and began entering GPS codes into his laptop, forty-seven of them, for the trucking company was a big and busy one. Soon forty-seven bright dots appeared on the laptop screen, several of them heading north just outside Chicago's Loop on Interstate 94, then northwest on Interstate 90, and Jack set out in pursuit, keeping to the speed limit. No point in getting hauled over for speeding. Besides, he didn't need to. He knew his quarry would be sticking to the limit.

Mile by mile passed by through northwestern Illinois and southern Wisconsin, and the stream of dots on Jack's laptop thinned as truck after truck pulled off the interstate and headed to its destination. Soon the dots had dwindled to a glowing trio, then two as a truck split off and headed west, and finally one was left still heading north.

Vacationers to Porcupine County from Chicago as well as truckers get there by three routes. The easternmost follows Interstate 43 from Milwaukee to U.S. 141 at Green Bay, then north on 141 to U.S. 2 at Iron River, Michigan, then west to U.S. 45 and finally north to that highway's terminus at Porcupine City. The westernmost route follows I-90/94 to a point north of Madison, Wisconsin, where it splits off on I-39 and heads past Wausau, where it becomes U.S. 51 and goes to northern Wisconsin. The central, and shortest (if there is not a lot of traffic) route is U.S. 45, picked up at Milwaukee after a 90-minute run north from Chicago on I-94.

Jack had reasoned that an eighteen-wheeler driver heading for Porcupine County would probably take the U.S. 45 route when traffic was light, because the mileage was shortest, and if he did not have customers to service on the way up. Because it would take all day — eight hours on the road — to get to Porcupine County, Jack thought, the driver would stop for the night at a motel somewhere and then make several service calls over the next day or two.

There would be at least three, maybe four or five, stops for Tancredi's twelve-thousand-gallon tank truck. Typical underground tanks in Upper Michigan can hold as few as two thousand gallons at Mom-and-Pop filling stations or as much as twenty thousand gallons at big service plazas. In practice, most gas station entrepreneurs kept the levels of their tanks as low as possible, taking in only enough fuel to last a few days until the next truck comes. Unsold stored gas is unprofitable. Often a driver will drop off as few as fifteen hundred or two thousand gallons and move on until his truck is empty.

Jack was right on both counts. Tancredi took U.S. 45 and stopped once, at Eagle River, for a late lunch and to refuel his truck, and kept on going until the glowing bug on Jack's laptop finally pulled up at a familiar point on Michigan State Highway M64 along Lake Superior between Silverton and Porcupine City.

"He's stopped at the Eagle Rest Cabins," Jack said on his cell. That was the same motel where I had directed the campers before the storm a week earlier. "Bet he'll overnight there."

"Do you need extra eyes?" I said.

"Probably, but not just yet," Jack said. "I'll put mine on him and we'll take it from there, okay?"

"Okay."

An hour later Jack pulled up at the motel, a dozen one-room cabins around a wide U-shaped asphalt driveway, the office in a larger building in the middle of the property. Tancredi's tanker truck was parked on a gravel patch to one side. Cars sat in front of three of the cabins, where lights glowed over the entry doors, showing that they were occupied. A lamp also burned outside a fourth cabin. There was no car in front, but the cabin was the one closest to the truck.

"VACANCY," said the neon sign in the window of the office.

Jack strode inside, and the clerk behind the desk raised his eyebrows in surprise. He was the owner of the place. Phil Esterhazy is a Hungarian who had emigrated from Budapest after the fall of the Iron Curtain and bought the old mom-and-pop motel, a deteriorating dump, and turned it into a comfortable country lodging that had become popular with vacationers, hunters and skiers. Phil is a member of the local volunteer search-and-rescue squad, and I'd officially deputized him a couple of times when we were hunting a fugitive in the woods. He's an intelligent guy, quick to pick up on events, and trustworthy as the day is long.

Jack put his finger to his lips, winked, and cocked his head toward the eighteen-wheeler.

"Need a room for the night," he said.

Phil nodded, winked back, and said, "Any preference?"

"Who's in Twelve?" Jack whispered.

Phil checked the register. "Joe Tancredi," he said just as quietly. "From Indiana. Drives that tanker. He's been a regular here for more than a year."

Jack peered out the window and said, "Put me in Eleven."

In three minutes the agent had entered the cabin. It was perfect for surveillance of Twelve. A side window in the tiny bathroom looked out onto the front stoop of Tancredi's cabin just five yards away. Closing the bathroom door would shut out the light from the lamp in the bedroom while it softly illuminated the yard out front. Jack pulled in a chair, parted the bathroom window drapes slightly, and sat in the dark while he listened to classical music on his iPod. As a young FBI agent he had earned the sobriquet "Iron Ass" for his ability to sit unmoving for hours on a stakeout.

"Eyes on the prize," Jack said on his cell.

"Think he's had supper?" I said.

"Probably later. I'll follow if he goes out. He didn't stop for lunch until about two Central time, so he won't be hungry for a while."

For two hours Jack sat and watched. Nothing appeared to his eyes except a few cars and pickups speeding by on M64. His buttocks began to grow numb — Iron Ass was, after all, in his sixties — and he stood up from the hard chair several times to scratch and stretch. By nine p.m. the shadows of the tall hemlocks and white pines along the highway had fallen over the cabins.

A scraped and dented fifteen-year-old Saturn pulled up in front of Cabin Twelve just as dusk rolled in. A tall, slim, wild-haired woman in her forties got out and walked to the door, already being held open, and disappeared inside. Before she could do so Jack had photographed her face and the car's license plate with a telephoto-equipped Nikon.

Quickly, while still at the window, he took the memory card out of the camera, plugged it into his laptop, and emailed two photos to me. When Jack called my cell, I was at Ginny's, following my resumed routine of dropping by her house for supper and maybe her bed. Just in case anybody was watching, we wanted everyone outside our little law enforcement circle to think we all were just leading our normal lives. The truth was that we were all coiled like compressed springs, antsily waiting for a trigger into action.

"Borrow your puter for a sec?" I asked. The photos

were on my iPhone, but the screen is small.

"Be my guest," Ginny said, and followed me to her kitchen desk.

In a minute both photographs Jack had sent were on Ginny's monitor. Immediately I recognized the woman. She was the one I had seen in the door at Caleb Pennington's place the year before when Annie and I had paid our visit to him. I did not recognize her car, but called Joe Koski, on overnight duty as dispatcher and corrections officer at the sheriff's department. I gave him the plate number and asked him to run it. In less than a minute he called back.

"Plate belongs to a '91 Saturn abandoned to a junkyard downstate," he said. "The plate tag's expired. Probably somebody bought the hulk and fixed it up without registering."

That sounded like the Penningtons, the kind of backwoodsmen who obey as few laws as they can get away with. I called Jack back.

"I've seen that woman," I said. "She apparently lives with the Penningtons. We don't know exactly who she is. Probably Pennington's daughter, maybe a niece. Remember, the Pennington men had an alibi for the night before Billy Gibbs' body was found. But she wasn't with them. That means she could be Tancredi's accomplice. After all, they're all neo-Nazis."

"Okay," Jack said. "I'll keep watching, see what they do and where they go."

"Thanks," I said and hung up.

Half an hour later the pair emerged from Cabin Twelve and drove west on M64 in the Saturn. Quickly Jack followed in his pickup.

Just six miles later Tancredi and his companion pulled up at the restaurant that was part of a chain motel in Silverton, and entered. Jack waited five minutes, then went in himself.

The pair sat at the crowded bar, nursing Bud Lights, munching burgers and fries, and darting knowing glances at each other. Fueling up before the night's activity, Jack thought. But he doubted that it involved anything illegal. He sat on a stool next to them and listened, trying to make out their conversation over the jukebox din. Neither had ever seen him before, and the beard he had grown helped him blend right in with the others at the bar.

It was so noisy in the barroom and the couple's voices so low that Jack could understand few words, but he was able to catch "niggers," "kikes" and "beaners," among other unpleasant things.

Toward ten o'clock, well before closing time, the two left the bar and drove back to the Eagle Rest. Jack followed in the night a few hundred yards behind and pulled in just as the couple entered Cabin Twelve. He took up his station in Cabin Eleven's bathroom.

After fourteen minutes by Jack's watch, the ceiling light went out in Cabin Twelve. But Jack could see television flickering through the curtain in the side bedroom window. Although the front of the cabin was softly bathed in light from the overhead door lamp, the side of the cabin was well shaded. Although he already had a pretty good idea of what was going on in the cabin, Jack decided to see if he could observe the action. The old G-man had both attended and testified at hundreds of criminal trials, and he knew that eyewitness testimony with plenty of vivid detail would trump any defense attorney's suggestion that he was making unfounded assumptions.

Jack was also very good at stealth. He changed into dark trousers and a black windbreaker, put a black balaclava over his head and face, then turned off the overhead lamp on the cabin door before opening it quietly and slipping into the shadows with his camera. In two minutes he crept out of the brush behind the cabins and approached Cabin Twelve's side window. A sliver of curtain had opened to the interior. A low light flickered from a television screen and Jack could hear moaning within.

The light was from a porn video, which surprised Jack at first. Phil Esterhazy was not the sort of innkeeper who subscribed to cable-television adult movies, as do so many nameless hotel chains, in the expectation that their clientele can't fall asleep without this stuff. He did equip his cabins' televisions with DVD players and maintained a small library of G- and PG-rated movies in the office, free for the asking. Doubtless Joe Tancredi had brought in his luggage a supply of his preferred form of video entertainment. That appeared to be group sex involving industrial-strength BDSM.

Jack changed his angle of view slightly. The woman stood by the bed, nude except for absurdly high spike heels and a leather helmet that covered most of her face and gave her a Hannibal Lecter grin. With a wooden yardstick she was busily belaboring the naked buttocks of Joe Tancredi, who was fettered with steel handcuffs, his neck ringed by a wide leather slave collar, and his mouth gagged by a leather ball. Under his protruding belly he had a rampant erection, and as Jack snapped a photo through the curtain, the woman kicked Tancredi to his knees with one sharp heel, and he ejaculated copiously on the bedspread.

"That was all I needed to see," Jack told me on his cell a few minutes later, after he had returned to Cabin Eleven. "I can testify in plenty of detail about those activities. I don't need any more of that *Fifty-one Shades of Grey* stuff."

"Weren't there only fifty?" I said.

"They must have invented one more."

Sexual deviance of all kinds was part of every police officer's library of knowledge. But although I knew all about it, I wasn't into it, and, frankly, the details did not interest me at all.

"Okay, Jack, I'll read about it in your report. You *are* going to file a report?"

"Of course. Now I'm going to get some shuteye. I'm a light sleeper and will definitely hear the Saturn start up if it leaves tonight, let alone a big eighteen-wheeler tractor."

At about one in the morning the lovers finally ran out of steam. A few minutes later, as Jack watched, the woman emerged from the cabin and drove off in the Saturn. Jack could have put a GPS bug under its bumper, but we dared not wake Judge Rantala for a warrant. We already had a pretty good idea where that car and its occupant was going: Caleb Pennington's place in the woods.

TWENTY

"WHAT WAS THAT all about?" Ginny asked as I laid my cell phone on her night table.

"Oh, nothing," I said. "Just a little kinky sex."

"You seem to work the most interesting criminal cases," she said, utterly unfazed. "Tell me about it in the morning."

After blueberry pancakes with my blasé bedmate, who surprisingly did not ask for details about Jack's midnight call, I was off to the sheriff's department. As soon as I arrived I called in Chad, showed him the photographs of the woman and Joseph Tancredi, and gave him a heavily edited but still frank version of Jack's reports from the previous evening.

"Find out who she is, willya?" I said. "Call the Southern Poverty Law Center. They probably know."

An hour later Chad returned to my office, notebook in hand.

"The woman in question is Anne-Marie Hutchinson, age forty-three," he said. "She's the daughter of Caleb Pennington. Grew up in lower Michigan, had two years at Kalamazoo College, then married and divorced a white supremacist named Alex Hutchinson. After the split three years ago she moved from Dayton, Ohio, to the family place near Ewen.

"She writes what she calls 'investigative journalism' under several pen names for quite a few neo-Nazi websites and magazines. In fact, the people at Southern Poverty say, she's one of the biggest single sources of hate literature in the country. If you've read a printed screed against Jews or African-Americans or Latinos anywhere, it's probably her doing.

"The divorce record was never sealed, and the Dayton police faxed me a copy. Among the grounds was sexual incompatibility. Hutchinson told the lawyers he couldn't keep up with his wife's 'unnatural demands,' quote unquote."

"Why am I not surprised?" I said.

"There's more," Chad said.

"Go on."

"On a long shot," he said, "I had the traffic cam archives checked to see if a '91 Saturn with her license plates had been photographed anywhere in Houghton County at the time Gibbs was killed. No dice, but I did turn up a traffic violation on LEIN. Anne-Marie Hutchinson was ticketed by a deputy for speeding on a county road just outside Freda two days before Gibbs' body was found near St. Ignace. The deputy evidently was in a hurry and didn't run the plate. Probably thought a beater that old couldn't be a stolen car. That was lazy."

"You're getting to be as bad as Alex," I said. Chad clearly had adopted the trooper's storytelling narrative style, starting at the beginning and building to a climax. "But that puts Hutchinson within a mile of the cabin Gibbs had rented in Freda. I will bet Tancredi killed him there with Hutchinson's help, and the two carted the body to Mackinac County for a reason we don't yet know."

"If they did that," Chad said, "maybe they stashed the corpse in the trunk of Hutchinson's Saturn and the staties can find blood or DNA or possibly trace evidence of the body in it."

"Very good deduction, Deputy Garrow," I said. "Couldn't have put it better myself."

"Now what?"

"We bring in Anne-Marie Hutchinson for

questioning."

"Think she'll talk or lawyer up?"

"We might be able to get something out of her before she does."

"How? I mean, why do you think so? She's not stupid. She probably knows the law."

"Just a feeling," I said. "I'm going to call Lieutenant Hemb."

Jack had arrived at the sheriff's department and had opened his laptop at one of the vacant deputy's desks. He was following the GPS transmitter on Tancredi's truck. It was parked at a gas station in Greenland twelve miles southwest of Porcupine City, apparently his first stop of the day. There are about a dozen independent filling stations in Porcupine County, and if he serviced only half of them, it would take all day before he could start back to Whiting. He might even overnight somewhere in the county or the next, and it stood to reason that his girl friend would meet him there, perhaps for another round of Marquis de Sade whoopee.

"She's very likely going to come out of that dump in the backwoods sometime today, probably in the afternoon," I said. "Time for a stakeout and a pickup."

An hour later Chad and Annie took up station in both Expeditions on the county gravel road off M28 just south of Ewen. I've instructed my deputies to use two vehicles, if possible, when making a traffic stop that is likely to lead to an arrest. One deputy places his vehicle immediately behind the target car and approaches the subject from the left, attracting the driver's attention in the left-hand mirror. The other officer parks behind the first deputy's car and approaches unseen from the right side, sometimes with gun drawn and pointing downward.

Chad and Annie parked their vehicles on a sandy turnaround screened from the road by thick brush, but had a clear view of anything passing by. Annie climbed into the passenger seat of Chad's mount so that she could see better and help pass the time.

The sun rose and the cool nighttime temperatures climbed into the seventies. At noon Chad pulled out his lunchbox. He is a thrifty soul and prefers to eat a homemade sandwich at his desk, if he's not driving, or in his vehicle, if he is. Annie, who always goes to Merle's for lunch because she "has nothing else to spend money on and besides the food is much better than anything I could ever fix for myself," leaned over and said in a mock flirtatious tone, "Halfsies?"

Chad was familiar with Annie's mealtime proclivities and in fact was expecting the question. The big deputy always packed a big lunch for himself, bigger than he really needs. "All right," he said, "but that's another favor you owe me."

"Good man," Annie said. "Of course."

At one p.m. Tancredi was making his third stop of the day, at an independent station on River Street in Porcupine City. As the gasoline flowed from truck into ground tank, Anne-Marie Hutchinson emerged in her Saturn from the woods thirty miles to the south and turned onto M28. The two sheriff's vehicles quickly followed, and as she slowed for the only traffic light in Ewen, Chad flicked on his blue-and-white flashers. Annie kept hers off.

"License and registration, please," said Chad at the driver's door in the universal weary tone of a cop making a stop for a traffic violation. Annie took up station in the blind spot at the right rear fender of the Saturn as Chad examined the driver's license. Her gun hand gently brushed the butt of her Glock.

"What did I do?"

"You're Anne-Marie Hutchinson?"

"Yes. What is this all about?"

"Step out of the vehicle, please, and open the trunk."

THE RIDDLE OF BILLY GIBBS

"You think I'm carrying dope?"

"Are you?"

"No!"

"Please open the trunk anyway."

If she refused, Chad was ready to produce a warrant obtained earlier that morning, but he liked to gauge how cooperative a subject might be. Or how ignorant of the law.

"Oh, all right!" She popped the trunk lid. It rose with a protesting squeak.

Annie stepped forward and peered inside, playing her Maglite into every nook and cranny. The trunk gaped empty except for a doughnut spare tire in the bottom and tire tools in one corner. A nearly invisible brown stain the size of a serving platter colored the center of the tan carpet. An almost successful effort had been made to scrub it out. Annie took a close look at the seams of the carpet. It had been carefully vacuumed, but black grains that looked like sand were caught in the weave.

Annie stood up and nodded to Chad.

"Miss Hutchinson," Chad said in a quiet and polite voice, "we are detaining you temporarily for questioning in a criminal case. We will take you to the sheriff's department in Porcupine City for an interview. We will park your car at the gas station across the street and we will bring you back to pick it up after the interview."

Always keep them thinking. Don't say "arrest." Say "detain." Keeps the subject off balance.

"What criminal case is that?" Hutchinson said in a demanding tone.

"The sheriff will tell you," Chad said. "Please get into my vehicle."

"Oh, all right," Hutchinson said. "I guess I don't have any choice."

That surprised Chad. He was all ready to slap the cuffs on and stuff her into the caged back seat of the

Expedition. He was sure she did not know what the "detainer" was all about. If she had, he doubted that she would be so cooperative.

He held the back door open and she slid inside. They set off for Porcupine City while Annie stayed behind. When Chad's vehicle faded from sight, she drove the Saturn into the gas station and into a service bay, where it would be hidden from outside view. Then she called Alex, who was already on his way to Ewen from his headquarters at Wakefield, and told him about the stain in the trunk. When he arrived he'd give it a quick test for blood. If the result was positive, he'd call me and cut out a chunk of the carpet to send to Marquette for DNA analysis and the black grains tested as well.

While this was going on, I put that call in to Sue Hemb in Lansing. Fortunately the forensic psychiatrist's shingle was out, and she answered immediately.

"Sue," I said without preamble, "is sadomasochistic behavior connected with neo-Nazi and fascist beliefs?"

"Why do you ask?" she said, surprised.

I explained, telling her what we knew about Anne-Marie Hutchinson and attempting to keep my description of Jack Adamson's report as PG-rated as possible, and failing miserably — but not by Sue's standards. As a shrink she already knew everything about kinky sex and nothing surprised her.

She chuckled. "You're blushing, aren't you, Steve?"

I could almost see her grinning. One of the reasons law enforcement officers all over Michigan are fond of her is her wry sense of humor. She finds much of human behavior to be faintly comic in its absurdity, and often chooses layman's language to explain it. She works with cops, after all, and cops like things kept simple and understandable.

"Anyway, to answer your question, there can be

such a connection, especially in pornographic literature and movies. But marching to the beat of 'Horst Wessel' and whipping your bedmate with a limber yardstick is not always connected. We have to accept that perfectly respectable folks often enjoy bondage, domination and sadomasochism, usually in their fantasies but sometimes they act them out with willing partners. Legally speaking, kinky sex can be perfectly innocent, especially if both parties — or all parties — consent. Of course, this view may not agree with one's particular moral code, but in a court of law that is neither here nor there.

"BDSM doesn't necessarily lead to 'Heil Hitler.' But 'Heil Hitler' *can* lead to BDSM. People with fascist beliefs are fiercely authoritarian and often conflicted about it. They can praise sexual purity in public but practice the opposite in private. That could be a therapeutic escape from the stresses of their actions. I'll go out on a limb and say that it's entirely possible your Anne-Marie Hutchinson was pretending to be the Bitch of Belsen and imagining Tancredi as a Jewish prisoner, and he was acting out deeply buried feelings of guilt by allowing himself to be whipped."

"That sounds *painful.*"

"People get their jollies in various and sometimes puzzling ways. In any event, although what that pair was doing was not against the law, the impulses that led them to it may also have affected other actions. At their extreme, the sadistic fantasies of neo-Nazis can sometimes lead to actual violence, especially if the actors lose all sense of reality.

"What's more, ideologues of this kind think they're smarter than everybody else, except maybe for Jews, whose historical reputation for superior intellect and culture often frightens them. In my experience, neo-Nazis tend to be glib parrots, not original thinkers. They think they can bluff their way through a confrontation. But many of them seem to be emotionally fragile and can often be manipulated by authority, especially when their arrogant bluster is challenged. Deep down, they're surprisingly weak."

"You know all that for a fact?" I said.

"Of course not. But it's what I think."

"Thanks for furthering my education," I said. "I'm not sure I needed to know all that, but some of it is very helpful."

Soon Chad arrived with Anne-Marie Hutchinson. She was not cuffed, I noticed, but Chad walked half a stride behind her, arms loose, ready to pounce if she tried to bolt. He directed her to the kitchen and held out a chair at the cracked linoleum table. She sat, and he took up station leaning against the refrigerator a few feet away.

"Sheriff will be out in a moment," he said. "Sorry for the delay."

We had a video camera—largesse from the Pentagon—trained on the kitchen table, and I watched as Hutchinson fidgeted. One of the principles of interrogation is softening up the subject by delaying the beginning of an interview, giving interviewees time enough to work up a nervous sweat wondering what the cops have on them.

"What's going on?" Hutchinson said after ten minutes, a tense whine in her voice. "Why are we waiting?"

"Sheriff's busy," Chad said solicitously. "He'll be here as soon as he can."

The big deputy knew exactly what I was doing, but his patience had limits, too. Just as *he* was beginning to fidget I walked into the kitchen, case file in hand.

She glared up at me and I took a good look at her. She was an Aryan wet dream. Everything about her was *long:* long legs on a skinny torso, thin matchstick arms, long straight blonde hair, a long, high-cheekboned, thin-lipped and aquiline face that was still pretty in its early forties but in a few years would droop into horsiness. Her blue eyes were intense but very light, almost washed out.

She looked fetching in a tight black short-sleeved jersey over black jeans and black riding boots. Her only jewelry was a long braided gold chain with a pendant in the center, a runic sculpture of the numerals "88." The eighth letter of the alphabet is "H." Double that and you get "HH," or "Heil Hitler." That piece of jewelry is a common symbol of recognition among neo-Nazis. Convicts often have "88" tattooed on their shoulders.

Her haughty expression dripped self-assurance and contempt for the company in which she unwillingly had found herself. I took a deep breath and reminded myself of the adage "Beauty is skin deep, but ugly goes clean to the bone."

After another beat I said in as apologetic a voice as I could muster, "I'm sincerely sorry to keep you waiting, Miss Hutchinson. I was tied up with another case. You know how it is."

"No, I don't," she said. "What's going on?"

"First of all," I said, ignoring the question, "I want to show you a picture."

I opened the file, selected a photograph and slid it in front of her. It was a mug shot of Gibbs, taken in the sheriff's department when he was charged with sexual assault.

"Do you know this man?" I said.

"Never saw him before," she said.

Mistake number one. Everybody in Porcupine County knew who Billy Gibbs was, what he looked like, and what had happened to him. As Sue had forecast, Hutchinson's ideological arrogance had led her to underestimate my intelligence. People like her tended to think bare-faced denial would see them through an interrogation. In reality, it just dug their hole deeper.

"Okay," I said. "Do you know *this* man?" I slid a head shot of Joseph Tancredi before her. The Southern Poverty Law Center had faxed it to me.

"No," she said. "Who is he?"

Miss Hutchinson, you are lying to me," I said, switching my tone from casual and friendly to stern and sepulchral, and carefully placed between us the photo of her meeting Tancredi on the stoop of Cabin Twelve. She stared at it in open-mouthed dismay. Then I lowered the boom.

"Can you explain this?" I said, placing Jack's second photograph in front of her, the one he had shot through the curtain of the cabin side window. In it Hutchinson was striking Tancredi on the buttocks just as he reached orgasm. Though the photo was not evidence of a crime, it did place them together and in a situation she almost certainly would not want made public. It also showed that we knew a lot more about her than she would want anyone to know. She gaped in shock, and behind her Chad took a step forward.

"You black bastard!" she snarled, rising from the chair. With his huge hands on her shoulders Chad sat her back down.

"I'm actually an Indian," I said. " 'Native American' in *polite* company."

"Same thing," she said, still in a fury. "Human trash!"

"Miss Hutchinson," I said, ratcheting my Bringer of Doom tone several notches upward, "we have firm evidence that you were in Freda, Michigan, the day Billy Gibbs was murdered. We know that you received a citation for speeding just outside town. We believe that you helped Joseph Tancredi murder Mr. Gibbs there and helped him dispose of the body near St. Ignace. We found human bloodstains in the trunk of your car. Their DNA is being tested right now, and if it matches the DNA of Mr.

231

Gibbs, you are looking at least thirty years in prison for conspiracy and being an accessory to murder."

We did not yet have enough evidence enough to charge her with first-degree murder, the maximum penalty for which is life without parole, but I wasn't about to tell her that. Not yet.

I slid a fifth picture under her nose. It was a morgue shot of Gibbs lying naked on the slab, an enormous blood-encrusted hole in his chest.

"I want a lawyer. Now!" she said.

"That is your right," I said. "You are now under arrest. You don't have to say anything more." I pulled out the Miranda card and carefully enunciated every word so that she could fully understand the fix her lies had landed her in. She sat rooted to the chair, trembling in dismay.

"If you help us *now*," I said after a moment, returning to a quiet and reasonable tone, "there's a chance we may be able to get your sentence reduced. It's your call."

Of course she could have and should have waited for an attorney before waiving away her right against self-incrimination. A good lawyer might have been able to negotiate a plea bargain more substantial than the vague offer I was waving across the table.

But almost instantly she broke. I had half expected her to — as Sue Hemb had said, the backbones of neo-Nazis tend to be as robust as kitchen matches — but I was still startled at the speed with which she grasped the tiny straw I proffered. Sue's speculation had been right on.

"All right," Hutchinson said, quivering, tears running down her cheeks. "What do you want to know?"

"Let's begin at the beginning," I said, then announcing the time, date, place and names of the persons present for the benefit of the official voice recorder. "Tell us how you first met Joseph Tancredi."

Sergeant Tancredi, she said, had noticed her byline atop several of the screeds she wrote for a variety of hate websites and magazines that he accessed from and read in his barracks at the Bagram air base. Over several months he sent her a few fan letters praising her deep understanding of the enemies of white America and her insights into the cause to which Adolf Hitler, Heinrich Himmler and Hermann Goering "had sacrificed their lives and fortunes," as she put it. So had his barracks mates Ioannis Cacoyannis and especially Michael Ahern, who had asked Hutchinson for advice on writing and publishing "the same subject matter I advocate."

Even though she was confessing, she still seemed to believe in the toxic sludge she had shoveled into the mails and the Internet. At trial she very likely would try to justify her actions by demanding to take the stand and deliver windy speeches praising Great God Adolf and his modern minions. That would give both defense counsel and presiding judge a throbbing headache, and it would not impress the jury either. The media would roll its collective eyes and boil her grandstanding peroration down to a sentence or two.

The online exchanges between Hutchinson and Tancredi soon turned from raw politics to mutual attraction, and when Tancredi was discharged from the army they met in person for a long weekend in a resort on the shore of Lake Michigan at New Buffalo. I did not ask about their activities at the resort—she volunteered them.

"We spent the whole time in bed," she said. "We barely went out to eat. It was amazing. We did things we'd never done with other people. We did things other people probably have never done."

I didn't ask specifically what those were. If confined to a bedroom, they were probably not illegal. And at the moment they did not seem germane to the murder case. If they turned out to be, we could always re-interview her.

233

"What happened after that?" I asked.

"I'd just been divorced," she said. "My ex was incapable in bed. Couldn't get it up very often and when he did he wasn't very hard. Joe came along at just the right time. I needed somewhere to live for a while and decided to come back to Daddy's compound outside Ewen while Joe found a job and got himself established. That took a while. I was going to move in with him later this year. We were going to make ourselves the leading tellers of truth to white America."

"Mm," I said noncommitally. "Now what about Billy Gibbs?"

"Joe told me almost as soon as we met at New Buffalo all about what the two niggers did to him and his buddies at Bagram," she said. "He was very angry about it. He said he was not only going to get his share of the money but also the whole thing. And he was going to make sure those black bastards never screwed a white man again."

"What about the others? Cacoyannis and Ahern?"

"Both of them pussies," she said. "Joe said they didn't deserve a share. All they ever do is goose-step around the room like sniveling babies. They're cowards."

"Did you ever meet them?"

"No, and I don't want to."

In the months after their military discharges Tancredi had lost track of Gibbs' whereabouts and had neither the skills to locate him nor the funds to hire a skip-tracer. When the newspapers and television stations announced Gibbs' arrest for sexual assault, Hutchinson immediately recognized the name and phoned Tancredi in Whiting.

"He came up to Ewen and stayed with Daddy and me while we discussed what to do," she said.

"Did that include coming up with a scheme to kill Gibbs?"

234

"Yes."

"Your father was included?"

"Yes, and my brothers. We all talked about the best way to get him alone and do him. We couldn't do that when he was in jail waiting on his trial."

"What if he had been convicted?"

"Oh, that would have been easy. All we would have to do is get word to the Aryan Brotherhood and they'd pump him for the location of the money before slipping him a shank."

The Aryan Brotherhood is a violent and highly dangerous group of white supremacist inmates that rules the roost in many state and federal prisons. The FBI says its members constitute only one per cent of the federal prison population, but are responsible for as many as twenty per cent of the murders behind bars. They are also drug traffickers, extortionists, pimps and killers for hire.

"Did you ever think that Gibbs might be exonerated?"

"He never should have been," Hutchinson said, sneering. "He was guilty as the day is long. The jury was too lily-livered to do the right thing. The prosecutor was incompetent and the judge looked the other way. For Joe it wasn't just getting his money. He wanted justice. He wanted it *all*, in fact."

"The money, you mean?"

"Yes. Joe said he never could figure out how two darkies could be smart enough to get all that money home from Afghanistan without getting caught. He wanted it all because he didn't think Cacoyannis and Ahern deserved a dime of it."

"How much was all that money?"

"I'm not sure. Once Joe said six million. Another time he said two million. I don't think he knew for sure."

"So what did you and Mr. Tancredi do?"

"We watched the trial and after it was over we

followed Gibbs to a friend's house. We wanted to do him there right then, but there were too many people helping him celebrate. We parked along the highway in the middle of a bunch of cars and watched the party. All those nigger lovers! Can you believe it?"

Rage and disgust distorted her pretty features.

"Then, about one o'clock in the morning, when just about everybody had left except two or three people, Gibbs came out of the house with a couple of suitcases, got into his truck and headed toward Houghton on M28. The others went home at the same time."

Hutchinson and Tancredi followed Gibbs to Freda in her Saturn and watched, their lights out, as their quarry unlocked the door to a cabin in the center of a dozen similar cottages.

"There were just too many people around," she said. "We couldn't execute him then. So we slept in the car and waited until morning. We went to the office and asked to rent the cabin Gibbs was in, just to find out how long he would be there. The owner said sorry, the cabin had been rented for a month. So we went home."

Back at the ranch, if Pennington's hovel could be called that, the pair discussed what to do. Caleb Pennington and his three sons offered a host of suggestions, most of which had to do with explosives and rocket-propelled grenades, none of which the strange family possessed but thought they could procure from a friendly crooked arms dealer somewhere. Finally Hutchinson and Tancredi worked out a less noisy plan, and three weeks after the trial, drove back to Freda.

For two days they watched through binoculars as Gibbs went through his daily routine. Each morning he ran two miles in both directions on the black-sand beach, Hutchinson said, and his route skirted a large double outcropping of rocks into the lake that blocked the view from both east and west, forcing him to splash through ankle-deep water before he reached the beach again.

"We decided to take him there, and we lay in wait. Joe had a shotgun and a three-foot-long piece of twine with wooden handles at each end. I had a length of clothesline. It was about four p.m. when Gibbs came around the first rocks and Joe stepped out with the shotgun and told him to stop.

"Gibbs didn't seem surprised at all. He said, 'So you finally caught up with me.' He wasn't scared.

"Joe said, 'Where's the money?' and Gibbs said 'Fuck you.'

"Joe said, 'You cheated me, you black son of a bitch,' and he went on like that for a couple of minutes. Gibbs kept shaking his head 'No.' Then Joe made him put his hands behind his back and I stepped over and tied them with the clothesline."

If Michigan still had the death penalty, I mused, those words would have put Anne-Marie Hutchinson right onto the gurney awaiting the needle. Her actions had progressed beyond simple conspiracy all the way to Murder One. I knew Garner Armstrong would demand a life sentence, no matter what promise we had made to her—and I had carefully avoided spelling it out, our strategy in hinting that there could be a plea deal.

"He made Gibbs get on his knees, then lie on his stomach, on the sand," she said. "Then he jumped on Gibbs' back and wrapped the twine around his neck and pulled and pulled on those wooden handles. Gibbs bucked and twisted but Joe is pretty big and strong and he stayed on Gibbs' back. After a couple of minutes Gibbs stopped moving.

"I thought that was the end of it, that we'd drive his body to an old stone quarry and dump it there. But no, Joe wasn't finished. He dragged the body to a sand bluff and leaned it against the bluff face forward, on its knees. Then he stepped back, raised the shotgun and fired twice. There was a lot of blood.

"I asked Joe why he did that but he didn't respond. He just said 'Help me clean him off.' We dragged him into the water and washed away the blood and sand. Then we carried him to my car a hundred yards away on a dirt road in the woods and dumped him into the trunk."

"After that?" I said.

"Joe wasn't finished. He said, 'He's got to be strung up in a tree like the nigger he is.' What I don't understand is why we had to drive all the way to St. Ignace to do that."

Possibly, I thought, Tancredi figured that putting plenty of distance between place of murder and place of discovery of the body would help cover their tracks.

"Then when we got there and I watched from a few yards away, Joe put a noose around Gibbs' neck, threw a rope over a limb, and pulled up the body. I was surprised he could do that. But Joe weighs about two hundred fifty pounds, you know, and he's strong."

"Then what happened?" I said.

"We drove back to Freda and got there at about four a.m., and we searched Gibbs' cabin. We were careful to put everything back the way it was, to fool the police, but there really wasn't much. There was no money. We had been worried about the blood on the beach, but the lake had kicked up that afternoon, and the waves had washed everything away.

"Joe had taken the keys from the body before stringing it up, and he drove Gibbs' truck to the quarry. We followed in my car, and we went to the quarry at Torch Lake, where Joe parked the truck. We slept a few hours in it, and then Joe pulled apart the interior looking for the money. There wasn't any there, either. Joe lost it and went into a rage for ten minutes, smashing all the glass with a tire iron and using up all his ammunition shooting holes all over with the shotgun and with the rifle he'd also brought. I tried to make him stop, because he was making

238

so much noise that I was afraid people would come. But
nobody did. Finally Joe calmed down. He started the truck,
put it into gear and let it go over the cliff into the water. He
said it would never be found."

"Go on," I said. "What did you do then?"

"We drove back to Ewen in my car. The next day
the TV said Gibbs' body had been found, and we decided
to stay out of sight and go about our business as if nothing
had happened. Joe went back to his job in Whiting and I
stayed with Daddy, helping out around the house and
working on my articles."

"There's more, isn't there?" I said.

"Yes. We wanted to search Gibbs' trailer outside
Porcupine City, but we knew the police would be
watching. They could have put video cameras all over the
property. Didn't you?"

I shrugged noncommittally. Theoretically we could
have, but we had neither money nor manpower for that.

"Then when the big snow came a few months later,
Joe came up to Ewen and he and I went out to search the
place for that money. It had stopped snowing, but the
drifts were still high. We came in on snowshoes through
the woods on the other side of the trailer. When we got
inside we cut open all the furniture and pulled the
paneling off the walls. Yeah, we messed up the place good.
Of course we didn't find anything. Then Joe left a gasoline
bomb with a timer set to go off six hours later. Didn't you
find it?"

I did not answer, but everything she had told us
matched what we already knew.

"Did Mr. Tancredi say anything about Keyshawn
Banks?" I said.

Hutchinson gasped slightly. She now knew we had
put together the whole story.

"Yes," she said. "A couple of weeks after he killed
Billy Gibbs, he called me and told me he'd taken care of

Banks in Flint. Those were his words."

"Did he say how?"

"Shot him from the window of a building half a block away. He used a pimped-out military rifle."

"You will testify to all this in a court of law?" I said.

"Yeah. You know everything anyway. Will it help me?" She was almost pleading.

"We can try."

"Thanks."

"That's all for now," I said. "You will be placed in a cell overnight, and tomorrow morning we will take you to court to be arraigned. If you don't have your own lawyer, the judge will appoint one for you."

"Can I get my phone call now?"

The lack of a Michigan statute granting an arrestee the right to make a phone call gives law enforcement plenty of leeway in the timing of such a call. I wasn't going to let Hutchinson tip off either Tancredi or the Penningtons that we knew everything now. We still had things to do and people to see, as we say in the Upper Peninsula.

"We'll book you in a few hours and you can then make your call," I said. "Chad, please escort Miss Hutchinson to her quarters."

As soon as they left the kitchen I strode into the squad room and asked Jack, who had been there all afternoon watching his laptop and listening to our interview, where Tancredi was.

"Bruce's," he said.

Bruce's—actually Bruce Crossing, but Porkies habitually shorten the name, just as they often say "Porky" instead of "Porcupine City"—is just twenty-eight miles and about thirty-two minutes southeast of Porcupine City down U.S. 45 at the speed limit.

"He just got there and is pumping out what's probably the last of his load," Jack said. "I figure he'll be gone in half an hour."

"We'll be there in less than that," I said. "Probably twenty or twenty-five minutes. We can grab him up there, or stop him down on 45 on the way to Watersmeet. Sheila, call the tribals and ask them to block the highway at Watersmeet just in case we're not able to stop the truck before it leaves Bruce's. I'll call Alex and ask him to get the ESU to help him round up the Penningtons sometime tonight. Chad, Annie, Jack, you're with me. Let's go."

TWENTY-ONE

A POLICE-EQUIPPED Ford Expedition with a 365-horse
engine can do a hundred fifty miles an hour on a pristinely
groomed test track, but only an idiot would take it over a
hundred on a gravelly and cracked Upper Michigan
highway. The Porcupine County Sheriff's Department
officially limits its two Expeditions to ninety and only on
perfectly straight and smooth stretches of state or federal
highway, and I prefer that my deputies keep theirs at
eighty or below for non-pursuit dashes to crime scenes or
emergency sites, even with sirens. Of course, breaking the
speed limit on the way to lunch is a firing offense — at least
Gil says so.

"Faster, faster," I urged Chad as we sped toward
Bruce Crossing under our red-and-blue turret flashers,
using the siren only when we overtook a vehicle or one
approached from the other direction. The speedometer
topped eighty-one, then eighty-two, then eighty-three
miles an hour. The big deputy glanced skeptically at me in
the right seat.

"Boss," he said. "What's the hurry?"

"It will be safer to take Tancredi if he's already on
foot," I said. "If we have to flag him down in his truck
we'll be standing next to a ten-thousand-gallon tank of
flammable gasoline and fumes. What if he turns around
and puts an incendiary bullet into it?"

"You worry too much," said Jack from the back seat.
"Who carries incendiaries these days besides combat

soldiers?" Next to him Annie giggled.

"Even a regular lead bullet could punch a hole in the tank and put us into the middle of a lake of gas," I said. "That can be awfully unhealthy."

Twenty-one minutes after we had left Porcupine City, we approached the abandoned railroad right-of-way that gave Bruce's half its name, and Chad slowed to sixty, then forty as we neared the sprawling filling station and supermarket on the corner. Finally he pulled into the broad asphalt truck park, large enough to accommodate a dozen overnighting eighteen-wheelers. Tancredi's tanker was still parked next to the filler pipes to the underground fuel tanks. He was nowhere in sight.

"Probably inside getting a sandwich or taking a piss," said Jack. "I'll go look."

Jack was the only one of us not wearing the uniform of a lawman. Technically I wasn't, either, but my ball cap had a sheriff's star, and I'd left my Cubs chapeau in the other SUV. Going bareheaded was not an option. In the countryside, hatless men are as noticeable as tuxedoes on a nude beach, as Chad probably would say if you asked him.

"Okay," I said. "Chad, Annie, take up places on either side of the front door."

The two quickly stepped over to the market's double sliding doors and took up position out of sight of anyone emerging, casually leaning against pillars and looking bored. I stood behind a gasoline pump, my cap turned back to front, studying the fine print on the state permit while keeping an eye on the doors. In less than a minute Jack walked out and nodded, pointing to his crotch. We stood by, coiled and taut, ready to explode into action. I nodded to all three of my deputies and held up a finger. On my signal.

Tancredi stepped out of the doors, still adjusting his zipper underneath the flab of his belly. He looked even worse dressed than naked. Sloppy, I thought, and when I spotted the pecker tracks dotting the front of his trousers, even sloppier. What a guy.

I casually strode forward and stopped four feet away. "Joseph Tancredi? Porcupine County Sheriff's Department."

Quietly Chad and Annie approached from either side and Jack from behind. Jack motioned to the back of his own jeans. Tancredi was armed. The two deputies drew their Glocks and trained them on his head. Point blank.

"What's this?" he said. "My tags are current. I wasn't overloaded."

"Very carefully," I said, "take that pistol out of your pants between your thumb and forefinger and hand it to me muzzle down. My deputies have you covered from both sides and a FBI agent from the back."

Tancredi stared at me with naked hate and menace. I'm only an inch shorter and just as broad, and a stagey stink eye never impresses me. His puffy face and protruding belly told me I could take him easily if he lunged. But he didn't. Not with two gun barrels three feet from his temples.

"I've got a carry permit," he said, trying to bluster his way out of the jam. "You can't nail me for that!"

"No," I said, taking Tancredi's revolver, an old .38, from his loose grasp, "but I can for something else."

"What?" His expression told me that he knew exactly what.

"The murders of William Gibbs and Keyshawn Banks. Put your hands behind your head and interlace your fingers."

Immediately Jack reached up, yanked Tancredi's hands down by the wrists, and snapped on the cuffs he had carried ever since he agreed to be a deputy. He knew the old routine. Never go on duty unarmed or unequipped.

All the way back to Porcupine City Tancredi said

not one word from between Jack and Annie in the broad back bench seat of the vehicle. Arrestees often babble nervously, trying to fill in the vacuum of quiet and talk about anything but the reasons for their arrest, as if changing the subject would also change the awful reality. It never has. Neither has a stony, silent glare straight through the windshield.

In the kitchen at the sheriff's department I opened proceedings, this time with the Miranda recital. Tancredi sat rigid, eyes straight ahead, staring over my shoulder, and did not answer. Chad stood behind his chair and Annie a little to the side. Jack leaned against the stove.

"I'll take your silence to mean yes, you want a lawyer," I said. He did not blink. "You'll get one tomorrow morning, unless you already have counsel."

Still he did not speak.

"Before we put you in a cell," I said, "we are going to explain our evidence to you, whether you want to hear it or not." The Miranda rules may give arrestees the right not to talk, but they don't take away the police's right to talk. Besides, arrestees are entitled to know the evidence against them anyway, and sometimes outlining it thoroughly during the first interview softens them up for the second with a lawyer present. Cop Psych 101.

Carefully and in plenty of detail I told Tancredi what Jack had found during the search of his apartment and gave him a step-by-step, blow-by blow account of Hutchinson's confession.

"In short, we've got both testimony and concrete evidence that will put you away for life," I said. "If the bullet found at the scene of Mr. Banks's murder matches your rifle, and the DNA in the blood found in Miss Hutchinson's car matches that of Mr. Gibbs, those things will just be gilding a very large and very ugly lily."

"God damn you, you'll never find the money

either!" Tancredi shouted.

"Again I must caution you against self-incrimination," I said in as pompous a tone as I could muster. "But what you've said has already done the job. If I were you I'd shut up until I had a lawyer."

"Fuck you."

"In your dreams. By the way, we've already found the money. Quite a bit of it, too."

With a snarl Tancredi rose and tried to lunge at me over the table, but Chad and Annie quickly wrestled him back into the chair.

"Where?"

"That you will find out in due time," I said. Let him wonder. Let him sweat. Let him fret in a puddle of hate and frustration.

"Off to the rubber room with him," I said. We housed our unruly prisoners in the padded detox tank, at least until they calmed down enough to behave.

"Alex?" I said on my cell. "Sit rep?"

"ESU choppering up from Traverse City as we speak," he said from his office in Wakefield. "Six guys. They'll be at the airport by eight p.m."

Alex had suggested the use of the state police's special weapons unit to grab up the Penningtons. That family had shown considerable potential for violence when Annie and I visited them during the previous year. The highly skilled Emergency Services Unit was much better than a clutch of deputies at neutralizing such subjects. Besides, if I showed my face outside Caleb Pennington's door again, he very likely would try to shoot it off and I would have no choice except to respond in kind.

"No argument," I had said. "But tell them we want those guys alive. We're going to charge them with conspiracy, not with Murder One."

246

"Will do," Alex had said. But we both knew that ESU troopers would do what they had to do to protect their own skins, even if that meant shooting to kill. I hoped the Penningtons would realize that, too.

At seven-thirty Annie and I drove out to Porcupine County Airport to meet the incoming flight. In the still of evening, half a dozen members of the local radio-controlled airplane club were putting their models through their paces. I always enjoyed watching them, having once been an active pilot. I let my FAA medical certificate expire after the county made us get rid of the department's old Cessna because it was too expensive to maintain. But I still yearned to fly. Maybe someday I'd join those modelers.

"Incoming police flight from Traverse City in ten minutes," I told them. Without being asked, they quickly landed their airplanes and started to line them up on the grass in front of the small airport office building, expecting to resume flying as soon as the area was clear.

"Guys, we're going to need the office," I said. "Headquarters for law enforcement activity tonight."

Without a word of protest or the need for further explanation, the pilots gathered up their models, put them into their vehicles, and prepared to drive off.

I strode over. "Keep this under your hats till tomorrow, okay?" I said. I knew all six men, and knew that they'd comply. They knew they were lucky to be able to fly at the little-used airfield and they'd do nothing to jeopardize the privilege.

At precisely seven-thirty Alex and a State Police corporal arrived in two Tahoes just as a nearly brand-new Bell 407 Long Ranger helicopter, "MICHIGAN STATE POLICE" emblazoned on its side, landed with a clatter and a storm of dust on the ramp in front of the building. Half a dozen troopers emerged, carrying canvas bags containing their weapons. I strode over and shook hands with their leader, Lieutenant Ted Olson, a compactly built veteran of

THE RIDDLE OF BILLY GIBBS

the U.S. Army Special Forces. He and his men had assisted us on more than one occasion.

Introductions all around, then I ushered the troopers into the small office building. Alex was already setting up a whiteboard and easel. From memory I drew a rough approximation of the Penningtons' property and house, adding the access road and outbuildings as accurately as I could. Annie, who had also been there, made a couple of small corrections as the troopers jotted the information into notebooks, actually to burn it into their memories.

"We didn't get a chance to go inside," I said, "but old cabins like that usually follow a standard layout. One big room downstairs, kitchen to one side, bedroom in the back, outhouse outside. Sleeping loft upstairs. Probably old man Pennington sleeps in the bedroom and the three sons in the loft."

"We've got eyes for that," Lieutenant Olson said. "That'll be no problem."

"How do you want to do this?" I said.

"As soon as it's dark we'll go out to Ewen and park off the road. Then we'll take up station around the cabin and hit it at exactly two in the morning. I'll keep in touch by radio. Also cell, if we can get enough signal strength."

"The land's flat," Alex said, "but the nearest cell tower probably won't give you more than one bar."

I wished Annie and I had tested our cells when we were out there, but we hadn't. It didn't matter. Radio would work.

"You think they'll suspect anything if the woman hasn't come back?" Olson said.

"No," I said. "They'll expect she's spending the night with the guy we also arrested this afternoon. Word has not gotten out about the busts. We made sure."

Olson nodded.

"Okay," I said, shaking his hand. "Good hunting."

In ten minutes the troopers had piled into the two Tahoes and were off. I returned to the department and settled in for a long night.

As soon as I entered my office I called Ginny and told her I wouldn't be by that night, that we were wrapping up a big case. She knew exactly what I was talking about, although I didn't spell out the details.

"See you, Steve," she said. "Love you lots."

Half an hour later she rolled into the squad room with a five-gallon percolator of her best Colombian coffee, a huge tureen of pea soup with ham, and several loaves of French bread she'd baked herself. Jack, Annie and Chad beamed in delight, and so did Sheila, who never goes home when the game is afoot. Only Gil remained expressionless, but he did raise one beetling eyebrow in appreciation when he took the lid off the soup and sniffed. Joe Koski came in from the cell block and lifted both his brows over a broad smile.

"What can I say?" I said. Ginny just gazed at me fondly.

"Thought you'd like some company," she said.

"Oh, we do," Chad said before I could, and immediately we all dug in. If it weren't for the mission being executed at Ewen, the atmosphere would have been festive. As it was, the spread allowed us to relax a little while events followed their course.

At midnight Alex called on the radio. "Team in place," he said in a whisper. "Undetected."

"Where are you?" I said.

"Just outside the gate to the Pennington property. Hiding in a bush with the fancy eyes."

He'd document the operation as best he could with the camera, but he also had another task: to determine exactly where the four Penningtons were inside the cabin by their heat signatures, readable on the thermal imaging scope that served as the camera lens. That was a five-thousand-dollar piece of equipment I'd love to have but would never be able to get the county commissioners to agree to. That didn't really matter if ESU had one.

We waited. And waited some more as the clock in the squad room slowly ticked toward two a.m. Chad and Jack dozed in chairs. Gil busied himself with accounts in his office, now and then peering at the clock. Annie and Ginny sat at a desk, heads together, occasionally glancing over at me and giggling. I wondered what they were talking about. Men and their shortcomings, I was sure. Not the soup and bread. Both had disappeared quickly.

At one-fifty-nine Alex radioed again. "One subject in the back bedroom downstairs. Three upstairs. Nothing moving. We're ready to go. Out."

Two o'clock. Two-oh-one. Two-oh-two. Two-oh-three. The silence in the squad room was so intense my ears were thrumming. Two-oh-four.

At two-oh-six the radio crackled. "All subjects in custody," Alex said.

At the appointed hour, three of the troopers had thrown M84 "diversionary devices," as the army officially calls them, through windows on both floors of the cabin. These stun grenades pack a two-and-a-half-million-candlepower flash and a 175-decibel bang. If you're in the room when one goes off, your senses instantly will be addled, and it'll take you long minutes to recover.

An instant later Olson had shouted, "The Michigan State Police special weapons team has you surrounded. Walk out the door backwards with your hands up and empty."

One by one all four Penningtons did as ordered. They lay quietly and flat on the ground in front of their cabin while the troopers cuffed their hands behind their backs, and stayed prone for the moment.

"Uh, Steve," Alex finally said. "We need two more

vehicles to get these guys to the jail."

We had not prearranged that transport, for we didn't know whether we'd need SUVs or a quartet of hearses.

"Chad, Annie," I said. "On your way."

Shortly after four a.m. the convoy of SUVs pulled up in front of the department and the four sullen Penningtons were marched in and clapped in cells immediately. Even Caleb remained tight-lipped and silent, though his eyes flashed with rage. We'd have to move some of them to another jurisdiction later in the day because we'd run out of cells. We'd do the bookings after catching a few hours of sleep. It had been a long night, but a fruitful one.

"I love it," I said to Ginny, "when we close a case without shooting anybody."

Right there in the middle of my office with everybody watching, she gave me a huge warm hug. But I wasn't in the least bit embarrassed. My crew was clapping, not only for us but also themselves and the state cops and ESU troopers lounging around the squad room.

"We all done good," I said.

Five days later most of our prisoners had been farmed out to other jails and we again had the "Vacancy" sign up. Only Tancredi and Hutchinson remained in Hotel Porcupine County, and we lodged them far apart, one in the women's cells on the other side of the block.

Tancredi refused to talk, even to his court-appointed lawyer, a local attorney next up in the public defender rotation. It didn't matter one whit. The DNA of the blood in the Saturn matched that taken from Gibbs' body. The black sand in the car and on Tancredi's boots were identical to that on the beach at Freda. And the round taken from the window frame at the site where Keyshawn Banks was killed matched the rifle found in Tancredi's apartment. There was also the undeniable matter of those size eleven Field & Streams. And, of course, the damning testimony of Anne-Marie Hutchinson.

On the advice of her court-appointed lawyer she had pleaded not guilty at her arraignment, despite her confession. This would allow her to strike a deal with the prosecution to get a charge lesser than first-degree murder if she testified against Tancredi. That would give her a chance to get out of prison before the end of her natural life.

Caleb Pennington was no more forthcoming than Tancredi. He also lawyered up early and declined to answer questions, even when I told him what his daughter had said about the family's involvement in the conspiracy to murder Gibbs. All he would offer was a steady stream of ugly invective about his daughter's betrayal as well as my Indian ancestry.

Two of his sons, Ezekiel and Gabriel, also clammed up. Azrael, the third and youngest, followed his sister's example and admitted everything, but he seemed to show some sense of contrition and did not parrot her white-supremacist credo. His involvement clearly was minimal and even reluctant. Garner told him that if he agreed to testify, the charge against him would be reduced to the barest minimum and if the judge went along with the deal he'd probably get no prison time.

Slam dunk all around. The sheriffs and prosecutors of all three counties involved in the case agreed that the trial would commence six months hence in the district court at Porcupine City, Garner prosecuting and Judge Andrea Cunningham presiding, for Judge Rantala would be retiring at the start of the new year. The media had come, done its thing, and gone. At long last we could go back to normal, serving warrants, prodding citizens into cleaning up their lawns and fixing their roofs, busting speeders and patronizing cookie-and-lemonade peddlers. The only sour news that day was that the county commissioners would not let me hire a new deputy to replace Chad after he moved up into the undersheriff's office. No money in the budget, they said. Surprise.

Something else had happened. For the better part of the week Joe Koski and Sheila fielded a citizen's phone call seemingly every five minutes. Instead of complaining about their neighbors or reporting a stray dog, they all said they wanted to congratulate law enforcement in general and the sheriff in particular on a job well done. Just two callers railed against us, one of them saying we were "spending nigger-loving money to put good white folks in prison." They refused to identify themselves. That was no surprise, and we didn't bother to trace the calls to find out who they were. They just weren't worth the trouble.

"Amazingly, finding the killers of black men seems to be good news to almost everybody," Joe said. "Last night at Merle's and Maxie's, all anybody could talk about was 'how justice finally has been served' and 'the memory of two good men has been honored.' If you ran for re-election today, Steve, you'd win ninety-nine point nine per cent of the vote."

I put that into perspective by reflecting that much of the country had reviled the Reverend Martin Luther King Jr. before his death but afterward named a national holiday for him. Like Dr. King, Billy Gibbs was no saint, and neither was Keyshawn Banks. Dr. King had a weakness for women but transcended his shortcomings, and Billy in particular was a charming rogue who could have risen above his own flaws if he had lived. If, in the end, the soldiers' crime turned out to be paltry compared to those committed on grand corporate scales in Afghanistan and elsewhere in the world, it still had led to their demise.

I have no illusions, either, about my fellow Porkies. Many of them are still racist at heart, as they often show when they think they are alone with like-minded folks, for old prejudices die hard. But they can sometimes rise briefly above their human pettiness.

As for Gibbs' gold, it belongs to the government of the United States, and that is where it eventually will go. The chunks cut from the truck frame are still being held as evidence in a vault the Marquette state police post rents at a local bank, and when court proceedings are over, it will be melted down and sent to Fort Knox along with the confiscated jewelry Gibbs mailed home to his mother.

One more thing to do that day. It was Gil's last day at work and Chad's first as undersheriff of Porcupine County. We sent Freddie Fitzpatrick down to Merle's to pick up a cake so that we could throw a little retirement party for Gil in the squad room that evening. Before Freddie could get back Sheila said, "We'll have to move the party to the courthouse. So many law enforcement officers have said they're coming that there's no room in this little bandbox."

"Who?" I said.

"Just about the entire Wakefield state police post. About twenty more troopers are coming from Marquette, Negaunee, Sault Ste. Marie, Gladstone, Iron Mountain, Calumet, and St. Ignace. Oh yes, Selena Novikovich and a deputy or two from Mackinac County, and in fact the same from every sheriff's department in the Yoop and several in northern Wisconsin. Gonna be a hot time in the old town tonight."

"Jesus. How are we going to feed and water all those cops?"

"Ginny is organizing everything. She's ordered fried chicken, potato salad, beer and pop from the deli at Frank's. She'll bring it all to the courthouse."

And foot the entire bill, I was sure.

"She said to tell you something else," Sheila said.

"What?"

"Quote, 'This is "Just Soup" all over again.' "

"Yeah. That means that once more she's saved my

a— I mean, hide."

"You were right the first time. She saved your *ass*."

So many police cruisers and SUVs crammed every nook and cranny in the courthouse parking lot that dozens of alarmed citizens called the sheriff's department and asked what was going on. After Joe Koski told them, some of them said they wanted to come out and help send Gil off.

"I asked them not to," Joe said. "I told them that it's a private party, there isn't any room anyway, and if they showed up, there'd be a competition to arrest them."

"Did they laugh?" I said.

"Most of them did. I had to explain to a couple of not-too-bright ones that it was a joke."

I chuckled myself and headed for the fried chicken. Ginny stood at the serving table chatting with Sheriff Novikovich, who had just arrived. Selena peeled away and headed directly for me.

"Now how about that hug?" she said, in a voice that carried.

Grinning widely, I opened my arms, and as the sheriff of Mackinac County floated into them, she planted a wet one right on my kisser.

"You hot piece of man ass, you!" Selena said with a wicked grin that stretched across the room and into the night. Quickly I glanced at Ginny, who was laughing uproariously along with three-quarters of the law enforcement of Upper Michigan.

I wasn't the only red-faced one present. Two detectives with the Ontario Provincial Police we had once worked with sent an enormous bouquet of roses to Gil, embarrassing and confusing him.

"Guys don't do that for other guys, do they?" he said.

"In Canada they do," Alex said, as if that explained everything.

Tommy Standing Bear couldn't get away from his studies at Michigan State but sent a long email he asked Chad to read to the assembled LEOs. In it he talked about how Gil had been an important presence in his life and mentioned his "grace" and "charm" and "wit," words I doubted had ever been used before to describe a fearsome former drill instructor who exuded all the sex appeal of an armored vehicle. Everybody cheered, and I could swear I saw a bashful tear course down the cheek of that creased old mug.

I thought about a small bit of unfinished business: the Stenfors family. Deena had gone back to Michigan Tech, but after a few weeks dropped out and moved to Los Angeles, Tommy said, adding that he had heard she was serving tables at a pizza emporium and living with three other young women in a shabby apartment. Gene and Carla had sold their house for a song and moved to Topeka. I wondered if forgiveness ever would reunite that family.

I knew that we would never find out exactly what had happened deep inside the minds of Deena Stenfors and Billy Gibbs during that fateful sexual encounter at his trailer. Two human beings can experience, and recall, the same intense event in subtly different ways, almost as if each was living in a parallel universe. I will go to my grave believing that both Deena and Billy told the truth as they had lived it.

Later, as the revelry wound down and the last troopers and deputies filed out, Ginny and Sheila set to cleaning up, and the sheriff of Porcupine County, who definitely knew his place in a land where women ruled, rolled up his sleeves to help.

As I picked up a broom I asked Gil, "Where you gonna go?"

"Nowhere," said my now former undersheriff. "Going to stay right here in Porcupine City."

"What you gonna do?"

"Nothing. Sit in my rocking chair and read and maybe do a little hunting and fishing. But mostly nothing."

I glanced at Jack Adamson next to him. The old FBI agent and the erstwhile undersheriff just grinned. Nothing, indeed.

Somehow I didn't feel quite so short-handed anymore.

THE RIDDLE OF BILLY GIBBS

About the Author

Henry Kisor is the author of five previous Steve Martinez mysteries, *Season's Revenge, A Venture into Murder, Cache of Corpses, Hang Fire,* and *Tracking the Beast.* He and his wife Debby spend half the year in Evanston, Illinois, and the other half in a log cabin on the shore of Lake Superior in Ontonagon County, Michigan, the prototype of Porcupine County. He is also the author of three nonfiction books, *What's That Pig Outdoors: A Memoir of Deafness; Zephyr: Tracking a Dream Across America,* and *Flight of the Gin Fizz: Midlife at 4,500 Feet.* He retired in 2006 after thirty-three years as an editor and critic for the old *Chicago Daily News* and the *Chicago Sun-Times.* In 1981 he was a finalist for the Pulitzer Prize in criticism.

THE RIDDLE OF BILLY GIBBS

A F T E R W O R D

Adventures in Self-Publishing

IN THE AUTHORSHIP game, I'm like a journeyman ballplayer who bounced around the big leagues for a few years before being sent down to the minors for good.

In the 1990s, major New York publishers—Random House, HarperCollins, and Farrar, Straus & Giroux—issued my first three books, all nonfiction. Reviews were good (the New York Times Book Review praised all three) and sales were modestly successful (one book made enough to send a son to a private college for four years).

When I switched to mystery writing in the early 2000s, the first three whodunits in the Steve Martinez series—*Season's Revenge, A Venture into Murder, and Cache of Corpses*—were issued by a competent second-tier publisher of genre fiction, Tom Doherty/Forge. They were well reviewed but not heavily promoted, and sold modestly.

In 2008, when the Great Recession had thoroughly staggered the publishing industry, Forge let me go. Though my notices had been good, sales of regional mysteries—especially mine—had just been too meager. I joined a host of similarly orphaned novelists struggling to find new publishers.

Finding a fresh vendor wasn't easy. Publishing houses are loath to take on a fiction series in midstream.

Because they don't own the earlier books, they can't depend on revenues from them to support taking a risk on new ones, hoping their writers will someday become best-sellers. And so for more than three years *Hang Fire*, the fourth in the Steve Martinez series, languished in limbo until Five Star/Gale, a specialty house that markets genre fiction chiefly to libraries, rescued it for the 2013 publishing season.

Five Star has been a good choice for young writers seeking to break in as well as older ones hoping to keep their careers afloat. In 2016 it also published *Tracking the Beast*, the fifth Martinez novel. Both novels did well enough to earn back the tiny advance payments and generate additional royalties.

At the beginning of 2016, however, Five Star suddenly decided to stop publishing mysteries entirely, and focus instead on romances and Westerns, both booming genres in the library market. Five Star did not say why, but it was easy to guess the reason: Mysteries were no longer doing so well in its market.

The Riddle of Billy Gibbs had been acquired but not yet contracted for, and so Five Star set it adrift along with a number of other mystery novels.

Rather than ask my agent to shop it around for months and even years, I decided to publish *Billy Gibbs* myself and get it out into the sun sooner rather than later. Although I couldn't give myself a fat advance, the royalties I could pay myself down the line might not be so bad.

But isn't this *self-publishing*? Only a decade ago, when I was the book review editor for the Chicago Sun-Times, there was a real stain to the idea. Professionals looked down on the wares of "vanity presses" as beneath their notice. Reviewers assumed that a book that hadn't met the demands of an agent and the ministrations of a genuine publishing house couldn't possibly be worth reading. Selling such a book was nearly impossible without reviews, and countless authors ended up with hundreds of unsold copies on skids in their garages.

As the recession has slowly lifted, some things clearly have changed. Self-publishing is no longer considered such a mug's game. The advent of easy-to-produce ebooks and publish-on-demand paperbacks have eased the task of creating a book by oneself. Of course, nothing can replace the skill and experience of a good agent and a veteran publishing house, but the alternative is a lot sunnier than it used to be.

I'd had some experience in the book game on the production side as well as the writing. In 2009 the rights to my first book, *What's That Pig Outdoors: A Memoir of Deafness* reverted to me, and I decided to bring it up to date and see if I could get a university press interested in the project. That happened, and the University of Illinois Press republished it in 2010 as an academic paperback.

My agent was then attempting to sell *Hang Fire*, and I thought its chances to find a new publisher would be helped if the earlier books had reappeared and were building an audience. And so I won back the rights to the earlier novels and brought out *Season's Revenge, A Venture into Murder*, and *Cache of Corpses* as $3.99 ebooks on Amazon.com and Barnesandnoble.com in 2011.

The big job, as with *Pig*, was scanning the original hardcovers into electronic form and cleaning up the text. I still had the original electronic manuscripts, but the publisher's considerable edits had been done on paper. It was simply easier to scan than to hand-insert the changes.

Next came interior design — not difficult for an author of several previous books — and then the front covers. I didn't think I'd ever make enough royalties to justify hiring a jacket artist, so did them myself. They've been through two iterations so far, and they're still not quite right, though they're good enough for government work.

The total cost: Nothing, except for my own labor. Amazon and B&N don't charge a dime — they just take a modest cut of sales. And I don't need to keep an inventory of copies.

At first those three reissued mysteries brought in only enough money to take Debby out to dinner once a month (twice if it was a good month), but sales have slowly increased to the point where I can now treat her twice a week. I have done no real marketing for those titles, except for a few library presentations, but Five Star's publicity efforts for *Hang Fire* and *Tracking the Beast* piqued reader interest in the earlier books.

In 2012 I decided to get back the rights to my other two nonfiction titles, *Zephyr: Tracking a Dream Across America* and *Flight of the Gin Fizz: Midlife at 4,500 Feet,* and reissue them as ebooks.

The same year I discovered Amazon's CreateSpace "independent publishing platform," its print-on-demand paperback scheme. Print-on-demand is wonderful for authors because we don't need to keep a sizable inventory in our garages — unless we choose to.

For someone with the skills I've learned over the years, it's an easy way to produce actual printed books of reasonably high quality. Many readers, especially older ones, would rather have volumes they can hold in their hands rather than peer at ebooks on an electronic reader. Two months after the ebooks appeared, *Zephyr* was also reborn in CreateSpace form. Not *Gin Fizz;* the market for old aviation books is too small to be worth the effort.

This time I had the sense to use actual photographs as book covers rather than scratch out amateurish art. The toughest part was deciding on the fonts for the title and cover text.

These two forms of self-publishing have been highly fulfilling, for they enabled me to use — and hone — the skills I had learned not only as an author but also as a newspaper editor with experience in computerized page design and graphics production.

Gin Fizz has languished, for books on aviation no longer command sizable audiences. The rail buff community, however, loves books about trains, and *Zephyr* has stayed afloat among it, especially since I'm able to promote the book on railfan web sites and Facebook pages.

In 2016 I republished the first three Steve Martinez novels as one omnibus ebook and as a single print-on-demand paperback called *Porcupine County*. The latter is a 726-page doorstop of a volume, and despite its $9.99 ebook tag and $25.95 paperback price, sales have been modestly heartening.

I followed that later in the year with three separate $12.95 paperbacks for readers uninterested in an omnibus.

The toughest part of this enterprise, of course, is winning the attention of potential readers. I still have to go out and peddle the product, mostly in presentations at friendly libraries. With one or two exceptions, bookstores have not seemed interested in selling print-on-demand paperbacks, let alone ebooks.

Getting reviews is still difficult. Book review sections have dried up with the rest of the newspaper industry. A few surviving magazines, including those geared to libraries, still review books — but most don't touch self-published efforts. Neither do most literary blogs and Web sites devoted to mysteries (some will, but only for a fee, and I refuse to pay). Fortunately the five previous novels in the Steve Martinez series provide a built-in readership for every new novel, thanks to my Steve Martinez page on Facebook and my web site, henrykisor.com. Yes, the web site is self-published; I had to teach myself HTML coding.

Now you are holding the latest example of my efforts — *The Riddle of Billy Gibbs*.

Being a one-man publishing house has been a

gratifying pastime during my retirement years. I certainly am not making a living at it, but it keeps my aging brain limber — and it also keeps all my books alive, gaining new readers every day.

75679630R00147

Made in the USA
Columbia, SC
25 August 2017